SUFFERANCE

Other Works by Thomas King

Fiction
Medicine River
Green Grass, Running Water
One Good Story, That One
Truth and Bright Water
A Short History of Indians in Canada
The Back of the Turtle
Indians on Vacation

DreadfulWater Mysteries
DreadfulWater
The Red Power Murders
Cold Skies
A Matter of Malice
Obsidian

Non-Fiction
The Truth About Stories: A Native Narrative
The Inconvenient Indian: A Curious Account of Native People in North America

Children's Illustrated Books
A Coyote Columbus Story, illustrated by William Kent Monkman
Coyote Sings to the Moon, illustrated by Johnny Wales
Coyote's New Suit, illustrated by Johnny Wales
A Coyote Solstice Tale, illustrated by Gary Clement
Coyote Tales, illustrated by Byron Eggenschwiler

Poetry
77 Fragments of a Familiar Ruin

SUFFERANCE

A NOVEL

THOMAS KING

HarperCollins*Publishers*Ltd

Sufferance
Copyright © 2021 by Dead Dog Café Productions Inc.
All rights reserved.

Published by HarperCollins Publishers Ltd

First edition

The book's epigraph is from Nunnally Johnson's screenplay of *The Grapes of Wrath* (1940),
adapted from the John Steinbeck novel of the same name.

HarperCollins books may be purchased for educational, business or
sales promotional use through our Special Markets Department.

HarperCollins Publishers Ltd
Bay Adelaide Centre, East Tower
22 Adelaide Street West, 41st Floor
Toronto, Ontario, Canada
M5H 4E3

www.harpercollins.ca

Library and Archives Canada Cataloguing in Publication

Title: Sufferance : a novel / Thomas King.
Names: King, Thomas, 1943- author.
Identifiers: Canadiana (print) 20210124377 | Canadiana (ebook) 20210124407
ISBN 9781443463102 (hardcover) | ISBN 9781443463126 (ebook)
Classification: LCC PS8571.I5298 S84 2021 | DDC C813/.54—dc23

Printed and bound in the United States of America
LSC/H 9 8 7 6 5 4 3 2 1

To the memory of what we have lost
and what we continue to destroy

"Then who *do* we shoot?"

—1940 film adaptation of Steinbeck's *The Grapes of Wrath*

M orning.

The light takes the river by surprise and sets fire to the ice. Crows gather in the trees. Canada geese huddle together in the open pools of black water. On the far bank, a red fox sorts through the broken snow and brittle grasses.

A dead mallard is frozen up against a bristle of wolf willow, its feathers bright and glowing under a sharp sky. The bird will be gone by midday. If the fox doesn't find the duck, the current will cut the body loose and carry it away.

The overnight temperature has stayed below freezing. Winter is leaving the land, but the cold is retreating at a tourist's pace, strolling along, taking in the sights, lingering over lunch at a restaurant recommended in the guidebook.

I have no grievance with the season. Winter is winter. What does anyone expect? Spring will be cool and wet. Summer will be humid and hot. Fall, brisk and colourful. Then winter will return. Just like the moon and the sun. Just like night and day. Life and death.

Well, not like life and death. Life doesn't come rolling around again as though it's strapped to the spokes of some cosmic wheel.

Life. Death. Life, death, life, death, life, death.

Life is motion. Death is not.

The fox on the bank. The duck in the river.

LAST NIGHT, a storm rushed in, rattling the roof of the old residential school and shaking the walls. Lightning. Thunder. Rain and wind. Bluster and bluff.

Today, the sky is clear, the river path into town quiet.

Except for the crows. They're on the move now, keeping pace with me, jumping from tree to tree, calling out to one another, playing games in the bright sunlight.

Marco.

Polo.

They're having a good time at my expense. Making fun of this enormous, flightless bird, this featherless lump tethered to the earth.

Marco.

Polo.

I show the crows that I can be a good sport. I jump into the air, fling my arms about, and this sends the birds into paroxysms of screeches and shrieks. I leap up a second time and come down wrong on an ankle.

Nothing serious.

But it's the end of my performance.

Up ahead, Iku Takahashi is dragging her newly arrived puppy along behind her. The dog is an Australian labradoodle. Iku has decided to call the dog Koala, slightly disingenuous for an animal who looks more like a dust mop than an arboreal marsupial.

Swiffer would be a better name.

I don't want to talk to Iku Takahashi, and I don't want to pet Koala.

"Mr. Camp," Iku calls out. "You're limping."

I smile.

"Have you met Koala?" Takahashi touches the pair of binoculars that hangs around her neck. "She's a purebred, out of Nicole and Teddy, and carries for chocolate and parti as well as gold and black."

Who talks like that?

"How are the renovations going?"

The binoculars are green and heavy, an expensive brand that is popular among birdwatchers.

"I hope you saved the wainscotting."

Joggers pass us on the fly, and Nicole and Teddy's little princess bursts into life, leaping about on her leash like a trout on a line, annoying the whole of creation with her sharp, firecracker yelps.

I couldn't own a dog. Or any animal for that matter.

"She's in training," Takahashi says, by way of explanation. "Everything is still new. Everything excites her."

I begin a slow drift away from the woman and her dog.

"Have you thought about the binoculars?" Mrs. Takahashi holds them up so I can see the lenses. "Keizo said that with them, you could see the world."

I don't want to see the world.

"And when you have the big open house," Takahashi calls after me, "don't forget to invite us."

IN THE SUMMER, especially on market day, the town plaza fills with people. Pickups and vans ring the small park, tables and tents take over the square, with vendors selling everything from locally grown vegetables to jellies and jams to handmade clothing and local crafts.

Lump-of-clay coffee mugs and beer-bottle wind chimes.

On those days, if you're so inclined, you can have your fortune told or your face painted. Or you can dip wands into buckets of soapy water and lob huge bubbles into the air and dance in the grass.

Today, the plaza is deserted, the bubble and dancing season somewhere out on the horizon.

As I pass the Plaza Hotel with its beaux arts facade, I run into Bob Loomis coming out the front door. Loomis looks slightly startled, as though he's been caught voting NDP.

"Jerry."

Loomis thinks reducing my name to a diminutive makes us friends.

"Just the man I want to see."

Bob Loomis is tall and slender, pale, with wispy hair that floats around a thin face. A long nose that hooks in like a beak and soft blue eyes that bulge just a little. He stands on the sidewalk with a hip thrust forward, his right hand hanging at his side, as though he expects to find a sword strapped to his waist. More than anything, he reminds me of the characters from *commedia dell'arte*—Pantalone, Pierrot, Scaramouche—with their elaborate costumes, obscene gestures, and unsettling masks.

"So, have you thought about it?"

Loomis owns Gleaming Realty. He's also the town's mayor and is running for re-election.

Bob's the One.

In many ways, it's the perfect political slogan. Equal parts endorsement and accusation.

I look at my list.

Pick up eggs.

Check out the tomatoes.

Get spaghetti sauce.

Avoid Mayor Bob.

"The land's just sitting there." Loomis finds an easy smile. The glare off his teeth is blinding. "And you know what they say."

And fruit. If I can find anything that hasn't spent the last month on a boat.

The mayor puts his hand on my shoulder, as though he is bestowing a blessing.

"Until we understand what the land is," he says, his voice becoming deep and resonant, "we are at odds with everything we touch."

Wendell Berry. *The Art of the Commonplace: The Agrarian Essays.* 2002. Someone has been watching the History Channel again.

Loomis hands me his business card. "And you know what that means."

The mayor leaves his hand on my shoulder. "That land claim is never going to see the light of day," he says. "It's been what? Seventy? Seventy-five years?"

Loomis has his back to the Plaza, so he doesn't see Maribelle Wegman step out into the spring air, and she doesn't see us until it is too late to duck back into the hotel.

"And cemeteries can be moved." Loomis takes out a second business card. "Why don't you come by the office? Give us a chance to talk. *Mano a mano.*"

"Jeremiah Camp and Bob Loomis." The widow Wegman gathers herself, pats at her hair, and comes forward on cue. "You two look as though you're up to mischief."

Wegman's voice startles Loomis, and he drops the card.

"Mrs. Wegman," he says quickly. "What a coincidence."

"Surprise, surprise." Wegman smiles and holds her hands up, palms out.

Maribelle Wegman is known as the widow Wegman. Married four times. Three dead husbands. Not her fault, but having managed the hat trick already, she has been given the trophy to keep.

"Mr. Loomis and I sit on the city's preservation committee," says Wegman. "Do you know the history of the Plaza Hotel?"

I don't care about the history of the Plaza Hotel.

"And has the mayor talked to you about the matter of the crosses?" asks Wegman. "Quite a few people have called my office with concerns about the crosses."

Loomis has recovered completely. He holds out an arm cocked at the elbow, lets the watch catch the sunlight. "My god," he says. "Look at the time."

The watch is a thick, ugly thing. White face. Blue ring. Numbers running in all directions. It's an expensive piece that looks happy on his wrist.

Wegman brushes the hair away from her face. "I hope we can get the matter of the crosses settled amicably."

The mayor pats his stomach as though it's a close friend. "I have a lunch meeting at the club."

Wegman nods. "And I have to get to the gym."

Across the square a black SUV, newly washed and polished, floats in against the curb, while near the bandstand a man picks his way through a garbage can that looks like a hippo with its mouth open.

"One of these days," says Loomis, "you'll have to tell me how you managed to purchase that property. Didn't know you could buy a residential school."

The windows of the SUV are tinted. No one gets out.

"I'm guessing friends in high places." The mayor stoops down and picks up the card. "Am I right?"

Loomis waits for an answer, and when he doesn't get it, he heads off in one direction, while the widow Wegman trots off in the other. Neither one of them breaks stride or looks back.

THE SUCRE BLEU BAKERY is two doors along from the Plaza Hotel. This is where Swannie Gagnon presides over brownies and lemon tarts, Danishes, and macarons.

Swannie is from Quebec City and, according to Eddie Ott, who owns the Bent Nail, this is why Swannie is somewhat abrupt and occasionally rude, and why she doesn't shave her underarms or her legs.

I stand in line behind several people and watch the yellow jackets in the display case crawl across the eclairs. Today, Swannie has made her famous sausage rolls, and the woman in front of me buys six.

"I should get a discount for quantity," the woman tells Swannie. "Buy five, get one free."

Swannie shrugs and takes her money. "Then the business, she would be gone. Poof." Swannie makes a popping sound with her mouth. "And the sausage rolls? Poof."

I can see that the woman is not convinced, and I can see that Swannie doesn't care.

I step to the cash register. As soon as she sees me, she rolls her eyes and gives me an exaggerated shoulder. "The brownie? Yes?"

I nod.

"Always the same." Swannie goes to the case and picks up a brownie with the tongs. "One brownie. But perhaps one day the brownie will be gone. Poof. What then will you eat?"

Swannie raises her arms over her head, stretches to one side and then to the other.

"The *tarte au citron*? The *gâteau basque*? The *pain au chocolat*?"

The hair under her arms is impressive. I can see why Eddie is jealous.

The man is still at the can. He's up to his waist in the hippo's mouth. The SUV has disappeared.

I cross the plaza, head to the far edge of town and the Piggy café, a one-storey brick building, backed against a grove of cedar. The Piggy started life as a bank. The Gleaming Bank and Trust, founded in 1922 by Arnold S. Overholt. There's a cornerstone with the date and Overholt's name on it.

Arnold presided over the bank for thirty-five years, before he passed it on to his son, Seymour, who looked after the bank for the next forty, before his son, Charles, took over and promptly ran the business into the ground.

And when the 2008 financial crisis rattled the windows of the world economy, Charles gathered up what was left of the bank's negotiable assets and disappeared into Cuba.

Or Argentina.

Or Mexico.

FLORENCE HOLDER is standing in the gloom of the Piggy, next to the espresso machine.

"That better be a brownie."

I put the bag on the counter. Stand in the room and let my eyes adjust. Florence gets two plates and cuts the brownie in half.

"You missed Roman."

Florence waits to see if I have anything to add.

"They let him out early. Stopped by to pick up his horn."

Florence puts a scoop of beans in the grinder.

"And you just missed the Three Bears."

Florence fills a cup with scalding water.

"Tonight, we're going to Venice. Seven sharp. Don't be late."

She turns the grinder on, and the café is filled with the shrieks of coffee beans.

"People keep asking me about you."

Florence dumps the water out of the cup and puts it under the basket. She lifts the lever on the machine.

"And I keep telling them that you're busy 'renovating.'"

I watch the espresso leak into the cup. At first, it's almost black, and then it turns a soft tan. Florence lets it run out.

"It sounds better than 'sitting on your ass.'"

I wait for Florence to steam the milk.

"Nutty thinks you should do a smudge. Chase the badness out of the school with smoke. But if you ask me, the only way to renovate that wicked place is with a can of gas and a match."

THE BANK SAT VACANT for a number of years, tied up in liens, in class-action suits, and by angry creditors. There was talk of turning the building into a museum, and there was talk of tearing the building down. But in the end, the Gleaming Bank and Trust was dusted off and put up for auction.

Sealed bid. No reservation.

Turned out no one wanted a building that had been a bank. Something about the renovation costs, all the marble and the teller cages, and the enormous walk-in vault. Something about the shadow of failure.

Except for Reggie Clarke and his partner, Florence Holder.

Reggie managed a small restaurant in Toronto's St. John's Ward. Florence was a high-school history teacher.

Their bid wasn't the best of bids. But it was the only one.

As soon as title cleared, Reggie rounded up a truckload of used restaurant equipment—gas stove and grill, refrigerator/freezer, sink, prep table—along with an espresso machine and a Rock-Ola Bubbler, and moved in.

There was some local interest in calling the place the Overholt Café for historical reasons, but Reggie had his own ideas, and seven months after he and Florence bought the place, the Piggy Bank was open for business.

I GO TO THE TABLE in the corner by the jukebox. I sit with my back against the wall. From here, I can see the big-screen television and the front door.

Florence joins me. She brings a fork with her. In case I can't finish my part of the brownie.

"You know why I like espresso and brownies?"

Florence has told me this more than once.

"Because they're the perfect combination of bitter and sweet."

No argument there.

"And because we're all the same lovely colour."

Florence slides the cup to me. The dollop of foam floats on the macchiato like an iceberg in a dark sea.

"News, blues, and comfortable shoes," she begins. "Lead story in Europe is the death of Fabrice Gloor, head of Suisse-Baer Group. Gloor was killed in a single-car accident near Cap d'Ail. Was headed into Nice when his Maserati went off a cliff."

Florence lives on the internet. News outlets, Facebook, blogs. Each morning over coffee, she brings everyone up to date on what they might have missed.

"In Texas," Florence continues, "police have exonerated themselves in the shooting death of a woman who was killed as she was getting her baby ready for bed." Florence shakes her head. "Woman was Black. Cops were White."

I don't need anyone to tell me what is happening in the world, and I don't want to know. But that doesn't stop Florence.

"I'm guessing the baby was packing a semi-automatic rattle."

I take a sip of the coffee. Perfect. The brownie is just as good.

"While in local news, Mayor Bob and the city council will be having a meeting about the reserve at the end of the week. Closed-door session."

The Cradle River reserve. About forty families, give or take. The mayor and the city council want to move the band and acquire the land, so the river frontage can be "properly" developed.

"But I expect that Louis and Enola and Ada and the gang are going to show up anyway."

No one called it the Piggy Bank. It was just the Piggy. Breakfast and lunch. Reggie did the cooking, assaulting Canadian fears and prejudices with Caribbean flavourings, breaking down culinary barriers with cou-cou, pudding and souse, conkies, cutters, and black cake, and adapting traditional recipes to accommodate fresh trout, wild game, back bacon, and fried potatoes.

Shelagh Rogers interviewed him for CBC. Margaret Atwood stopped in for breakfast one day and tweeted her appreciation. *Toronto Life* featured the café in their annual edition of where to eat in Canada.

Before long, Reggie had a large and passionate following, with people stopping in from around the world to eat at the Piggy.

And then he died.

Florence takes a deck of tarot cards out of her apron and slaps them on the table.

"Shuffle and cut," she says.

Florence doesn't believe in tarot. It had been Reggie's obsession. Every morning, he would start his day with coffee, toast, and the cards.

"Day he had his heart attack," Florence tells me for the ump-teenth time, "he got the Nine of Cups. Happiness, wish fulfilled, physical well-being, love of sensual pleasures."

Florence kept Reggie's deck, along with the guidebook that explained what the cards meant.

"Nine of Cups. Lot of good it did him."

Today, I pick the Seven of Disks. Failure.

Florence holds the card up to the light. "It's reversed," she says, "though it ain't much good either way."

The card is an ugly thing. A dark grey pile of grass with holes.

"Despondency, deterioration, cut your losses, avoid gambling," says Florence. "Maybe you should have stayed in bed."

Yesterday, I picked the Ace of Swords.

"Nutty's under the weather." Florence puts the cards back in her apron. "Might consider stopping by and saying hello."

I finish the coffee. Then I lean back and close my eyes. I feel Florence push out of her chair.

"That old school ain't going to protect you," she says, her voice sad and flat. "You can close the windows, lock the doors, and the world is still going to come calling."

I stay where I am, push brownie crumbs around on the plate, and let the shadows fill in around me. There's no place I need to be, so here is as good a place as any.

By the time I leave the Piggy and get back to the plaza, the town's transient families have begun to filter into the park.

The Neighbours.

They've spread their sleeping bags on the grass and are making themselves at home. Wes Stanford and Autumn Dare are sitting on a blanket with their three children.

Autumn is passing out sandwiches and apples. Wes is watching for trouble to arrive.

At the bakery, Swannie Gagnon is busy setting up tables on the sidewalk, so customers can sit in the fresh air and pretend that they're in Paris on a trendy street in the Marais or the Latin Quarter, or at a small café just off Canal Saint-Martin.

On the far side of the plaza, Dino Kiazzie and his son Javi are putting out boxes of fruit and vegetables in the hopes of coaxing warmer weather out of its hidey-hole, while the front of Matthews Hardware is awash in wheelbarrows and garden hoses.

Even the Bent Nail has a festive look to it. Someone has hung a Canadian flag in the window of the bar.

A reminder of the close relationship between patriotism and drinking.

I stand at the corner and take my time. Delivery truck, couple of bicycles, people on the move. A dog licking itself in the shade of the bandstand. Four motorcycles with custom paint jobs, wide tires, and ape-hanger handlebars parked in front of the Nail.

I don't see the SUV.

And I don't see the guy at the hippo can. Either he's moved on or he's fallen in and can't get out.

At one time, Gleaming and Cradle River First Nations were distinct communities, but over the years, Gleaming has grown, and now the only thing that separates the town from the reserve is the old riverbed.

"If the houses don't have wheels and you got concrete under your feet," Ada Stillday will tell you over coffee at the Piggy, "you're in town."

Just above the reserve and the town, the Cradle River used to split into two branches. The main branch ran alongside the reserve, while the smaller branch cut in between the two communities.

The earthquake of 1944 changed that.

It was not a strong quake, but it altered the level of the riverbed, and overnight, the branch that had separated the reserve from the town vanished.

Like a moat that had been drained.

"And if you're standing on dirt in the middle of a beat-to-shit trailer park, you're on the reserve."

For as long as memory, the reserve had been a loose collection of split-plank houses, heavy tents, and half a dozen seasonal tipis. And then Indian Affairs decided to modernize the community. Shiny new trailers were brought in from Quebec, and the plank houses and the tents were bulldozed and hauled away.

Only the tipis were left standing. Part of the provincial master plan to encourage tourism in the area.

The trailers had arrived one hot July. A ministry official came in from Ottawa, made a speech about the band's bright future, cut a ribbon, and opened the door of the first trailer.

That's when things started to go sideways.

The trailers reeked. The ministry official assured everyone that the smell was temporary and posed no health hazards, that leaving the doors and windows open for a few days would solve the problem.

Then she had her picture taken with the chief and council.

Then she got back in her car and left.

But the problems didn't stop with the off-gassing. By the end of the first week, the band discovered that the hydro service to the reserve needed to be upgraded in order to manage the trailers with their new electrical appliances. And while there was municipal water, there wasn't enough money to pay for all the hookups.

The council wrote a long letter to Indian Affairs detailing the problems, and Indian Affairs wrote back asking that the band fill out a survey so the ministry would know how they were doing and in what ways their services might be improved.

Two years after the trailers arrived, they began to leak. By the end of the third, the mould appeared.

NUTTY MOOSONEE IS sitting outside in her red recliner. She's wrapped up in a quilt, enjoying the sun. Nutty's trailer has a blue tarp slung over the roof and tied down with rope and bungee cords. There are official-looking stickers stuck to the side of the trailer that warn against entering the premises.

The tarp is new. The stickers are not.

I set the grocery bags on the ground.

"That peanut butter I hear?" Nutty's voice is raspy, and her breathing is laboured. "And pie cherries?"

I fish the jar and the can out of the bags, hold them up for Nutty to see.

Nutty licks her lips. "Put those good things in the icebox."

The air inside the trailer is old and swampy. Brown stains climb the walls and fan out across the ceiling. The linoleum floor moves underfoot, an uneven surface of bubble-wrap lumps. The counter around the kitchen sink has begun to lift off at the seams, and there is a thick line of mould that runs out along the windowsill.

I'm tempted to get a knife and lift it off in one piece. Like skinning a snake.

I open the refrigerator. There's a can of instant coffee on the top shelf along with two hard-boiled eggs, a carton of vanilla yogurt, and three rolls of toilet paper.

I get a bowl from the cupboard and a spoon from the drawer. I move slowly so that I can conserve energy and get out of the trailer without having to take another breath.

NUTTY HASN'T MOVED. I put the bowl on the table next to her.

"Harold and Ester are leaving. Going up to Croker." Nutty stirs the cherries into the yogurt. "Ester's cough ain't getting better."

I pull up one of the orange plastic chairs.

"Roman's back," she says. "Figures he'll fix my roof."

A skinny crow lands on the garbage can with a thud.

"That's Slick," says Nutty. "Bon-Bon's kid. Flies okay, but he's still working on the landings."

Nutty takes a peanut out of her pocket and holds it up. The crow begins to squawk and dance about along the rim of the can.

"He hasn't learned patience just yet."

Nutty tosses the peanut. The bird catches it in mid-air, gives it a shake, shits on the edge of the can, and flies off.

"Manners need some work, too."

Overhead the sky is clear, but the air remains unsettled. Nutty puts the bowl on the table, pushes the quilt to one side, and finds her cane.

"Come on," she says. "Let's take a wander."

I grab my grocery bags and follow Nutty as she makes a slow circuit of the reserve. The trailers look sad and tired. Nutty stops at one that is pitched to the side, threatening to tip over.

"Those Indian Affairs people promised to put them all on blocks, nice and level. Finish them off properly with wood skirting. Like in the pictures."

That didn't happen, and over time, the tires have gone flat, the rubber has rotted away, and the trailers have slumped onto their axles and rims at alarming angles.

"Ada figures that the government never had any intention of

making the trailers permanent. Wants to keep the reserve mobile. In case we get in the way and they have to move us somewhere else."

Nutty stops at a white single-wide with red trim and an official-looking seal across the front door. "Empty," she says. "And those two over there. Empty."

The ground is rough and broken. I walk close to Nutty, in case she stumbles and starts to fall.

"Empty trailers are bad luck. Government sees empty trailers and pretty soon they'll start thinking we don't need the land we got left."

Nutty leads me through the rows of trailers to the large double-wide that serves as the band council office, to the circle of open ground that's used for powwows and ceremonies. There's an arbour and a wood bench at the far side.

"Powwow was supposed to be at the end of the month."

Nutty makes her way to the bench, sits down, stretches her legs, turns her face to the sun.

"But we got no money for prizes. Don't even have money for the drums."

Somewhere in the cluster of trailers, a portable generator kicks in, its rackety clack disturbing the peace.

Nutty leans on her cane. "Tell me what you hear."

Other than the generator, the powwow grounds are quiet. The trailers are quiet.

"Children," whispers Nutty. "You should hear children."

On the far side of the powwow grounds, I see Ada Stillday erupt from a row of trailers. She's a substantial woman, but she moves quickly and with purpose.

Like a boulder falling off a cliff.

Nutty taps her cane on the ground. "Be nice to hear a baby cry. Be nice to hold something soft and sweet-smelling."

Ada's shadow arrives before she does. It's long and heavy and pushes through the air with unexpected force.

"Nutty Moosonee, we got to talk." Ada looms over Nutty, blocking the sun. "You hear what that lump for a mayor is up to now?"

Nutty waves Ada to the bench under the arbour.

"Not enough that he wants to have us moved. Now he wants to put those hippies in our trailers."

The Neighbours. The transient families in the park.

"Don't think they're hippies," says Nutty. "They're just poor. Like us."

"This is Indian land," says Ada. "Cradle River First Nations land."

"Nothing wrong with being generous."

"Since when have Whites been generous with us?" Mrs. Stillday rocks from side to side. "You tell me that."

"Not about what other people do," says Nutty. "It's about what we do."

"World's falling apart." Ada shakes her head. "Crazy man living in our school."

Nutty pats my hand. "Jeremiah's family," she says. "He was born here. Just like you."

"Him being Ruby's boy don't make him family," says Ada.

"Ruby was your cousin," says Nutty. "You two grew up together. That's blood."

"So why'd she leave off?" Ada doesn't look at me. "You tell me that."

"Had her reasons."

"Takes off. Waltzes back in all pregnant, hangs around looking for tea and sympathy, then takes off again? What does that tell you?"

"Tells me some folks don't have it easy like us," says Nutty.

"And she never came back."

"People come and go all the time," says Nutty.

"I hope this ain't about my daughter." Ada clenches her hands. "Emma ain't in Winnipeg 'cause she wants to be in Winnipeg."

"Thought you said she was coming home," says Nutty.

"What if she is? Ain't nobody's business. And if she does come back, what's she going to do?"

Ada pauses for a breath.

"Hippies trying to steal our homes. My daughter's a lawyer and she's working at a restaurant in Winnipeg? What the hell is that? You know how many times I've seen my granddaughter?"

Ada holds her position for a moment.

"Every winter, my water line freezes and the toilet backs up. Anyone care about that?"

And then she turns and stomps off across the powwow grounds, kicking up clouds of complaint as she goes.

Nutty watches her. "Ada means well, but she's got no stretch left."

To the southwest, clouds have begun to form at the edge of the escarpment. By evening, there could be rain, but there's little chance that the rain will last, little hope that it will fall out of the heavens without pause and flood the world. Still, a second apocalypse is a pleasant thought, and I roll it around in my mouth, try to make the taste last as long as possible.

"Better get back." Nutty sets the cane in front of her and stands up. "There's a baseball game on television. Spring training. Ada likes to watch that baseball, but she don't like to watch it alone."

I walk Nutty to Ada's trailer. The ball game has already started. I can see the television through the sliding glass door. Ada is sitting on her sofa, a pot of tea and two cups on the coffee table.

"I'll be fine," says Nutty. "Ada likes to bark, and she chews a bit. But she don't much break the skin."

I figure I'll wait until the two women are settled, until tea is served, and a new inning begins.

Nutty slides the door open. "If you see my grandson," she says, "you might ask him about the roof."

3

The residential school was built in 1903 and given over to the control of the Catholic Church. It was in operation for sixty-two years, before it was abandoned to time and the elements, before a fire destroyed everything except the main building.

I didn't buy the property. But now, it's mine.

At its peak, the school housed some 124 students, ages eight to sixteen. Eighty-five boys. Thirty-nine girls.

In 1929, a young priest, Father Edward Hinch, was put in charge, and he remained in charge until the school closed thirty-six years later.

Now, all that remains of the facility is a large, two-storey building, fifteen rooms in total. Kitchen, dining hall, bathrooms, classrooms, dormitories.

There is a large room on the second floor. In the southeast corner. Separate from what used to be the boys' dormitory. There had been an old spring bed-frame leaning against one wall, so in all likelihood, the room had been used by someone in charge of the floor. Not a guard watching prisoners exactly, but an overseer, a supervisor, a monitor to make sure that the children did not mistake the grant of civilization for assault, or the gift of christianity for punishment.

It would have been an easy mistake to make.

Now that room is my living quarters. A bed, a rug, an easy chair, and a floor lamp. A desk and a bookcase. My mother's old Lone Ranger lunch box on the windowsill. Ruby Camp. "R.C" is scratched into the edge of the lid.

The room is small, but I can sit in the chair and see the river, watch the crows as they arrive each morning to discuss their plans for the day.

THERE IS THE STORY of a farmer in Saskatchewan who decided that he would shoot crows, knowing that if he shot one, others would come to be with the injured bird.

So it would not die alone.

And when they did, the farmer shot those birds as well. When he finally got bored and went in for the night, he had killed over two hundred crows. The local newspaper sent out a reporter to do a story on the massacre, and the farmer became a minor celebrity.

A week later, he woke to find his truck and his farm equipment covered in crow shit. He sat out all that night in a chair with a shotgun on his lap, waiting for the crows to return.

But they didn't.

The next day, he went to town, and when he came home and pulled into the yard, he found that the crows had returned, had picked up rocks and dropped them from height on his greenhouse, smashing the glass panels.

A few days after that, the farmer went to help a neighbour with a tractor that had become stuck in a field, and the crows used his absence to break into his house through an open window. The flock tore at his furniture and smashed the Hummel figurines that the man had bought his wife, one for each year that they had been together.

After the massacre, the farmer never saw another crow on his farm, but all that year and the next, in small and large ways, the crows wreaked havoc on the man and left his farm in ruins.

Crows see everything, and they remember everything. They can be the best of friends, but they do not forget. And they do not forgive.

WHEN I GET BACK to the school, I lug the bags into the kitchen and put the groceries away. Butter, eggs, bread, bananas. There were no grapes at Dino's, not even the balloon variety that is shipped in from Chile. The broccoli from Mexico was already on the wilt, and the hothouse tomatoes were soft and translucent. There was a bin of cabbages, but I don't trust a vegetable that can be shredded and boiled without changing its disposition.

I'm exhausted even before I finish arranging the food. It's probably just age. Or something equally serious.

When I arrived at the old school, there was a cat in residence. An orange tabby, lean and watchful. She disappeared the moment I stepped through the front door, but slowly, by degrees, she has made her presence known.

And her needs.

Now we're friends, or more to the point, we're able to inhabit the same space at the same time.

If she has a name, I don't know it.

The cat is mostly a night cat. Every so often, when I get up to go to the bathroom, I'll hear her on the prowl in a downstairs classroom, her claws clicking on the wood floor. Or I'll catch a glimpse of her outside in the graveyard in the moonlight, gliding through the pale crosses like heavy smoke.

Normally, we only see each other first thing in the morning and last thing at night. Shift work, if you will. But today, as I put the groceries away, there she is, sitting on the windowsill, staring at me with an intensity that could burn through plate steel.

I check the bowls. She has enough food and water, so that's not it.

The cat jumps down off the chair and brushes up against my leg. This is the first time she's done this. Perhaps she's decided that a little affection wouldn't be a bad thing. A long leisurely scratch, perhaps. A tummy rub? A warm lap to sit on?

The knock at the door is sharp and unkind, someone with little regard for old wood. I stand in the kitchen with the cat and try to think of who might be foolish enough to risk my porch. I turn back to ask the cat if this is why she has made an appearance, to warn me about the complications of community, but she's disappeared.

The second knock is louder and more forceful than the first. I consider leaving whoever is standing on my porch to remain there until they tire of knocking and go away.

Still, curiosity is a powerful emotion.

It would be handy if the heavy door had a peephole. But it doesn't. I take a deep breath, in case I'm able to smell who is on the other side.

And then I open the door.

The knocker is a cashmere overcoat, wire-rim glasses, and a dark grey homburg, the hat made famous by Edward VII.

"Lovely to see you again."

There's nothing lovely about finding Oliver Flood on my porch. He's not happy to see me. I'm not happy to see him.

"I'm hoping we might have a word."

There is nothing exceptional about Flood. He is, in most ways, ordinary, an off-the-rack, one-size-fits-all corporate assassin. Except for his eyes. They're amber brown with specks of gold. The eyes of a wolf.

"Is it true that you don't have an email account or a phone of any sort?" Flood makes a puffing sound with his lips.

I don't have a television, either.

"How is that possible?"

The black SUV from the plaza sits in the shadow of the trees. Up close, I can see that it's a Tesla. The X model. The one percent's answer to global warming. Master of Nordschleife, zero to sixty in 2.7 seconds.

"And so, we've come in person."

Two men stand by the vehicle. A matched pair of hunting dogs, sprung and silent. Flood makes a small gesture with his hand, and one of the men opens the trunk, takes out two folding chairs, and arranges them in the dirt at the entrance to the graveyard.

Oliver Flood. Majordomo of the Locken Group. An international conglomerate with strong interests in biochemistry, marine biology, molecular biology, genetics, biophysics. Speciality in military technologies.

Flood steps off the porch and walks to the chairs. "Join me."

Oliver Flood. Ex-military. Stanford MBA. Director of Difficulty Resolution. Vice-President of Persuasion.

"What is it Mr. Locken used to call you?" asks Flood.

Thomas Locken. The seventh generation of Lockens. Heir to an empire of immeasurable wealth and power.

"Forecaster? That's correct isn't it?"

Flood sits down in one chair. I sit in the other.

"I've come to tell you that Thomas Locken has died."

Thomas Locken died months ago. Oliver Flood didn't come all this way to tell me this. Flood waits. A moment of mourning. In case I care.

"As you can imagine, his death has caused ripples in the Realm."

Ripples that will dissipate quickly. Equilibrium before the end of the third quarter.

"And it has been decided that the Realm has need of your skills." Flood stands and straightens his coat. "I have already informed the powers that be that you will say no. But they believe you can be persuaded."

I glance up at the second-floor windows to see if the cat is watching from the shadows.

"To that end, your presence would be appreciated." Flood slips into the back of the SUV. "This evening. The Plaza Hotel. 8:30. I will meet you in the lobby."

This is not a request.

The car is remarkably quiet. I don't even realize the engine is running until the vehicle pulls away. And because I have nothing better to do, I sit there in the folding chair, the school at my back, the graveyard at my shoulder, and watch my past drive away into the cool, spring day.

4

Forecaster.

A name I haven't heard in years. Not since I left the city and the corporate world behind.

The cat sits on the chair with her feet curled up beneath her to let me know that she's comfortable and not to be disturbed.

I take a handful of kitty treats and drop them on the floor. This is our game. If the cat is on the chair, I put the treats on the floor. If she's on the floor, I put them on the chair.

The cat stays where she is, pretends she has no interest in the lumps of flour and egg and salmon flavouring done up to look like little fish. That's what I like about the animal. She doesn't need to talk to me, and I don't need to talk to her.

The sound is faint, but it's enough. The cat explodes off the chair and is gone. It's just the mail arriving. I have removed the mailbox in an effort to discourage the postal folks, to suggest that the school might be deserted.

But it hasn't worked, and now the mail just gets dumped on the porch.

Most days it's flyers, and today is no exception. There's a special on chainsaws. An offer from a roofing company, with no payments and no interest for two months. A gym membership that comes with four free tanning sessions. A tri-fold flyer from a car dealership promising a car wash when you come in for a test drive.

Buy two pizzas, get one free.

There's also a brochure from Elections Canada on how to vote. Which might be useful if there was anyone on the ballot worth the effort.

I carry the remains of a perfectly good tree directly to the garbage.

Outside, the crows have gathered in the branches on the far side of the graveyard. They sit in a row, eyes on the old school, as though they've been hired to keep the place under surveillance.

The Locken Group. They could afford a crow reconnaissance.

Not that crows would have taken the job.

One of the crows in the tree begins bobbing its head, shuffling from side to side, and caw-cawing out a song. One by one, the other crows join in, and together they form a conga line of dancing, singing birds.

I head upstairs to my bedroom. As I've gotten older, I've discovered that I need naps, and now that I have time to take a nap, I do. I lie on the bed, stuff one of the pillows under my stomach, and wrap myself up in the quilt.

Outside, the crows are still singing and dancing. I want to believe that they're trying to cheer me up, but they're probably just excited by what they can see on the horizon.

I DON'T REMEMBER going to sleep, and now it's late afternoon. How did that happen?

I sit up. The crows have disappeared, and the tree is bare. The cat is nowhere to be seen. At some point, I'll have to conjure up a meal. Not that I'm hungry right now, but Oliver Flood's visit has made me restless and apprehensive.

Given my history with the Locken Group, there is only one thing that they could want.

THE SCHOOL HAS its own graveyard. Seventy-seven graves. Each marked with a wood cross. Originally, the crosses were white, but now the wood is grey and weathered, the graves all but forgotten.

Still, at the end of the day, when the shadows stretch out and bring the land into sharp relief, you can see the neat rows of indentations hammered into the earth.

I put on my boots, my jacket, my oilskin hat, grab my chisels. I've been pulling up the wood crosses and replacing them with limestone slabs that I pry out of the dry riverbed in the belief that the children buried here deserve better than having their graves marked with the talisman of the cult that killed them.

I dig up a stone, carry it to the graveyard, bury it flush with the ground. And chisel the child's name into the rock. None of the crosses have names, but Father Hinch kept excellent records, went so far as to create a hand-drawn map of the cemetery with each grave noted.

I think of my efforts as a reconciliation project, even though I don't believe in reconciliation any more than I believe in religion.

Mind you, removing the crosses has caused no small amount of alarm and anger. There have been complaints of sacrilege and disrespect, talk of indictments and hangings.

Each time I pull up a cross, I set it to one side in a pile. And when I have enough crosses, I plan to burn them.

When I first started, I wasn't very good with the chisels. But I've gotten better. And quicker. Even so, I've only replaced about a dozen crosses, and now Maribelle Wegman wants to save the rest, has gone so far as to create an ad hoc group to have the crosses and the graveyard declared a heritage site.

She also chairs the committee that is trying to get the reserve moved. Another place. Not here.

TODAY, I'M FINISHING UP Agnes Makwa's name, trying to get the legs on the *W* the same length. My hands have finally gotten used to the work, the blisters all but healed. The trick is to keep the tools sharp, but that's the trick to most everything.

I lean in to blow the dust off the stone, and that's when I see the girl. And in a blink, Agnes Makwa stands in the middle of the graveyard among the crosses. In a blink, I see the child who is buried here.

It's not the first time this has happened. Not the first time my imagination has stretched reality.

But it still brings me up short, and I have to sit back, wait for the moment to pass.

Enough for today.

I gather my tools. The late sun comes in low and bright. It flares off the windows of the old school and sets fire to the crosses. And, as I start back, I imagine I'm walking into an inferno.

5

Travel Night at the Piggy is a monthly event that tries to make up for the disparity between those who can afford to explore the world and those who cannot.

In the time that Florence has been hosting the event, neither Bob Loomis nor Maribelle Wegman has ever attended. Swannie Gagnon is a regular. Iku Takahashi is not. Dino Kiazzie and his wife, Giulia, never miss a tour. They sit at the back, in the darkest part of the room, with their Chianti concealed in a Save the Planet reusable water bottle.

Maidie Matthews, who owns the hardware store on the plaza, shows up depending on the evening's destination. Maidie likes France and Italy, dislikes Mexico and Peru. Likes Norway and Scotland, but wouldn't be caught dead in India or Africa.

The Three Bears always come early to help set up the chairs. Louis Bear, his daughter, Enola, and his nephew Wapi make sure that Nutty Moosonee and Ada Stillday have seats in the front row. So Nutty can see the screen without having to squint.

I STAND OUTSIDE in the shadows of the cedar grove and watch everyone file into the café. This is as close as I need to get. From here, I can see the people and the video through the window. I've been to Venice any number of times, so I know all about the Piazza San Marco and the Grand Canal, about the Doge's Palace and the Rialto Bridge, about the Basilica di Santa Maria della Salute and Chiesa di Santa Maria Assunta.

Venice is one of my favourite cities. To be sure, the tourists who invade it each summer and the ocean liners that steam through the lagoon are a problem. But Venice is also one of a handful of cities in the world where cars are not allowed, where you can escape the blaring of horns and the stink of exhaust and walk the streets in peace and quiet and safety.

Of course, there's the water.

The last time I was in Venice, the *acqua alta* had come hard and fast, the high water trapping a group of girls on the wrong side of the piazza. But as little is denied to youth, the young women simply took off their shoes, lifted their dresses up their thighs, and splashed barefoot through the flood to the opposite shore, laughing, delighted with their fearlessness and derring-do.

Tonight, the video on Venice has a short segment on MOSE, an unfinished $6.5-billion seawall that is supposed to protect the city from high tides. Sadly, the project is a giant scam. The wall remains unfinished and will, in all probability, never be put into service. However, in terms of enriching politicians, criminals, and construction companies, it has been an unmitigated success.

None of which will help Venice. The Adriatic will come. The city will sink. The patterns are clear. All you have to do is look.

I stay in the trees long enough to watch the tourists in the video stumble along on the raised platforms that the city erects in front of Saint Mark's Basilica each time the sea tides up and floods the piazza.

There is a moment when I'm tempted to slip into the Piggy and join the community. But instead, I stay in the trees and wait for the moment to pass.

Then I turn back to town.

THE SQUARE IS DESERTED, the bandstand empty. The Neighbours are gone, as are the motorcycles in front of the Bent Nail. But they'll be back. They have nowhere else to go.

I sit on one of the benches that faces the Plaza Hotel and try to guess in which room Mayor Bob and the widow Wegman are discussing the ins and outs of historical preservation. They would have a room at the back, overlooking the alley. They would not be concerned with the view.

The woman who steps out the front door of the hotel is elegant and completely out of place in Gleaming. She is quickly joined by two men who take up positions behind her and on either side.

The hunting dogs.

The woman stands in the night, looks into the sky to make sure that the stars are still there.

I look as well.

The door to the hotel opens, and a third man comes out.

Oliver Flood. He stands beside the woman, inside the perimeter created by the two men, and says something that makes her smile.

She turns back to the hotel, and Flood follows. Spot and Rover stay put. They stand on either side of the front door like stone lions guarding the approach to a drawbridge over a moat.

I check the sky once more to make sure nothing has gone missing.

"Hey, you missed the show."

The Three Bears.

"Another successful Travel Night," says Enola. "Florence really knows her history stuff."

"The video was pretty good," says Louis. "Wouldn't mind going. If we could afford it."

"Way things are," says Enola, "we can hardly afford to go home."

"Home," says Wapi.

Louis Bear is the current chief of the Cradle River reserve. His daughter works in the band office. Wapi is Louis's brother's son.

Enola is smiling. "I liked it when everything flooded, and you had to wade through the water with plastic bags on your feet."

"Bags," says Wapi.

Wapi holds up his tablet. It's covered with stickers. The plastic case is falling apart. There's a crack in one corner of the screen.

"Feet," says Wapi.

Louis's brother Sam and Sam's wife, Angie, were killed in a car accident. Wapi survived.

"Beats getting your shoes wet," says Louis.

The three of them stand in front of me and block my view of the hotel.

"We're going to South Island, New Zealand, next," says Louis. "Always wanted to go there."

"New Zealand's got Maoris," says Enola. "Sort of like Indians, only tougher."

"Hey," says Louis, "I'm tough."

"Then how come I can beat you up."

Enola puts her shoulder into her father with about as much effect as if she had tried to push a large mountain up a hill.

"You ever been to Venice?" asks Louis.

Both Enola and Wapi have a go at Louis. Enola takes him from behind. Wapi attacks his legs. With no better result.

"Or New Zealand?"

"Jeremiah doesn't go anywhere." Enola bends over, her hands on her knees. "He just hides out in that old school."

"School," says Wapi.

"I think Mr. Camp is lucky." Louis ruffles his nephew's hair. "Having a place to himself. Somewhere peaceful and quiet."

"Travel broadens the mind," says Enola. "Travel makes us more tolerant of difference."

This is a popular axiom that has never been proven. If you were to correlate the amount of travel we do with the level of intolerance manifested in our politics and social interaction, you might come to the opposite conclusion.

"Wapi needs a new tablet," says Enola. "He lives on the internet."

"Tablet," says Wapi.

"I don't know about that internet," says Louis. "Some of the stuff you see."

"You mean like that movie star who made a candle that smells like her—"

"Enola!"

"Come on, Dad. That's old news. No big deal."

"No big deal." Wapi swipes a finger across the screen. One of the corners of the tablet is dented.

Louis takes off his Blue Jays cap and puts it on Wapi's head. "Kids."

"Parents," says Enola.

Louis grabs Enola in a bear hug. "Guess the internet is like that genie. Once it gets out, there's no way to put it back in the bottle."

Louis has been around long enough to know better. There is no genie. There is no bottle. It's just one of the excuses we use to explain the consequences of expediencies and bad decisions.

Enola breaks away from her father. "Did you know that Mr. Camp doesn't have a computer?"

"Good for him."

"And he doesn't have a cellphone."

"Wish to hell I didn't have one," says Louis.

"Dinosaurs," says Enola.

"Dinosaurs," says Wapi.

"Come on," says Louis, "we need to check the generators before we call it a night."

"Check generator," says Wapi.

Louis lumbers out across the plaza towards the reserve, Wapi hard on his heels. Enola hangs back for a moment, hugging herself against the evening chill.

"Don't think I could live the way you do."

I stay on the bench, watch Enola cut through the grass and catch up with her father and her cousin, wait to see if the plaza woman will appear again.

When she doesn't, I get to my feet and make my way to the hotel.

O liver Flood is waiting for me in the lobby.

"You're late."

Rover and Spot swing in behind, tighten up against me. Flood leads the way to the elevator.

"Didn't your parents teach you to be punctual?"

The elevator in the Plaza Hotel is the original mechanism. As such, it is both ornate and cramped. If there's a weight limit, then we have certainly exceeded it.

"They don't make them like this anymore," says Flood. "Thank god."

We get off at the top floor. Halfway down the corridor, Rover stops me and Spot pats me down. He is not at all gentle but stops short of breaking bones. As it is, I'll only have bruises.

"I'm told," says Flood, "that Elvis stayed here."

Elvis never stayed at the Plaza. But a few years back, the local Rotary Club organized an Elvis-impersonator night to kick off the hockey season and to raise money for a dialysis machine.

Elvis on ice.

That night, twenty-seven Elvises, of varying skill levels, showed up at the local rink. One guy slipped on the ice and wrecked a knee. Another sprained a wrist.

The best of the Elvises, a nineteen-year-old from Saskatoon, won five hundred dollars and a night on the top floor of the Plaza. The *Gleaming Advertiser* declared the event a "stunning success."

And it was never repeated.

Flood stops in front of a door, holds the card key against the sensor, and waits for the light to turn green. Then in we go, leaving Spot and Rover to guard the empty hallway.

The suite is turn-of-the-century extravagant. High ceilings, heavy drapes, parquet floors, uncomfortable furniture. There is a long table against one wall with silver serving trays and an ornate coffee urn.

Flood goes to the connecting door. Knocks and waits, stands there like a statue, eternally patient.

And then the door opens.

The woman is the same woman I saw earlier. She's older than I had supposed. Late-thirties. Honey blonde. Blue eyes. Slender. No makeup. Casually dressed. Black slacks and a silver blouse.

"Jeremiah Camp."

She doesn't bother shaking hands, goes directly to one of the wingback chairs and sits. I do the same. Flood brings her a cup of coffee. I wait for him to bring me a cup as well.

"You knew my father."

Ash Locken. Heir apparent to the Locken fortune. Charter member of the Three Comma Club.

"With his death, responsibility for the Realm has fallen to me." Locken pauses, in case I want to offer my condolences. "Transitions

41

are never seamless," she says, "and several matters have come to light that need explanation and resolution."

I get out of the chair and wander over to the trays. Maple soy-glazed salmon. Wild rice with dried cranberries and pecans. Yamashita spinach. An avocado caprese salad with several dressing options.

"And in this regard, I wish to engage your skills."

By the time I've worked my way past the appetizers and the entrees to the chocolates and the fresh strawberries, I discover I'm no longer hungry. I leave my plate on the table, help myself to a cup of coffee, and go back to the chair.

"You worked for my father for almost thirty years." Locken tilts her head, as though this is a question. "And then you quit. Quite suddenly."

Flood slips into the adjoining room and disappears.

"My father thought highly of you, Forecaster. In particular, of your ability to predict the future."

I can't predict the future. Thomas Locken knew that. Ash Locken knows it as well.

"Of course, no one can predict the future," she continues. "But you have a unique talent. For seeing patterns."

Flood reappears, a manila envelope in his hand.

"When I went through my father's things, I discovered a set of files that he had kept separate from everything else. Nothing out of the ordinary, really. Special projects he was working on. Creative financial arrangements with other corporations, politicians. Countries. Most of it not unexpected."

Locken nods. Flood hands me the envelope.

"And then there was this."

Inside the envelope is a single sheet of paper.

"This was in a file by itself," says Locken.

On the sheet is a list of twelve names, each in a large, bold font. Easy to read. Double-spaced. At the bottom of the page is a hand-written note.

"I'm sure you recognize everyone."

I do. Thomas Locken and eleven other of the richest and most powerful individuals in the world.

"In fact," she says, "I believe you created this particular list."

Locken goes to the table and helps herself to a chocolate and two strawberries. "And given recent events, I'm sure you might expect that I would be curious."

I'm not curious. I'm bored. I stand up slowly, so as not to startle Flood, and move towards the door.

Flood moves quickly to intercept me.

Locken stays him with a gesture.

"You're right, Forecaster," she says. "It is late." The chocolate and the strawberries on her plate are untouched. "There's no rush. We can finish this conversation later."

I wait for the rhetorical turn, for the veiled threat to make an appearance. Instead, Locken walks back to the adjoining door, pauses at the threshold.

"It's been a pleasure," she says.

I can get home by myself, but Flood insists that Rover and Spot see me safely back to the school. Spot walks ahead on point, while Rover protects me from adulterous mayors and hairy bakers.

They take me as far as the porch. I don't thank them or say good-bye, don't invite them in for coffee and cookies, and so far as I can tell, this does not hurt our relationship.

A full moon hangs over the graveyard and lights the crosses. There is symbolism here if you believe in that sort of thing.

I don't.

In the moonlight, along the river, I can see the silhouettes of crows hunkered down in the trees. I know that they have not gathered here for my benefit, are not concerned about my safe return.

But they are a comforting sight, nonetheless.

7

Morning comes early and bright as a pearl, and all of yesterday is forgiven.

The simple life. The quiet life. The unattached life. The life that never quite works out that way.

Breakfast. Walk into town. Brownie. Coffee. Listen to Florence read the news. Go out to the edge of the escarpment and watch the river plunge over the edge of the world. Return in time for lunch and a nap. Replace another cross or two in the graveyard. Chisel a stone. Dinner and bed.

Repeat.

Today I'm feeling hopeful. For no discernable reason. Perhaps I'll nod to Iku Takahashi, consider her binoculars. I might even pet Koala. Pick up a *gâteau basque* along with the brownie and surprise Swannie. Try to explain to Florence what I used to do for a living.

Buy a television.

The cat is waiting for me when I get to the kitchen. She is sitting on the table, next to a pile of cat puke.

Okay. Reality restored.

I clean up the mess, pad my way upstairs, and get into the shower. Under the hot water, I work on the problem that has found me.

Oliver Flood.

Ash Locken.

Thomas Locken and the list of names.

I stay there until the water begins to turn, and I'm forced into the cool air and a cold towel. As soon as I step out of the shower, the cat appears, goes immediately to the drain, begins licking at the standing water.

I'm not sure that lapping up grey water and citrus-scented shampoo is a good idea, and I consider saying something.

But then she did puke on the table.

THE RIVER PATH is busy. I don't see Takahashi and her pooch, but I have to dodge bicycles and step out of the way of joggers, who pound by me on their way to plantar fasciitis, bone spurs, and compression fractures.

Several couples are dressed in matching running outfits. A dress code for exercise seems excessive, but exercise is, after all, big business. Why not look good while you sweat?

The bakery is crowded, the line snaking out the door. Swannie is behind the pastry display, stuffing sugary treats into boxes and bags. I check to see if there are any brownies left.

"Jerry."

Mayor Bob and his wife. Cathy or Taffy. A thick woman. Bottle blonde, rumoured to have had major renovations.

"You've met my wife, Paula," he says.

I nod. Up ahead, someone has taken three of the brownies. Now there are only five left.

"I'm going to make you an offer," says Loomis, trying to channel Vito Corleone, "that you can't refuse."

"Make sure he doesn't cheat you," says Paula.

I check the display case. Now there are only three.

The mayor puts his arm around his wife. "Don't know why you insist we come here," he whispers. "Timmy's has a better selection and better prices."

In addition to the real estate company, Mayor Bob also owns the two Tim Hortons in town.

"Sure," says Paula. "If you want frozen lumps of lard."

"Canadian company," says Bob. "Buy local."

"Company hasn't been Canadian since 1995," says Paula.

"You see those wasps." Bob pokes a finger at a trio of yellow jackets crawling across the eclairs. "That doesn't happen at a Timmy's."

"Woman makes the best pastries around." Paula points her chin at Swannie. "But I wish to hell she'd shave her underarms."

By the time I get in the door, there are only two brownies left, and I have to use all of my mental abilities to dissuade the people in front of me from taking them.

"Ha," says Swannie when I finally get to the register. "You see? Today the brownies, they are gone. Poof."

There's one left, hiding at the end of the tray. I point it out.

Swannie frowns and puts her hands on her hips. "Such the lucky one," she says, and drops the last brownie into a bag. "Today, you must buy the lottery."

Mayor Bob stops me at the door. "Come by the office," he says. "Take a look at the model. Give us a chance to talk about the future."

THE SUN IS SHINING brightly, and for the first time in a long while, the air is warm. As I pass by the Plaza Hotel, I glance in the window of the dining room, and there she is.

Ash Locken.

She sits at a table, alone. No Oliver Flood. No Spot. No Rover. Today, Locken is wearing a print dress with a dark jacket. It is probably a trick of light through glass, but she looks younger now than she did the night before.

And softer.

A pleasant mouth. Impatient eyes. Long, elegant fingers that glow in the muted light of the restaurant.

Standing on the sidewalk looking in at Locken, I sense something familiar. Something shared. An echo in the body.

If I wait long enough, perhaps what it is will come to me.

Behind me, there's a low sound, and when I turn, I see Roman Moosonee. He's in the bandstand. With his horn. He's playing "Smile." Softly. A step lower than normal, the notes on the bottom sounding like moans. He sways from side to side, as though he's trying to find a balance.

I come back to the window, but now Locken is gone, the table empty, the chair pushed back, the napkin dropped on the plate as casually as a child might drop a toy on the floor.

Sadness. That's what it was. The echo. A deep, unyielding sadness.

Roman leans against the railing, tips the horn up to the open sky.

The music spills out into the sunshine like warm rain thrown into the air. I stand on the sidewalk and listen as he chases the song through a landscape of silences and long notes before turning effortlessly and finding his way home.

THE PIGGY IS BUSY. The Three Bears are at the back table. Enola and Wapi are looking at something on Wapi's tablet. Nutty Moosonee and Ada Stillday are huddled together by the window.

"You're late," Florence calls out as I come in the door. "That better be my brownie."

I try to look contrite.

"When my sisters and me did something we weren't supposed to do," says Florence, "we'd put on that same face."

I give remorseful a try.

"My father would line us up and ask who was responsible. Course we kept our mouths shut. He'd pace back and forth, hoping to wear us down."

I take the brownie out of the bag. So Florence can see that no crime has been committed.

"'Monuments of Injured Innocence.'" Florence shakes her head so her cheeks flop about, and she lowers her voice. "My father had a flair for the dramatic. 'Monuments of Injured Innocence.'"

After Reggie died, everyone thought that Florence would stop teaching and carry on with the restaurant. Breakfast, lunch. Breakfast, lunch. Just as before. She had helped out at the Piggy on weekends, so she knew the recipes, knew the business.

But that's not what happened.

LOUIS TAPS THE TABLE with his spoon. "I'm telling you," he says, "another twenty-five years of global warming, and Venice won't be there."

"Global warming," says Wapi.

"Along with Key West, Bangladesh, the Seychelles, Tonga, and the Maldives." Louis ticks each place off on his fingers. "As well as large parts of Miami, Vancouver, New Orleans, and Halifax."

"Global warming," says Wapi.

"Course," says Louis, "there are still a lot of people who don't believe in global warming."

What happened was Florence closed the Piggy. The restaurant was Reggie's dream, she told everyone, not hers. There was speculation that she would sell the place and move away. But that's not what happened either.

"Global warming doesn't care if you believe in it or not." Enola slaps Wapi's shoulder. "Right, little bear?"

"Global warming," says Wapi.

Louis holds his cup up in a toast. "We have met the enemy, and he is us."

I stand at the counter and cut the brownie in half. Florence waits for the machine to get back up to temperature.

"News, blues, and comfortable shoes," she says, her voice filling the room. "In Barcelona, peaceful demonstrations have turned into running battles with the police as activists continue to press for Catalan independence."

"You're too slow for a running battle," Enola tells her father. "Best you could manage is a walking skirmish."

"I can move when I need to move."

Florence doesn't break stride. "In California, a scientist has suggested that the arsenic-resistant bacteria and nematodes at Mono Lake may be from outer space."

"What I hear," says Louis, "most of California is from outer space."

"Outer space," says Wapi.

"While in Toronto, the body of Amanda Cho was found in her suite at the Four Seasons."

Florence wipes the milk residue off the steam wand.

"Cho was the head of the Phoenix and Dagon Consortium. According to her publicist, she was in Toronto on a shopping trip. Foul play is not suspected."

I stand at the counter and wait for my macchiato.

"Here at home," says Florence, "Indian Affairs has agreed to deal with the mould problem in the trailers."

"About time," Ada pipes up from the back. "Maybe they'll actually do something for a change."

"That's the spirit," says Nutty. "Little optimism never hurt nothing."

Florence slaps the deck of cards on the counter next to my elbow. "You think good thoughts," she says, "you get a good card."

I shuffle the deck and turn over the Nine of Cups. Happiness.

"If I were you," says Florence, "I'd consider picking another card."

AFTER REGGIE DIED and the Piggy closed, Florence took early retirement from her job at the high school and moved into the back of the restaurant.

To hide away from the world, to live in memories of the past.

But Nutty and Ada were having none of that. They had gotten used to the good times at the Piggy, so in spite of the sign in the window saying the restaurant was closed, the two of them would arrive each morning with the expectation that, if they couldn't get fed, they could at least get coffee.

Each day Florence would shoo them away, and each morning they would return, until finally she let them in and cranked up the espresso machine. And while she had no interest in restarting the restaurant, she discovered that she did enjoy morning coffee in the company of friends.

I FINISH MY COFFEE and eat my share of the brownie, while Enola and Louis and Wapi debate alien nematodes and global warming. Florence joins Nutty and Ada.

I stand at the edge of the conversations and work through the new patterns that have appeared. Thomas Locken. The arrival of his daughter. Fabrice Gloor. Amanda Cho. The list.

And then I follow the shadows to the door and slip out into the day.

Matthews Hardware is an institution in Gleaming.

The business was started by Old Man Matthews, who had emigrated to Canada from Scotland. Old Man wasn't his first name, but that's what everyone in town called him, and if he did have a first name, it got lost somewhere along the way.

According to Nutty, who knows these things, Old Man Matthews's oldest son, Vincent, took over from his father. Vincent's boy Ian was next in line, but Ian decided he had better prospects raising farmed salmon in British Columbia than selling hammers and garden hoses in Gleaming.

And so, Matthews Hardware passed from Vincent to his daughter.

MAIDIE MATTHEWS is stacking twenty-pound bags of sheep manure in a pile on the sidewalk in front of the store.

"End of next week, there won't be a bag left," she tells me.

Dino Kiazzie calls Maidie "Kri-Kri," because, he says, she reminds him of the feral goats on Crete.

"So, if you want a sack of the good shit, you better get it now."

According to Dino, kri-kris are all bone and horns, with no soft spots to pet and a constant need to bang heads.

"Just don't come crying to me when it's all gone."

I'm not in the market for manure, good or otherwise. What I need is a pry bar for wresting the limestone slabs out of the old riverbed and a cart of some sort to get them back to the school. I've been carrying the stones one at a time and have decided that this is neither smart nor efficient.

"How those chisels working out?"

I find a cart that looks like a kid's wagon with steel mesh sides and a lever that allows you to dump the load.

"That's the new and improved Little Elephant Garden Wagon."

I spend several minutes pushing the cart back, pulling it forward, working the lever.

"Truth be told, it ain't all that new, and the biggest improvement is in the price."

I buy a pair of leather gloves as well.

"Your cousin wandered by," said Maidie. "Him and his horn. Looked like he'd spent the night in a sack of rats."

I put the gloves in my new garden cart.

"And the Lock-Mould came in. Ten cartons of the stuff."

I'm not sure what Maidie is talking about, so I wait.

"For the mould in the trailers." Maidie shakes her head. "Government folks are supposed to come in the next week or so to show everyone how to use the stuff. Suspect they'll make a bunch of speeches, shake a bunch of hands, take a bunch of pictures, get all weepy about reconciliation."

I wait some more.

"Looks a whole lot like whipped cream, but you take one sniff and you won't be putting it on your pumpkin pie anytime soon."

I debate between a Stanley Wonder Bar and a longer demolition bar and decide on the shorter of the two. I pay cash and get the five-percent discount.

"You be sure about that wagon," Maidie cautions me. "I don't take returns."

I PULL THE CART back to the school. I'm hungry, but I take my time, pretend I'm walking a large dog.

"Hello," I could say to Iku Takahashi, if I happen to run into her on the trail, "this is Brutus." Or Daisy. Or Max. Or Lucy. Maybe my dog and Koala could be friends. Go on walks together. Chase each other around trees.

Buddy and Koala.

Koala and Chester.

By the time I get to the turnoff for Broken Bough Falls, I'm smiling and humming the tune about who let the dogs out. I even throw in a couple of dance steps. I'm sure I look like an idiot, and I'm glad the crows aren't around to see me.

WHEN I LEFT THE CITY, I decided I would stop talking. Completely. That was easy enough. I also decided to stop paying attention to what was happening in the world.

That was harder.

At the Locken Group, I was paid to collect the flotsam and jetsam of humanity. Collect it. Sort it. Process it. And finally, to squeeze out patterns from the distillate.

A great many people are fond of saying that information is power. It's not.

Thomas Locken knew that information by itself was worthless, that the only value was in the patterns that information revealed. Understanding those patterns, being able to predict how and where they would form and the effect they would have, that was power.

Seeing the patterns. Recognizing their significance. Forecasting. That was my job.

THE KITCHEN IS EMPTY. No cat. No Oliver Flood hiding in the cupboard. No Roman Moosonee and his horn lurking under the stairs. Today, lunch will be a hard-boiled egg, Swiss cheese, sliced tomatoes, cottage cheese, and a piece of toast. This is my lunch every day. What it lacks in variety, it makes up for in speed and nutrition.

Repetition is the rule for breakfast as well. Quinoa with a sprinkling of Parmesan and a large spoonful of cottage cheese.

Dinner, on the other hand, is a rotating medley of foods that can be cooked and refrigerated in bulk. Chili, stew, any number of casseroles, meat loaf, and soup. Cook once. Eat the same thing for the rest of the week.

The face of a routine.

There are a number of negatives associated with routines. They have the annoying habit of crashing on the unpredictability of life.

On the other hand, they provide structure and can take some of the stress out of everyday living.

My meal routines exist because I don't mind eating the same thing every day. They exist because I am determined to simplify my life. And they exist because I'm lazy.

I HAVE JUST SHELLED the egg and arranged the tomato wedges on the plate when I see the woman in the graveyard.

Ash Locken.

There's no reason for her to be there, among the crosses and the stones, but there she is.

I put the bread in the toaster and open the cottage cheese. If she wants to wander the graves, then she can wander the graves. Her presence is no reason for me to interrupt my lunch.

The cat appears out of nowhere, jumps up on the counter, sits on the window ledge so she can watch whatever drama might unfold. The list of names is on the kitchen table. I don't need to look at it, but I do anyway.

I FINISH MY LUNCH, rinse the dish and my fork, and put them away. I get into my work clothes, grab the hammer and the chisels, the new pry bar. Ready for a pleasant day of manual labour in the crisp spring air.

I go to the window. The graveyard is empty now. Locken has moved on, and it's safe to come out of the school.

Except it's not.

Ash Locken is waiting for me. She's standing by the corner of the building, next to my Little Elephant Garden Wagon.

"I had a wagon when I was a kid," she says, "but mine was pulled by a pony."

I put my tools in the wagon, pull on my gloves.

"I decided to go for a walk, and I wound up here." Locken looks around as though she's just discovered where she is. "What are the odds?"

I pull my wagon through the graveyard. Locken follows me.

"At the hotel this morning, you were staring at me through the window." Locken steps around a cross, looks down at one of the stones. "Do you stare at many women?"

Now that I have the pry bar and the wagon, I figure that I can move four or five stones at a time.

"Any thoughts?" she asks. "About last night?"

It is not a long walk to the dry riverbed, but it's across uneven ground. Locken is wearing shoes with spool heels, and they twist under her feet. There is the chance that she will tire of following me and leave.

But she doesn't.

"I'm not going anywhere, so we might as well talk."

I look around for the crows, but they are nowhere to be seen. That figures. First sign of trouble and they disappear.

"What did you make of the note at the bottom of the list?" she says. "Handwritten. Rather cryptic, don't you think?"

I bring the wagon to the middle of the riverbed, get down on my knees, and begin working on a stone buried in the silt.

"'We Exist at the Sufferance of Others.'" Locken flashes a smile. "Almost biblical."

I use the pry bar. The first stone comes up easily. I lift it into the wagon and go to work on a second.

"Amanda Cho." Locken lets the name hang in the air. "Fabrice Gloor."

The hard part is the chiselling. That will take much longer. On the other hand, the bonfire of the crosses will be satisfying.

"But I can see you're busy." Locken stands, smooths her dress. "And we're just getting to know each other."

Here, the dry riverbed is shallow, the bank not particularly high. Locken takes the slope at an angle, scales it easily.

"Let's do this again, soon."

I follow her retreat until she clears the graveyard and the crosses.

And then I go back to the digging.

9

I don't notice that the crows have returned until I put a large stone into the Little Elephant and discover that one of the birds has shit on my wagon. They're in a large cottonwood, sitting together in a row on a bare branch, and they all look guilty.

I clean the crow poop off my wagon with a handkerchief. My guess is that the culprit is Slick, and I'm willing to make allowances for youthful exuberance.

So long as it doesn't happen again.

I dig up three more stones, load them into the wagon, and head back to the graveyard.

FATHER EDWARD HINCH.

From all reports, a decent sort. Pious, idealistic, a young man who truly believed in the word of god and his omnipresence in the world, who trusted, without reservation, the church's claim as god's agent on earth.

"Guy was enthusiastic," Nutty told me. "Had a thing for religious stuff."

Father Hinch was a collector. Of holy relics. All the money he could scrape together went to the purchase of religious artifacts.

"Bought a couple pieces of that cross. Had a stone from some famous mountain and a tooth from one of the saints."

Buying or selling holy relics is simony, and it's a sin. But according to Nutty, Hinch didn't buy these things for his own edification. The money he spent was a donation in an ongoing effort to rescue spiritual artifacts from a temporal and skeptical world.

"Used to put all this stuff out on a table when he said Mass, so everyone could share in his happiness."

The problem was, Hinch didn't have the money to purchase chewing gum let alone a strand of the Virgin Mary's hair.

"Robbed Peter to pay Paul," said Nutty. "Took money from the school budget, when he should have been buying food and clothing and medical supplies for the kids."

Then came the winter of 1944.

THE CROSS THAT MARKS Jacob Potts's grave is rotted, and it breaks off when I try to pull it out. When this happens, I take the time to dig up the rest of the stake. I could ignore it, but I would know that the end of the stick is still in the ground, like a knife in a wound.

I should have brought my shovel with me. I try to dig the rest of the stake out with my hands, but it's buried too deep, and the ground is still hard. I drop the stone next to the hole as a reminder of what I need to do.

Then I move on to the next cross.

THE STORM OF 1944 started on December 12 and the snow didn't stop for four days. By the time the blizzard passed, Gleaming, the reserve, and the rest of the province were entombed under a mountain of snow.

Food at the school was scarce, warm clothing non-existent, and the children began to sicken. Father Hinch's answer to malnourishment and disease was to pray. He said Mass twice a day, had the children gather around his collection of relics for the protection he was sure they would provide. At one point, to keep the children's spirits up, he had everyone march around the chapel past the stations of the cross as he recited the rosary.

It wasn't until the snow abated and the weather cleared that anyone in the town or on the reserve knew that something was wrong.

Five children died during that snowstorm. Another four died within the following month.

Father Hinch was adamant that the situation could have been far worse had it not been for the relics and the power they contained, and that the children who had died had died in a state of grace.

By the end of the second month after the storm, the death toll had reached fourteen.

I PULL UP THE CROSS for Mary Rogers and the one for Susan Wabano. Both come out cleanly. I put the stones in place, digging around them, inlaying them into the earth, so that anyone who comes into the graveyard won't be stubbing their toes on the dead.

I wait for Mary and Susan to appear. But they don't.

TODAY, I DECIDE I will just deal with the gathering and the place-ment of stones, will leave the chiselling for another day. I make three more trips to the riverbed and bring back four stones each trip.

Twelve stones. One for each of the apostles, if I'm looking for religious symbolism. Or one for each month in the year, if I'm not.

Twelve crosses. Plus the ten already in the pile. More than enough for a handsome fire.

I'm thinking about the graves and the crosses when I see Roman step into the cemetery.

THERE WAS AN INQUIRY of course. The band pressed the diocese to have Hinch removed, citing the embezzlement and his incompe-tence in providing the necessities of life. But Hinch had stood firm. The actions taken, he argued, had been the correct ones, the use of the school budget justified, the purchase of sacred artifacts necessary for the spiritual health of the children.

The deaths, god's will.

Hinch stayed on for another twenty-one years, buying more trin-kets and charms, dispensing nostrums, tending the graveyard.

ROMAN IS CLEAR-EYED and shaven, his clothes clean, his hair combed. He smiles at me as though we're old friends.

"Cuz," he says. "You want some help?"

I flip a stone into place and begin the process of setting it into the ground.

"Nutty said you've been digging up shit." Roman turns and looks at the waiting pile of tinder. "Cool."

Roman and his cornet have been onstage with the likes of Neil Young, A Tribe Called Red, Nickelback, and Shania Twain. He's played at the Spotted Cat in New Orleans, Bimhuis in Amsterdam, the Rex in Toronto, and Ronnie Scott's jazz club in London.

"You like jazz, cuz?"

But when he's not playing, he generally winds up in trouble. One year, during the Remembrance Day celebration in the plaza, Roman showed up with the lyrics of an Edwin Starr song stencilled on a T-shirt and sporting a giant white poppy stuck to the side of a World War II combat helmet.

"Going to be at the Nail."

"War, what is it good for?" was on the front of the T-shirt. "Absolutely nothing" was on the back. Roman had stood at the edge of the crowd and played "Last Post" while the mayor was trying to read a speech about patriotism, valour, and sacrifice.

"Just got to get the lips back in shape." Roman kicks at the ground.

None of the people in the plaza that Remembrance Day would have admitted that they liked killing. All they wanted was to celebrate the traditions and pageantries of war, the bloodless rituals of flags and songs, without being reminded of the inherent slaughter.

"Jail don't help with the embouchure."

It was an illusion, of course. War was about killing, no matter how you dressed it up, and Roman, with his black T-shirt and white poppy, had called the question. And for that, the good folks of Gleaming did not forgive him.

Before the week was out, his trailer was vandalized, the tires on his pickup slashed.

"Let me know when you put the torch to the crosses." Roman turns towards the reserve. "That's something I'd like to see."

I FINISH SETTING the stones and call it a day. The bonfire can wait. The crosses aren't going anywhere, and I still have a great many left to remove.

The crows sit quietly in the tree, pretending that they know what is coming next. It's a trick they've learned over the years, and they're good at it.

I sit in the quiet of the graveyard, my back braced against the wagon. All around me, I can feel the children who are buried in this place, and I wonder if they know I'm here.

The Locken Group. Somehow, I thought I had escaped.

Ash Locken and the list. Somehow, I thought I was safe.

The crows come alive and begin squawking with delight. They're right. I should have known better.

10

For the rest of the week, life is a slow, quiet routine.

I get out of bed, feed the cat, pick up the brownie, listen to Florence and the news over coffee.

Even the weather has decided to co-operate, and I'm able to spend each afternoon in the graveyard, chiselling names into river stones. I pull up more crosses and put them on the pile, which is substantial now and should make for a remarkable blaze when the time comes.

But that is not today.

Today, the people from Indian Affairs are due to arrive on the reserve to meet with band and council. Nutty has asked me to be there. I don't want to go, but there's a good chance the crows will show up.

Maybe Slick will shit on the minister's car.

I wouldn't want to miss that.

I TAKE A SHOWER, shave, brush my teeth, put on a white shirt that I've kept from my days at Locken. The cat sits next to the toilet and watches me. I don't know if cats can smile or if they even have a sense of humour. I suspect that they're all sarcasm and mockery, and that this one is having a good time at my expense.

I avoid looking in the mirror. I have no interest in seeing what the cat sees.

I put on a light jacket and my oilskin hat. I'm not happy about leaving the school, not pleased with the prospect of standing around exposed, not excited by the certainty of pork-barrel speeches and fast-food ceremonies.

The acknowledgement that we're on fill-in-the-blank Nation's territory.

The assurance that the government has our best interests at heart.

The suggestion that things are not as bleak as they seem.

The promise that tomorrow will be better.

I TAKE MY TIME, walk around the long way, come into the council grounds at an angle. Nutty and Ada sit on folding chairs in the shade of the cedars. Florence stands behind them, her face flat, her lips set. Roman is at the big drum, along with Jake Somosi, Gordon James, and Benjamin Hunt. They sit there, drumsticks at the ready, in case a cavalry troop shows up unexpectedly.

The speeches are in full swing. The deputy minister, a young woman in a beaded leather jacket, is apologizing for the minister's absence, citing pressing duties in Ottawa and assuring everyone that this is, in no way, an indication of the importance the government places on the matter, and that when she speaks, she speaks for the minister. She stands tall at the podium, an RCMP officer in red serge at each elbow.

"Great," says Ada. "The big cheese don't bother to show up, so we get the Minister of the Moment and the Property Police."

"The Mounties look impressive," says Nutty.

"Yeah," says Ada, "if I were a piece of private property, I'd certainly feel safe."

Mayor Bob is hovering next to the microphone. With federal officials within spitting distance, he and Maribelle Wegman were sure to show up. The mayor welcomes the minister, even though the minister isn't here, and begins a litany of the co-operative endeavours in which the city council and the band council have participated.

Most of them are minor. All of them are over ten years old.

He does not mention the town's effort to move the reserve, nor does he touch on the band's ongoing problem with utilities and water service. Towards the end of his address, he spreads his arms as though he's about to embrace an old friend, and his coat flies open to reveal a beaded belt buckle. It's a handsome thing, red, black, yellow.

Photogenic and easily seen from a distance.

Louis and Enola wait by the side of the council office. If Wapi is around, I don't see him. The crows work their way across the roofs of the trailers, peer over the edge, wait to see who will go first.

I expect it will be Ada, but it's Roman. He comes off the drum and strides to the front of the portable podium with his arms folded across his chest.

"We don't have power, and we don't have water." His voice is clear and strong. "And we have mouldy trailers."

The Minister of the Moment's name is Joan Crankton, and she has an aide. A young man whose pants look as though they have been painted on his legs, and whose job it is to hand things to his boss.

"And that's why we're here," says Crankton. She nods at Tight Pants, and he hands her a large aerosol can. "After researching the problem," she says, raising her voice, "we believe that, in addition to proper ventilation, this is the most expedient and effective solution to the unexpected incidents of *Aspergillus* and *Alternaria*."

"What about *Stachybotrys chartarum?*" says Roman, the Latin rolling off his tongue like chocolate frosting.

Crankton and her aide have a quick whisper.

"This is Primo Pavella," says Crankton. "He's with the Ministry of Health. I'll have him answer that question."

Tight Pants steps to the microphone. The crows begin dancing on the roofs. Roman doesn't move.

"*Stachybotrys chartarum*," says Pavella, "commonly called black mould, is one of a number of mould varieties found in homes. While it is unsightly, it has not been shown to pose a substantial risk to healthy people with functioning immune systems."

Roman is smiling now. "So it just kills babies and old people?"

Pavella is unfazed. "There are a great many pathogens that are of concern to the very young and the very old."

"I think we've gone off topic," says Crankton, and she gently moves Pavella away from the microphone. "We're here today in our capacity as official representatives of the federal government to assist with the detection and remediation of the aforementioned difficulty, and to provide a solution to the immediate problem as well as a strategy to avoid a future reoccurrence."

Even Mayor Bob is stunned and left speechless.

Pavella has done this before. On cue, he goes to a table that has a cutaway model of a trailer window.

"Imagine, if you will, a window in one of your trailers. If there is mould present, it will, in all likelihood, form along the bottom edge of the sill."

Pavella takes a black velvet strip out of his pocket and lays it out along the window ledge.

"In most instances, the mould will look like this piece of black velvet. It will be soft and fuzzy. We do not advise you to remove the mould without proper respiratory equipment and training. Scraping at it could cause the spores to become airborne."

The gathering rumbles to life.

"No shit!" someone yells.

Pavella holds up a can and takes the top off. "This is Lock-Mould. It is an encasing foam that will trap and destroy mould. It's very effective and easy to use."

Pavella doesn't wait for questions. He shakes the can vigorously and then holds the nozzle to the inside edge of the mock window frame.

"Simply depress the nozzle and run a bead of Lock-Mould so that it covers the mould."

Roman holds up a hand. "What about compensation?"

Crankton smiles. "Compensation?"

The Mounties tense, as though they expect to be hit by something unpleasant.

"For the lousy trailers you gave us when you destroyed our good homes."

"Never had mould in my old house," Ada shouts from her chair.

"I'm afraid," says Crankton, "issues such as compensation are not within my mandate."

Mayor Bob, who has been sitting the whole time, leaps to his feet. "What we have to remember," he says, "is that we're all in this together. We are all Treaty People."

"Some more than others," shouts Ada.

Roman's face is a storm cloud. "And how are we all in this together?"

"The thing we need to do," says the mayor, "is try to make the best of an unwelcome situation."

Roman strikes his thigh with the drumstick. "That mean you're going to hook up our power and water?"

"Yeah," shouts Ada. "We need clean water and electricity. We don't need cans of whipped cream."

Pavella is amused. "Well," he says, "while it does bear some resemblance to whipped cream, I can assure you, you do not want to eat it."

"So, it's poisonous?" says Roman.

The smile slides off Pavella's face. "No, of course not."

"So it's just carcinogenic."

"Of course it's not carcinogenic."

"Then how come it smells so bad?"

The stuff does have a distinct odour. Even the crows notice it. They step back from the edge of the roof and turn away.

"There is some off-gassing associated with the foam," says Pavella, "but that will dissipate quickly."

"That's what they said about the trailers." Nutty reaches Roman's side and stands with him. "And look what that got us."

Crankton holds up her hands. "If you'll form an orderly line to the left of the table, Mr. Pavella will make sure that everyone gets a can."

Nutty takes Roman's hand and pulls him back into the heart of the gathering, away from trouble. Ada folds in behind them. A photographer appears out of nowhere and begins taking pictures of Crankton shaking hands with the mayor and of Pavella handing out the aerosol cans.

Each can comes with a ministry survey that Pavella encourages everyone to fill out and return to Ottawa.

As I start back to the school, I see them. Ash Locken and Oliver Flood. I can't tell if they have just arrived or if they have been here all along. They stand at the edge of the powwow grounds, looking like explorers who have just stumbled upon an unexpected civilization.

And then the drum starts up again, and the crows begin screaming.

11

The next day, I get to the Piggy early. Florence is sitting at one of the tables with her feet up on a chair.

"What happened," she says, without opening her eyes. "You forget to sleep in?"

I set the two brownies on the counter.

"Two?" Florence sits up. "Reggie used to do that. Whenever he messed up."

I find plates. Florence pads over to the espresso machine, heats the cups, grinds the beans. The sound reminds me a bit of the drummers and the crows.

"Missed all the excitement," she tells me. "After you left, Roman decided to experiment with that mould foam stuff."

Roman has not always been careful with the line between offensive behaviour and illegal behaviour. When Mayor Bob first announced his intention to talk to the department of Indian Affairs about appropriating the Cradle River reserve and moving the families somewhere else, Roman put forward a motion before the band council calling for the town to be moved instead.

"Sprayed it on the hood of that government car. Looked like cream frosting on a licorice cake." Florence takes a bite of brownie. "At first, they were good sports about it."

Roman's motion passed. The ensuing squabble between the band and the town was picked up by the national media, and within days, primetime news reporters with their TV trucks and canned sound bites had descended on Gleaming.

And for the next several weeks, the air was filled with accusations, counter-accusations, threats of lawsuits, ill-advised interviews, and a great deal of inappropriate language, leaving the town and the reserve exhausted and the mayor looking the fool.

"But then they tried to wipe it off."

Mayor Bob did not appreciate the notoriety or the embarrassment, and in short order, he instructed the city's public works to terminate hydro and water to the reserve, citing health concerns and public safety issues with the old pipes and the outdated electrical service, neither of which had been replaced since the plank houses had been exchanged for the trailers.

"It came off well enough." Florence is laughing now. "But so did the paint."

Roman might have waited to see if the band council, Indian Affairs, and the town could come up with a solution.

But he didn't.

Instead, he got a pipe wrench, a hacksaw, and a pair of heavy-duty wire cutters, and proceeded to "discontinue" electrical and water service to the homes of the councillors who had voted with the mayor.

"You know, Bob Loomis wasn't always such a dolt." Florence pokes at her brownie with a fork. "When Reggie was alive, he and

Bob were good friends. Bob and his wife came for breakfast every Sunday. Man had a sense of humour."

I try to imagine Bob Loomis with a sense of humour.

"And then he ran for mayor." Florence shakes her head. "What is it about public office that turns decent people into political cartoons?"

Louis, Enola, and Wapi roll into the Piggy just before nine. Louis sets a can of the Lock-Mould on the table.

"Going to try it on my rims," says Louis. "See if it will take the rust off."

"Rust," says Wapi.

"Did we miss the news?" Enola asks.

"Nope," says Florence. "Was waiting for you guys to show up."

"Yesterday was pretty depressing," says Enola. "Spray foam for mould?"

"No way that stuff is going to work," says Louis. "You get mould in trailers, you might as well burn them down."

"Burn them down," says Wapi.

Florence makes three macchiatos and a hot chocolate and sets them on the counter. "Okay," she says, "news, blues, and comfortable shoes."

Florence begins, as she always does, on the international front. An explosion has destroyed a decommissioned weather station on an uninhabited island in the Southern Ocean between South Island, New Zealand, and Antarctica, leaving authorities baffled.

In national news, the New Democrats win enough seats to form a minority government in British Columbia, while the Greens move ahead of both the Liberals and the Conservatives.

"And at the local level," says Florence, softening her voice, "today is Nutty Moosonee's birthday."

"She must be closing in on one hundred," says Enola.

"And those who don't stop by and wish that sweet old woman well can forget about coffee in the foreseeable future."

Louis taps the table. "Did anyone notice that we lost another one of our billionaires?"

Florence nods. "Always sad when that happens."

"Oleg Baranov? Russian oligarch?" Louis waits to see if the name rings any bells. "He went to Paris for cosmetic surgery, and bang, before you can say *rhinoplasty*, he's dead."

Enola snorts. "A nose job?"

"Nose job," says Wapi.

"Everyone dies," says Enola.

"Sure," says her father, "but this guy wasn't supposed to die."

"I had an auntie who lived to be ninety-eight," says Florence.

"That's genetics," says Louis. "The super-rich tend to live longer than the rest of us, because they don't have the same anxiety levels and because they can afford the best health care."

"Didn't work out so well for Mr. Nose Job," says Enola.

"Nose job," says Wapi.

"When I was at university," says Louis, "I had a class on the history of societal structures. You know what keeps the poor from killing the rich?"

"The police," says Enola. "The rich own the police."

"Elections," says Louis. "They give us hope and the illusion that we have some control over our lives."

"Nose job," says Wapi.

"And yet," says Louis, "the less democratic the nation, the safer it is for the ultra-rich."

I'm hoping that Florence will step in and move the discussion in another direction. Any minute now, someone is going to quote Aristotle.

"'Death is the solution to all problems,'" says Enola. "Joseph Stalin."

Louis leans back in his chair. "Why are you quoting Joseph Stalin?"

"We could quote Freud," says Enola. "Or Aristotle."

Florence sets the tarot on the counter next to me.

"Good news," she says. "Emma Stillday and her little girl are coming home. Ada's over the moon."

I shuffle the deck and pick the Hermit, one of the Major Arcana. The card looks as though one of the Cubists, Picasso or Braque, designed the thing. Lines and slashes and geometrical shapes. In one corner is a three-headed dog, which makes no more sense than the rest of the card.

"Caution, detachment from worldly things, healing, silence." Florence shakes her head. "Looks like the cards have got your number."

I take a peek at the next card down. The Ten of Wands. Oppression.

"Emma's going to have a hard time at first," says Florence. "Going to need some help getting settled. Daughter to look after. Place to live. Roman."

I look at the next card. The Ten of Swords. Ruin. I slide the deck back to Florence. Quit while I'm ahead.

Louis and Enola have moved on to religion and the concept of everlasting life and reincarnation.

"If you believe that there is life after death," says Enola, "you can endure the tribulations of living."

"The opioid of the masses," says Louis.

"Now we're quoting Marx?" says Enola.

"Your mother believed in god," says Louis. "Then she got cancer."

"Einstein suggested that religion provides an ethical framework for personal conduct."

"Don't need religion to tell us what's right and wrong," says Florence, joining the conversation. "Can figure that out on our own."

I can see that the conversation is about to implode and collapse on itself. I finish my coffee, float towards the door. Florence tries to hold me in place with a glare, but she's too late.

"You better remember Nutty's birthday," she calls after me. "You don't stop by and there's not a brownie big enough can save you."

The Neighbours are in the park. They've set up their daytime camp against the bandstand. The kids are busy with a pickup soccer game, while the adults relax in the sunlight.

As I cross the park, Wes Stanford waves me over.

"You know anything about the mayor's plan to stick us into those trailers? Good enough for Indians, good enough for us? That about it?"

Wes Stanford is a horse. Tall, with a long, heavy face. Hair tied back in a mane. Glasses that make his eyes seem even larger than they are.

"Is it true they're full of mould?"

And the smell. Not unpleasant exactly. Unexpected. Damp and decay. As though you had gone for a ride in a meadow on the edge of a swamp. Or slept too long in a barn.

"What the hell," says Stanford. "That fuck thinks we're going to let him put our kids in a gas chamber?"

Stanford worked the assembly line at the General Motors plant. And then it was closed and moved to Mexico.

"We been squatting in the old box plant."

Out past the Petro-Can. Bambridge & Moore made cardboard boxes until one of the big outfits in the U.S. bought the company and closed the plant.

"Lot of talk about converting B&M into low-income housing," says Stanford. "But now the mayor wants to tear down the place and build a new community centre and hockey arena."

Stanford watches the children race across the grass, laughing as they go. "It's not easy out here. Food's tight. Autumn's pregnant again, and Zoe rattles when she breathes. You think we like this?"

Stanford straightens his ponytail. "But the reserve don't want us any more than the town does."

I can't think of anything to say, so I don't.

"Hear you're fixing up that graveyard." Stanford jams his hands into his pockets. "You need help, you let me know."

NUTTY IS SITTING in her recliner. Roman and Ada are sitting on folding chairs. There's a chocolate cake on a dirty-white plastic table that looks as though it has been rescued from a curb. Slick is back on the garbage can. He's looking at the cake, his head bobbing up and down, but he stays put.

"Ada made the cake," says Roman. "It's pretty good."

"Of course it's good," says Ada. "I made it."

"Slick don't know what to do with it," says Nutty. Her cough doesn't sound any better.

"Long as he don't crap on it," says Ada, "he can continue to live."

"Mayor Bob came by earlier," says Nutty.

"But he didn't come to wish Nutty a happy birthday," says Ada. "Him and the law were looking for Roman."

"But they didn't find me."

I imagine Roman's new troubles have to do with the Lock-Mould and the car.

"They're saying I destroyed private property," says Roman. "Are they kidding? Their foam, their car."

"Said he's a menace to society," says Ada. "No mention of the trailers or the hookups. You should have seen the mess that spray made."

Nutty nods. "Roman probably saved our lives."

Roman runs a hand through his hair. "They damn well should arrest themselves."

"Billy Paul tried a little on one of his windows," says Ada, "and now he can't get it open."

"Probably saved our lives," says Nutty.

I get a plate and help myself to a piece of cake.

"So how old are you?" says Roman.

"Don't matter," says Nutty. "There's alive and then there ain't."

"She'll be here next year," says Ada. "None of us is going anywhere."

"And your daughter is coming home," says Nutty. "Can't wait to see that Lala."

Ada looks at Roman. "Maybe her father can lend a hand."

Roman shrugs Ada off. "Me and Emma got shit to work out."

Ada doesn't budge. "Try explaining that to a child."

Nutty tosses the crow a peanut. "Sweet little girl," she says. "Best birthday present I can think of."

The cake is good. Moist and tasty with a butter frosting. Slick doesn't know what he's missing, and I'm not about to tell him.

"No powwow this year," says Roman. "But I figure we'll have a protest in the plaza. Set up the big drum."

"You should have Jeremiah sit in," says Nutty.

Roman looks at me. "You know how to sing?"

"He can keep a beat," says Nutty. "And he's one of us."

"Not so you could tell," says Ada.

"Still family."

"Sure," says Ada, "but there's more to being Cradle River than having been born here."

"Let you use my old drumstick," says Roman. "Still got pretty good flex."

"Have another piece of cake," says Nutty, the cough worse than before. "Moving them stones can wear a body."

IT'S JUST AFTER NOON when I get back to the school. I could work in the graveyard or I could take a nap. I could walk the river or play with the cat. But I'm not sure I want to do anything. So, for the first little while, I stand at the kitchen window and look out.

There's nothing to see, but I know that if I stand here long enough, something is bound to come along.

12

As it turns out, I don't have to wait long.

I'm thinking about lunch when the kid appears at the far side of the graveyard. Not old enough to have shoulders. Or hips and a butt, for that matter. His clothes hang off him like wet laundry on a line. Jeans, grey hoodie, red tennis shoes.

The pack on his back weighs more than he does.

I run through the possibilities. Sales, home maintenance, charity. Buy our new phone service. Mow your lawn, paint your house. There's a starving child in Africa who needs your generosity.

He's not an evangelical. They're better dressed, and they travel in packs.

Not that it matters. He might get to the porch and the door, but he won't get any further. I send unfriendly thoughts into the afternoon to discourage him from even trying.

And then I see the camera.

THE LOCKEN GROUP found me at a job fair. They had what they called a "skills booth" set up. National competition. Four computer monitors on the back wall, a tumble of images, discordant music and sounds. One question. Thirty-second time limit. Give it a try. What do you see? Winners get a paid summer internship.

I did it in eleven seconds.

THE KID'S NAME IS Brian Busby and he's been hired by Maribelle Wegman and the Gleaming city council to photograph the graveyard.

"Do a lot of work for her committee," says Busby. "Mostly historic houses and buildings. This is my first boneyard."

Up close, Brian isn't as young as he looks.

"Telephoto lens," he tells me. "This way, I don't have to set foot on your property. Avoid any problems with jurisdiction or trespass."

THAT SUMMER at the Locken Group was not what I expected. I assumed that I would be shackled to a small desk in a large room, staring at a computer screen, under the scrutiny of a camp commandant.

Instead, on my first day, I was taken to a windowless room with nine other individuals, men and women. There was no pattern to gender, race, religion, or age. We were all strangers. We would remain strangers.

And except for that single day, we never saw each other again.

The morning was given over to Human Resources and their skid of paperwork, a seemingly endless parade of agreements, non-disclosure documents, personal history, health forms, and the like, all requiring signatures and blood oaths.

Lunch was brought in promptly at noon. At 1:15, Thomas Locken walked in the room and waited while two assistants handed each of us a thin manila envelope.

Inside was a single sheet of paper with a single question.

"You're here," Locken told us, "because you are smart. Just how smart is yet to be discovered."

Locken walked back and forth across the front of the room, slowly, as though he were waiting for his thoughts to catch up with his body.

"You will have full access to Locken's resources and research platforms. You will not discuss your work with the media or with any individual not previously cleared by Locken legal. This includes parents, spouses, significant others, friends, colleagues, along with enemies at home and abroad who seek to sap and impurify all of our precious bodily fluids."

It took a couple of beats before anyone laughed, even though it was obvious that we all knew the reference.

"You have one week to answer the question."

And with that, Thomas Locken gave us all a quick smile and walked out the door.

BUSBY SHOWS ME some of the shots he's taken. With the long lens shortening the distances and crowding the depth of field, the crosses look imposing and surreal.

"I could use a wide-angle lens," he says, "but then you get a completely different effect."

He lets me play with the camera, take a couple of shots.

"You have a knack," he tells me, as we check the display. "Good news is you don't have to shell out a bundle for a DSLR. You can take amazing photos with the new generation of cellphones."

Busby doesn't stay long. When he's done, he hands me a card.

"Check out my website," he says. "Heritage stuff and weddings pay the bills, but my first love is street photography. You know the Neighbours? I've got some really great shots of the Neighbours."

I don't tell him that I don't have a computer or a cellphone, that I'm not going to visit his website. Being anti-social is one thing. Mean is quite another.

So, the town is serious. Mayor Bob's real estate dreams, Maribelle Wegman's sense of heritage and authority. Buy the school. Move the graveyard. Appropriate the reserve. Have Busby photograph the families as they are herded into cars and onto buses, shipped off to a destination to be named later.

Nibble and chew until there is nothing left but bones.

I NEVER HEARD how I did on the question, but when the summer ended, I was offered a permanent position. After that first day, I didn't see Locken again. I did my research, filed my reports, made my recommendations.

And then I was summoned.

I came to work one morning to find a note on my desk that simply said, "2200. 9:30."

The twenty-second floor was Thomas Locken's personal domain. There were rumours that imagined Locken's office as an ornate collection of dark woods and Persian rugs, floor-to-ceiling bookcases and overstuffed chairs, an obligatory bar of single malts, Constables and Turners on the walls, a sanctuary reached only via a high-speed, private elevator with palm-print and facial recognition, and a full-body millimetre-wave scanner.

All guarded by a secretary from Newark, New Jersey, and a three-headed dog.

Instead, Thomas Locken's office was surprisingly bare. No desk. No computer. No bank of televisions. The furniture, what there was of it, consisted of two leather sofas facing each other with a long coffee table thrown in between them.

No executive bar. No landscapes on the walls. No dog.

Locken was at the windows, looking out.

"If you stand here long enough," he said, without turning around, "you might believe you're in charge of the world."

I waited, not quite sure what to do.

"Jeremiah Camp," said Locken. "Did you know that you still have the best time? In the job-fair competition?"

Locken turned to me.

"You predicted the S&L collapse."

That hadn't been particularly perceptive on my part. The patterns had been clear enough. But even after the collapse of Home State Savings Bank in Cincinnati in 1985 and Midwest Federal Savings & Loan in Minneapolis in 1989, the financial community had continued to pretend that these were minor aberrations in the business model, had persisted in ignoring the massive fraud and rampant greed that was at the heart of the debacle.

"Dot.com, Enron, China and India, Madoff, the collapse of Wall

Street. One or two of these might be attributed to luck. But you saw them all."

I hadn't seen 9/11 or Hurricane Katrina or the Gorkha earthquake in Nepal or the worldwide heat wave of 2015.

Thomas Locken came away from the window, sat on the far sofa, leaned back. "So tell me," he said. "What do you know about telomeres?"

AS SOON AS BUSBY LEAVES, the crows arrive. Today, they eschew the trees. Several land on the crosses to keep watch, while the rest walk the ground. They strut and hop among the graves, with no more regard for the dead than they have for the living.

They're cautious birds. They trust only what they can see and hear, and little else. Promises mean nothing to them. Friendships are rare, but routines are common. Feed crows, and after a while, they will come back each day to see if there is more food. If there is, the crows will eat it and fly away. If the plate is bare, the birds will fly away.

No harm, no foul.

No harm, no foul? I can't believe I said that. The crows continue their foraging, oblivious to my wit. Certainly, no one is laughing. I watch the birds for a while, in case they want to share funny stories or reveal what they know about the world.

And then my stomach reminds me that I haven't had lunch. I slip out of the graveyard, leave the crows to their own appetites, and drag mine back up the path to the school.

LUNCH ON THE TWENTY-SECOND floor of the Locken tower was catered. It arrived on a wheeled tray and was laid out on the coffee table with quiet ceremony.

"I'm told," Locken said, "there are complex organisms in the world that do not die."

I tried a bit of everything. The sushi was tempura shrimp and avocado, the chicken sizzling in a black bean sauce.

"*Turritopsis dohrnii*." Locken sat with his hands folded on his stomach. "It's a jellyfish. Small, transparent. Evidently, they're able to turn back time. They age and then they retrace their steps back to childhood. Amazing little beggars. They switch back and forth between life stages. Theoretically, and perhaps actually, these organisms can live forever."

There were pan-fried gyozas and vegetable spring rolls. Along with green tea and warm sake.

"And then there are *Hydra*. Here, instead of deteriorating over time, *Hydra* have the capacity for infinite self-renewal. A set of genes called Fox genes, found in all animals, plays a vital role in regulating just how long cells live. *Hydra* happen to have an overabundance of Fox genes."

I decided on the tea.

"Lobsters can repair their DNA thanks to a never-ending supply of an enzyme called *telomerase*, but they continually outgrow their shells. And the energy needed to create new shells is finally too much for the organism. The protective end caps on chromosomes, the telomeres, slowly get shorter and shorter, and when they're too short, a cell enters senescence and cannot keep dividing. And when that happens, the lobster dies."

Locken helped himself to the sake.

"You also have naked mole rats, a quahog clam named Ming, and bristlecone pines. Utterly fascinating. Humans have telomeres, but the levels of telomerase in most cells is not sufficient to rebuild the telomeres."

And then he went silent. We sat there in his office with the corner windows overlooking the lakeshore and picked at the food set before us.

"We spend our waking moments," he said at last, "trying to be successful, because we can't think of anything else to do."

And then Locken told me what he wanted done.

I STAND IN THE KITCHEN and consider lunch. I get as far as taking an egg out of the refrigerator and no further. I don't think I'm depressed, but that's the wonderful thing about depression.

It doesn't care what you think.

It was the cake. Nutty's birthday cake with the chocolate butter icing. I had a large piece. There's the reason for my malaise. Too much sugar. Along with the bother of finding young Busby mapping my home with his camera.

I'll recover, of course. My appetite will return. And if I look hard enough, I might even find something that passes for optimism.

13

Ever since Gleaming cut off services to the reserve, Cradle River First Nations has been operating on generator power and bottled water. There has been more than one meeting between the town and the reserve on the subject, but so far, the only things to have come out of these efforts have been hard feelings and bad language.

Along with the occasional confrontation.

After the city discontinued services, maintenance discovered that one of their utility trucks had been inadvertently left on the reserve. When workers went to retrieve it, they were told, in no uncertain terms, that they could not come onto Cradle River land and that the truck now belonged to the band council.

"Real standoff," Florence reported over coffee. "Almost had a hockey game on our hands."

For the next while, the truck was shuffled around the reserve in a running shell game. At one point, no one knew exactly where it was, it had been moved so many times.

"You never know just how handy a pickup can be," Nutty told me, "until you have one."

Almost immediately, the *Gleaming Advertiser* created a box on the back page of the paper to show the number of days the truck had been held hostage, and the band council countered, suggesting that while the *Advertiser* was at it, they might want to keep track of the number of years Cradle River had been waiting for their land claim to be settled.

"No winners," said Florence, "but it was a lot of fun."

Three weeks into the standoff, the truck was returned, dropped off in front of city hall in the middle of the night, washed, its gas tank empty.

THE AFTERNOON HAS WARMED beyond expectations, and I decide to leave the graveyard for another day. I'm not opposed to manual labour, find working with my hands more satisfying than sitting behind a desk, but sweating holds little appeal.

I'll pull up crosses and move stones tomorrow. Today, I'll simply wander. Head off in one direction or another and keep walking. Until I feel like stopping.

The river path is coming to life. None of the trees has its leaves yet, but nips of green have appeared against the dark branches. Along the bank, the grasses are returning, while the river itself is now free of ice. At the fork, I turn away from town and follow the path to Broken Bough Falls. Here, the river rushes over the edge of the escarpment and plunges a hundred feet into a deep pool.

And disappears.

The Cradle River's great claim to fame. A watercourse that vanishes into the earth and is never seen again.

The Cradle River is not the only such phenomenon. Devil's Kettle in Minnesota performs much the same trick, with the water hitting a rock outcropping and splitting into two streams. One stream keeps on going, winding up in Lake Superior, while the other side drops into a large pothole and is swallowed whole and complete.

The river trail ends in a small turnout with a bench where you can sit and listen to the water thunder over the edge and watch the spray rise into the air.

I see Roman before I hear the horn.

He's on the bench with his cornet, eyes closed, fingers working the valves, the sound drowned out by the falls. I catch snatches of the piece.

"Caruso" by Lucio Dalla.

Roman plays the song slowly, the horn aimed at the ground, as though he's trying to bury the sound. I take one step back. He sees me and sets the horn to the side.

"This is one of my favourite places," he says. "Used to come here when I was a kid. Throw shit into the river. Watch it go over the falls."

Roman leans back on the bench and stretches.

"Couple of times, I thought about going over myself. You know, get life over with rather than wait around to see what new crap it's going to dump on you."

The sun hits the fast water at an angle, fire and polished steel.

"But I didn't. Became a musician, didn't I. Damn good one, too. Played all over the world. Made good money. Big success."

I watch the water as it roars over the edge. I can see the attraction. Lean out. Let go.

"And yet here I am. Back on the reserve. Playing for a piece of the door at outhouse clubs where nobody can tell a cornet from a condom."

Roman runs a quick blues scale. "Funny thing is, I don't know which is the success and which is the failure. Not even sure it much matters."

The spray from the falls shifts directions and fills the air.

"So why did you come back?" Roman opens a spit valve and clears the horn. "Big-city job. Big-city money. Enough money to buy the old school. Enough money to be able to lock yourself away from the rest of us."

I can see that if we stay much longer, we'll both be soaked.

"How's that working out?"

Not that I mind getting wet. Worse things happen when you're not paying attention.

"Ada tell you my sad tale? Town council cut water and power to the reserve? No good reason. Just trying to drive us out, so they can take our land. So I cut off power to the council. Quid pro quo."

Roman slides into the high finish of "My Funny Valentine."

"They fucked the entire reserve and what happens to them? Not one damn thing. Whereas I cut off power to five people and get nine months in jail? Should have shut down the entire town."

Roman moves on to "Stardust," gets most of the way through the long introduction, and stops.

"My daughter's coming home." Roman puts the horn down. "You know, I went out to Winnipeg a couple of years back to see if Emma and me could get back together. You ever been married? Got any kids squirrelled away?"

Roman settles on the bench again, closes his eyes, and takes up "Stardust" where he left off, as though he's found a bookmark in a book.

"Don't even have a picture of my little girl."

I leave Roman where he is. The spray continues to swing around. Either he'll move or he won't.

THE GRAVEYARD is in slanted light. The long shadows of the trees drape over the crosses and settle on the stones. There are still two good hours left in the day, and as I walk through the dead, back to the school, I find myself unexpectedly drawn to the work at hand. A sudden flush of enthusiasm. A surge of energy that I hadn't anticipated.

The wagon is parked at the side of the building, along with the tools. It would only be a matter of moments to slip inside, change into my work clothes, head down to the riverbed.

"Forecaster."

Oliver Flood. Black slacks, black shirt. Camel sports coat. He's out of place on my porch. And unwelcome.

"You have an invitation," he says in his flat voice. "Tomorrow. A car will be here first thing in the morning."

Ash Locken.

"I accepted on your behalf."

Spot and Rover stand by the black SUV, their hands folded in front of them, as though they're waiting for me to ask them a question they can answer.

"Pack for an extended stay," says Flood, amusement colouring his

95

voice, as he walks to the car and gets in the back. "Think of it as a paid vacation."

I turn back to the graveyard. The shadows are longer and deeper now, the late light brightening the crosses with nature's grace. I imagine that I can hear Roman's horn off in the distance.

An illusion, of course. It's just the crows, singing out to each other as they come across the river to settle in the trees for the evening.

14

Spot and Rover and the Tesla arrive promptly the next morning. Rover is driving. Spot is the designated tour guide.

"Mr. Flood won't be joining us," says Spot. "He has other duties. He's asked us to see to your needs."

I have few needs. The main one is to be left alone.

Spot holds the door open for me. "Mr. Flood says to do your job, in and out, don't be an ass."

Then he shuts the door, and we're off.

I had expected that we would head for the highway, but instead, we drive to a field at the edge of the town. A flat field gone to weeds and short, rough bushes that hug the ground. The Tesla rolls across these, crushing them, and comes to a stop next to nothing.

And we wait. With no explanation.

But now I know what to expect, so when the helicopter arrives, I'm not surprised. A mid-sized Sikorsky in black and tan. It was foolish of me to think that we were going to brave the two-hour drive through lumbering herds of transport trucks and scuttling packs of family sedans.

Spot lets me out, and I walk the short distance to the helicopter with its whirling rotors. I can see that the pilot is a woman in a dark green jumpsuit.

A small surprise.

Gender equality is not common in the allocation of large toys.

The side door of the Sikorsky opens and a young man steps out, his hand pressed against his head to keep his hair from flying away.

"Mr. Camp," he shouts over the roar of the helicopter. "This way."

The way is apparent. There is only one field and one helicopter.

"Welcome to the Locken Group," says the young man. "May I have your cellphone?"

I wait.

"You'll get it back."

He's surprised and unhappy that I don't have a phone. This could be his natural state, or it could be the situation.

"We're expected for lunch."

The interior of the helicopter is appointed for executive travel. Soft, tan leather recliners on swivels. An upright, tall-backed chair at a desk by one of the windows. Three monitors. One for the stock market. One for a talk show on business. One for sports.

"George Dobbins," says the young man. "At your service. Coffee?"

Dobbins tells me how much he's looked forward to meeting me. How my reputation is well known. How he has admired my skills.

"They call you Forecaster," he says, "is that correct?"

I pass on the coffee. If it's not espresso, it's not worth drinking. I pass on the magazines and the newspapers, pass on watching a sports team in orange shirts and black shorts chase another team in magenta and silver around a field.

"If there is anything I can do for you," says Dobbins, "just ask."

This is rhetorical, and we both know it. I sink into the swaddled interior, close my eyes, and go to sleep.

I WAKE UP AS we begin our descent. At altitude, the city looks reduced, benign, vaguely artistic.

Michael Chesko's balsa wood renderings.

Meschac Gaba's sugar creations.

Edward Burtynsky's panoramic photographs.

And because everything is in miniature, there is a moment, before you drop into the cluster of towers and tight grouping of buildings, when you feel important and indominable, a moment when you might imagine that you see what only god can see.

If such a creature ever existed.

The helicopter rolls gently out of the sky and runs out along the lakeshore to where the newer towers are being built.

Sugar Beach.

A euphemism. Not a beach at all. A parking lot for the Jarvis Street slip until the city trucked in a triangular pile of sand to mask the industrial reality of the surrounding area. Pink umbrellas, white Muskoka chairs, an inflatable movie screen mounted on a barge to complete the illusion.

We're not going to the beach. Which is just as well. If I wanted to spend a day in sand, I'd go to Tofino and walk along Chesterman, or drop down the coast to Oregon and roam Ecola State Park.

My minder is up and moving. Dobbins points out the window as we make our final approach to a glass tower all aglow in the late-morning sun.

"The Lighthouse." Dobbins's voice softens in benediction. "Magnificent. If you had a cellphone, you could take a photograph."

The pilot makes a slow pass at the tower's helipad and then sets the Sikorsky down elegantly on the numbers. Dobbins is out the door the minute the wheels touch.

"Shall we?" he asks, as though this is a question.

The building proper is capped by a clear-glass circular dome that contains two high-speed elevators. A long corridor, also clear glass, runs from the dome to the edge of the helipad. This is the brainchild of a security savant, a way to isolate hostile visitors in a trap, a defensive time delay that allows for interventions in case of aggression.

"We call it the Igloo." Dobbins takes a fob from his pocket and points it at the outer door. "Polymer-infused plastic. It'll stop anything."

Dobbins is mistaken. Polymer-infused plastic is merely bullet resistant. A .454 Casull handgun would punch its way through the Igloo with impunity. Though I'm not sure such knowledge would change his life in any significant way.

The outer doors slide shut behind us. Dobbins walks to the elevator, stands in front of the control panel, and says his name. Then he looks into the black glass and waits for the computer to scan his iris.

I stand back and watch him perform the ritual.

"Your turn, Mr. Camp."

I stay where I am.

"You have to say your name," he says, "and look into the scanner."

That's not going to happen. Having decided not to talk to people, I'm certainly not going to talk to a machine. Dobbins doesn't have this behaviour variant in his playbook, and he's not sure what to do.

"Is there a problem?" His voice has lost some of its calm. The joy of being in charge is slipping away.

The Sikorsky is still on the pad, its rotors spinning.

"We can't get in unless you speak your name and allow us to scan you."

I turn and start back to the helicopter. I've only taken two steps when I hear the elevator doors hiss open behind me.

WE DROP WITH little sensation. Dobbins is no longer talkative. He is angry and reduced. I have little sympathy, so I don't pretend that I do. When the doors open, he stays behind in the elevator.

"Someone will take you from here."

Dobbins would hurt me if he could. I have broken the rules, and in his world, people who break the rules are punished. In his world, no one can be allowed to do this. But I no longer believe in rules or in the people who make them. This needs to be clear to everyone from the start.

The *someone* is a woman. Middle-aged, business suit. She is neither nervous nor impressed.

"Mr. Camp." The accent is Eastern. Prague, Budapest, Kiev. "If you would follow me."

This is a reasonable request.

"Do you have any food allergies?"

The floor we are on is not the top floor. It is somewhere in the middle. High enough to be defended. Low enough to be reached by rescue teams in case of a disaster. A compromise between status and safety.

We pass through a set of double doors into a space that has been purposed as a living room. The woman walks me to a long table, shows me a chair that faces the windows. So I can look out and enjoy the view.

"May I bring you anything to drink?"

I take the chair on the opposite side of the table. This doesn't faze her, as it would have Dobbins.

"I understand you enjoy espresso. A macchiato to be precise?"

I don't mind sitting with my back to the windows. I've seen the view before. If I don't see the city, I can pretend that it isn't there.

The woman passes behind me. I hear a door open and close. And now, for the moment, I am alone.

But of course, I'm not alone at all. I'm being watched. Cameras, microphones. My every move is being analyzed by technicians versed in psychological behaviour. Heart rate, blood pressure, eye movement, level of alertness, physical tells that can be crafted into a profile. Closing my eyes tells them something. Crossing my legs tells them something else.

I'm tempted to go to the middle of the room, squat into *utkata konasana*, and begin performing a *haka*, confident that the shadow watchers will dutifully record it, will spend the next week trying to make sense of what has just happened, dismissing the possibility of boredom for something more peculiar and clinical.

The psy-ops playbook, in a situation such as this, calls for a delay of at least half an hour. Five minutes in, I hear a door open followed by footsteps.

"I'm sure this is not your first choice of ways to spend a day." Ash Locken is dressed in a simple business suit with a cream blouse. "I appreciate your taking the time."

The tone of Locken's voice, like her attire, is soft, understated, and could be mistaken for sympathy.

"Do you know why we enjoy living in towers?"

It's a rhetorical question. We enjoy living in towers because we enjoy living in towers. Technically, the answer is a tautology.

"Because we like to imagine ourselves to be wizards."

The door at the far end of the room opens. Two women bring in a coffee service with fresh fruit, pastries, and a macchiato complete with a chocolate biscotti.

"I'd like you to stay with us, Forecaster."

This is not a question that is open for debate.

"A short stay. Give us a chance to have a proper conversation."

I try the macchiato. It's excellent.

"My father was a complicated man." Locken helps herself to a strawberry. "Though I expect you can say that about a great many people. Still, when you have the kind of money and power that my family has, you can pursue any whim, any passion."

I take some of the grapes. They're firm and cold.

"I have a friend whose passion is fashion. The newest style in clothing. The latest sports car. Another is keen on the environment, spends a good deal of her fortune on the conundrum of global warming. Still another lives for the arts, music, painting, literature."

And sweet. These grapes didn't sit on a boat, and they haven't been locked up in cold storage.

"For my father, it was longevity." Locken takes another strawberry. "No, that's not exactly correct. His passion was immortality."

I help myself to more grapes and the cheese.

"Death, the great leveller. The great destroyer. The one thing that the rich and the poor have in common. Everything you have become, everything you know, everything you've accomplished, gone. Lost forever. The same end. Sinners and saints alike."

Locken puts the stem of the strawberry on the edge of the plate.

"But my father didn't see death as part of some divine plan. He decided early on that 'gods in the universe' was a fairy tale, a story whose function was to give purpose and hope to misery."

The lighter cheese is fruity and sweet. The heavier one is a barnyard medley.

"But I'm sure you know all this already. I'm sure my father would have shared these feelings with his Forecaster."

He had. Thomas Locken saw death as a matter of biology and logic. If we could imagine immortality, he told me on more than one occasion, we should be able to achieve it.

"What I don't know is why my father had you create the list." Locken pauses, as though she has run too far too fast. "Or why people on that list are dying."

WE TAKE OUR TIME with the food, retreat into the safety of small talk. The weather. Life in the city. New restaurants. Political gossip. Locken walks me through the facility.

"This floor is essentially a guest house," she tells me. "Where our visitors can live and work."

Locken enumerates the points of interest.

"In addition to the living room, there's a bedroom, a bathroom, a small kitchen, as well as a sound-proof workspace with high-speed internet access. Along with a gym, if you can manage the tedium of exercise. I hope you'll think of it as home."

I wouldn't know. I don't have a home. I've never had a home.

"But enough for today. Let's get some rest, so we can start fresh tomorrow." Locken turns to go. "If you want anything, all you have to do is ask."

The space is well appointed, no expense spared. Full-length windows with a view of the lake, thick carpets, bespoke furnishings, locks on every door. Luxury living at its best.

And given different circumstances, it would easily double as a prison.

15

I don't sleep.

I try watching television, but it hasn't improved since I gave it up. Reality shows, a plague of farce and nonsense, have taken over, with the news channels close behind. Tonight, on Fox, a guy who was put up for adoption as an infant tries to find his biological father in a group of twenty-five strangers, while on CNN, a panel of four is debating whether or not the hot dog is a sandwich.

Is that really a question?

I turn the sound off and discover that the programs, *sine voce*, are less annoying, with no appreciable loss in comprehension.

There's a small library with a generous sampling of fiction and non-fiction, but I don't plan to stay here long enough to finish a book. I try meditation. I sit on the floor, relax, clear my mind. It's less insulting than watching television, but equally boring.

A little after midnight, I give up on entertainment and go to work.

Three women, nine men. All billionaires. All heads of major families who take their money and their privacy seriously. Names that do not appear on the Bloomberg Billionaires Index or *Forbes*'s roster of über-rich.

No one on the list has signed the Giving Pledge. No one on the list knows what it is.

Twelve names.

A combined net worth of over $600 billion.

I stare at the monitor for a while, and then I begin to arrange the individuals, their companies, and their subsidiaries into loose groups.

Similarities. Convergences.

Just for fun, I organize them by ethnicity, by language, by religion. Where they went to school. Who have yachts, who have planes. Which ones have charitable foundations, which ones don't.

Houses. Country club memberships. Wines, jewellery, cars.

Two monitors and a keyboard. Every key stroke watched by a Locken technician somewhere in the building. Every search engine scrutinized, every site I visit noted and analyzed.

At three-thirty, I run out of categories and call it a night. I curl up on the bed and don't wake until the alarm goes off at 8:00.

BREAKFAST IS WAITING for me in front of the panoramic windows. The sun is out, and it lights up the lake.

Ash Locken appears a little after nine. She helps herself to the coffee and a piece of toast, sits silently while I finish a cheese and onion omelette.

"I suppose you think you're funny," she says at last. "Grouping the names by their pets?"

The orange juice carafe has been chilled and the sides shimmer with condensation. Locken pours herself a glass.

"Do you really think that we haven't looked at all the commonalities, at every parallel, at each point of connection?" Locken doesn't sound as though she's gotten much sleep either. "When you're done stuffing your face, maybe we can get on with the real work."

THE REAL WORK BEGINS on the fifth floor, in a windowless room with reduced lighting.

"It simulates the quiet and peace of early evening," Locken tells me. "Supposed to be relaxing."

In the centre of the room is a large, oblong table. Most of the chairs are already taken with IQs over 135.

"Stop us at any point." Locken puts me at one end of the table. She takes the other end. "Ask any question you like."

After all this time, I don't plan to start talking now. Locken will figure it out soon enough.

"Or you can just listen."

And so it begins. First up is a young woman.

"Mona Bradley," she says, without preamble. "I have Fabrice Gloor. Gloor was Swiss. Sixty-three. Principal home in Zurich. Additional homes in Paris, Los Angeles, New York, and Monaco. Married three times. Two children by his first marriage.

"Mr. Gloor controlled the Suisse-Baer Group. Key holdings in robotics and artificial intelligence. He was driving from Monaco along the Moyenne Corniche on his way to have lunch with friends in Nice when his car went off the road."

The bank of monitors on the wall light up.

It could be a travel film. High cliffs, ocean views, lush vegetation, winding roads. And then police cars, roadblocks, ambulances, men running back and forth, a crane, a car dangling off the end of the cable like a fish on a line.

The car swings lazily in the sky, its front end a crumpled wad of metal, the windshield blown out, driver's door torn away by the impact.

"According to the official autopsy, Gloor was within the legal limit for alcohol and no drugs were found in his system. The inquest concluded that he either lost control of his Maserati or he went to sleep at the wheel."

Bradley brings up a series of documents on the monitors.

"Suisse-Baer had little interaction with the Locken Group. There are no outstanding lawsuits and the areas of competition between the two companies are not significant. Aside from the usual events and galas, Thomas Locken and Fabrice Gloor did not socialize."

Bradley takes us through everything from Suisse-Baer's stock market history to their newest acquisitions.

"The only overlap with Locken and Suisse-Baer is a biotech company called Ankh Technologies. We have no idea what the company does. No record that it is anything more than a name."

Mona Bradley sits down and is replaced at the podium by a Michael Zhao, who has been given Amanda Cho's dossier.

"Amanda Cho," he begins, "head of the Phoenix and Dagon Consortium. Fifty-two years old, Chinese national with strong ties to the Central Committee. Residences in Hong Kong, Singapore, Australia, London, and Vancouver. PDC is heavily vested in generic pharmaceuticals.

"Amanda Cho's death was ruled a heart attack. At the autopsy, there was an anomaly noted in the blood work, but Cho's family had her body flown to Singapore before a second test could be performed."

Zhao stands to one side as corporate documents appear on the screen along with a chart of quarterly profits.

"There is a series of emails that discuss investment possibilities in Ankh Technologies," says Zhao. "But it is unclear whether PDC ever took a position in the company."

FOR THE NEXT three days, Locken's geniuses take me through each of the names on the list. Two in the morning. Two in the afternoon. Three days of listening to researchers crawl through the lives of dead people. Three days of combing through expenditures, profits, annual reports. Three days of looking for something that all twelve had in common.

Three days of searching for the patterns.

On the afternoon of the third day, a tall Black woman in her early fifties takes the podium. Dr. Alisha Brown.

"Twelve names on a list," Brown begins, "and the only point of shared interest is an entity called Ankh Technologies. So far as we can tell, the company is simply a name. A ghost. We have found nothing to suggest that Ankh Technologies was anything more than a working idea, a suggestion that never took form."

Brown's presentation is short and succinct.

"Which brings us back to where we started. A list of twelve names, five of whom have died in the last year. Fabrice Gloor, Amanda

Cho, Jonathan Weston, Arjun Char, Oleg Baranov. Six, if we add in Thomas Locken."

Brown turns off the large screen behind her and brings up the room lights.

"Statistically, natural causes and accidents will not explain all these deaths in such a short space of time." Brown pauses, looks directly at me. "The evidence we currently have would suggest that, as improbable as it seems, a serial killer is targeting billionaires."

THAT EVENING, Locken joins me for dinner. She comes into the room with a tablet.

"I've made arrangements to have you taken home first thing tomorrow morning."

The sooner the better.

"But before you go, I want to share one last piece of information with you, something I have yet to share with the rest of the team."

Locken sets the tablet up on the table so I can see the screen.

An aerial view on the move. Coming in low over a jagged coastline of towering cliffs and thunderous waves beating against the margins, all under a bleak and hammered sky.

"Auckland Island. Five hundred kilometres off the southern tip of New Zealand. Average temperature between two and thirteen degrees centigrade. Rains most days. High winds much of the year. Home to albatross, penguins, petrels, sea lions, and fur seals."

Locken taps the screen and the image switches to a black-and-white still of a squat concrete building, late-1940s bunker style.

Practical and ugly. With a telecommunication array quivering on the roof in the wind like the quills of a porcupine.

"Mostly it's an uninhabited chunk of basalt in the middle of Ocean Nowhere. Main structure on the island is a decommissioned weather facility. This is an archives photograph, taken fifteen years ago."

Locken taps the screen again. "This is what it looks like now."

The building is gone, reduced to a pile of rubble.

"For the past eight years, the facility on Auckland has been leased by a subsidiary of the German conglomerate Oberste. Can you guess the name of the subsidiary?"

Ankh Technologies.

"Oberste is owned by the Vogel family." Locken lets the image of the blasted building linger on the screen. "Did you ever meet Gunther Vogel? He and my father were great friends."

Gunther Vogel. Blockish, bald, with a penchant for sailboats. Even in a world of impossible wealth, Gunther Vogel was memorable. A brutal narcissist who used money and power the way butchers used knives and cleavers.

"We have it on good authority that Vogel and his son Wolfgang were in the Ankh facility when it exploded."

The debris from the weather station is scattered in a wide circle. Natural or man-made, impossible to tell from this height.

"Gunther Vogel's training was as a geneticist. His speciality was deep-ocean organisms, with a focus on Siphonophorae. They're clever little creatures." Locken smiles as though she's just told a joke. "Evidently, they can live forever."

I watch as the video zooms in to show the extent of the destruction. It is difficult to imagine that the explosion was an accident.

"I know my father bought that property for you. The old school, the graveyard, the land. I don't know why he did it, but I have to guess that it was payment for a forecast. A forecast my father felt he needed."

Locken takes an envelope out of her jacket, slides it to me.

"Now I find myself in the same position. Like my father, I need a forecast, and like my father, I'm willing to pay for it."

Locken waits.

"Before he died, my father told me that a good forecaster could see into the heart of humanity, but that you could only look so many times."

Locken stands and straightens her jacket.

"Is that what happened? Did you look once too often?"

Locken waits. I wait.

"Someday," she says, "you'll have to tell me what you saw."

I DON'T STAY UP. I go to bed early. I don't dream, and I don't wake until the alarm goes off.

And when the helicopter arrives the next morning to take me home, I'm already on the pad waiting for it.

16

Oliver Flood and the Tesla are in the field when we touch down. He's alone. Spot and Rover must be off chasing rabbits. It's less than ten miles from here to the old school, and I seriously consider walking back.

"Don't be puerile," Flood tells me. "If you walk, you won't be able to tell me what happened."

Flood takes the long, slow way back to town.

"You ever drive an electric car? Great acceleration. Mind you, with the traffic what it is, there's not much call for it. But when you put your foot down, the damn thing flies."

I HAVE FLOOD drop me off in front of Swannie's bakery.

"You!" Swannie throws her arms over her head.

I can see four brownies left in the display case.

"You are sick? Four days I am waiting. The brownies are here, and you are not."

I buy two of the brownies.

"Four days we wait. Poof. Poof. Poof!"

I buy the other two as well.

"And now you see," says Swannie, "the brownies, they are gone. Poof."

AUTUMN DARE is in the plaza with her kids and a couple of dogs.

"Wes got some day work at the lumber yard," she tells me. "It's not much, but anything's better than nothing."

One of the kids kicks a ball to me, and I kick it back.

"Mayor met with the band council. About putting us in the empty trailers." Autumn scrubs at the side of her face. "Didn't go all that well."

I give Autumn three of the brownies. She breaks them into pieces and places them on the blanket.

"And a construction crew has started to put up a fence around the old box factory. In a week or so, we're going to have to find somewhere else to live."

There's a shout. Two of the kids are on the ground. The boy has a bloody nose and is starting to cry. One of the older girls tries to comfort him, dabs at his nose with a piece of paper towel. The dogs crowd around for moral support.

"Kids and dogs," says Autumn. "They look after one another. More than can be said for adults."

THE PIGGY IS NOT the same place I had left. Someone has scrubbed the restaurant clean, put plastic cloths on the tables, and turned on the lights. Even the jukebox looks as though it's been run through a car wash.

On the end of the counter is a stack of menus.

Florence is in her usual place, and the espresso machine hasn't moved, so perhaps not all is lost.

"About time," she says. "We thought you'd fallen down a hole. Sent Roman by the school to make sure you hadn't decided to drop dead."

There's a blackboard menu on the wall. The special today is eggs with cou-cou and bacon.

"Ada's girl is back from Winnipeg," says Florence. "She wants to get the café up and running again. Going to start off with Reggie's old recipes and move forward."

Or you can have cornmeal porridge.

"Not sure I like the idea, but I figure I'll give it a try."

I set the brownie on the counter.

Florence gives me a nod. "Guessing you'll be wanting a macchiato."

Louis and Enola and Wapi are sitting at a table with their coffee and hot chocolate. Wapi is folding napkins.

"What do you think of the new look?" Louis pats the checkered tablecloth. "If you didn't know better, you'd think the place was a restaurant."

"Grand opening is in a week," says Enola. "Wapi and me are the official menu tasters."

"You got to try the jerk goat," says Louis.

"Jerk," says Wapi.

Florence grinds the beans and packs the basket.

"But Emma's lamb chili's even better," says Louis. "Three kinds of beans. Anaheim and jalapeno peppers. You don't expect that lawyers would know how to cook."

I wait for the macchiato to arrive. It's going to take a little time to get used to the new-look Piggy.

"You went into the city, didn't you." Florence tries to turn me to stone with a stare. "Thought you gave that up?"

The macchiato is a shock.

"Emma's trying out a new bean."

I've only been gone four days.

"The perfect blend of bitter and acid, fused with the sweet notes of blackcurrant and a vanilla aftertaste."

I stop in mid sip.

"That's what the bag says." Florence leans on the counter and lowers her voice. "As you get older, change can be difficult."

The new macchiato is not the old macchiato. It's not bad. But it is different.

"Wait till you meet her little girl," says Florence. "Melt your heart."

I'm not sure that I like the new Piggy. It's a bit too bright and a bit too clean. I miss the shadows and the gloomy corners, the sense that you've crawled into a cave. A dark shelter. A quiet sanctuary.

And the new Piggy could well develop a more abundant and vigorous clientele.

"The widow Wegman came by." Florence waits for me to fall over. "She's got a petition going. Save the crosses. Already got over five hundred signatures."

"We didn't sign it," says Louis. "We want to see the bonfire."

"Bonfire," says Wapi.

"And the mayor is back at it." Louis brings the empty cups to the counter. "Just after you disappeared, he shut down the garbage service for the reserve, even though we still have two years left on the contract."

Maybe Florence can keep two espresso blends on hand.

"Says he has public safety concerns," says Louis. "Now he wants the Ministry of Health to inspect the reserve."

That way, people would have a choice.

"Says that we're a 'hazard unto ourselves.'"

Two espresso blends wouldn't be unreasonable.

"Unto ourselves?" Louis gives a quick snort. "Who the hell talks like that?"

THE NEIGHBOURS are still on the grass. I stay to the far side of the plaza. I don't need any more human interaction. I've had enough. All I want to do now is get back to the school and lock the door.

The walk along the river path helps. There is no one else in sight. Even the crows are off doing whatever it is that crows do. The sun is shining. The air is warm. I'm starting to regain my equilibrium.

And then I get to the graveyard.

Florence was right. Maribelle Wegman has been busy. Someone has wrapped yellow crime-scene tape around the perimeter and posted signs declaring that the site is now protected under a heritage bylaw. The crosses I had left in a pile at the edge of the graveyard are gone.

I don't waste time. The tape comes down easily enough. I pull up all the bylaw signs and stack them in a pile. Then I pull up half a dozen crosses for good measure.

I sweat as I work. I don't have my gloves, and the rough wood chafes my hands. I pull up one last cross, and when I do, I see the girl standing among the graves. If I had Father Hinch's map on me, I might be able to figure out who this is.

A Moosonee, perhaps. Or a Kenosha. Or a Stillday. Maybe even a Camp.

I take a book of matches out of my pocket. The ghost child watches me patiently as I ruin half a dozen while trying to get one to light. The old phosphorus-headed matches had been easy enough, but the new and improved safety matches are almost impossible.

What is the point of having a match that you can't light.

I finally get one to work, set the match to the corner of an official notice. The city's caveats and cautions make excellent starter, and the flames hit the new wood and the old crosses like a lightning strike.

I want to reassure the girl that there is no danger, that all of this is a useless gesture, that all the fires in the world will not burn history clean.

But when I turn back, she is gone.

17

I stay in the graveyard until the signs and the crosses have been consumed. It doesn't take long. The wood is dry. The flames are hot. I half expect the widow Wegman and her historical preservation committee to show up in red helmets, swinging axes and dragging fire hoses along behind them.

But through the whole of the conflagration, I'm an audience of one.

And then the crows show up.

They don't land in the trees, as you might expect. Nor do they hop around on the ground. Instead, they circle overhead, calling out to one another. They don't know what to make of me or my bonfire, and even after the fire is little more than a smouldering pile of ash, they stay in the sky, out of harm's way.

Now, I stink of smoke. And I notice that some of the sparks have burned tiny holes in my jacket.

The wages of sin.

The price of enthusiasm.

The cat is not going to be pleased with my return to school in this condition, but here I am.

The prodigal son.

The return of the Native.

I stop on the porch to get the mail. There's not much, and it's all junk, including an official-looking letter from the Gleaming town council. If I had thought about it, I would have stopped here first before I started the fire.

The old school is quiet and cool and dark, and as I walk down the corridor, I find that I'm suddenly and utterly exhausted.

Dead tired.

I leave the mail on the kitchen counter, head upstairs. And I'm asleep before I remember getting into bed.

THE CRADLE RIVER RESIDENTIAL SCHOOL.

Originally, the school and the graveyard, along with twenty-five acres of farmland and river frontage, had been part of the treaty that Cradle River had signed with the federal government. But in the early 1900s, Ottawa unilaterally split the property off from the reserve proper and gave it to the Catholic Church with the understanding that they would build a school where Native students from the surrounding area would be educated.

And given spiritual guidance.

After the school closed and the Catholics had moved on to more lucrative ministries, the property had sat abandoned. The band petitioned the federal government to return the land, and after due consideration, the petition was ignored. So the band began a formal land claim, arguing that they had never agreed to the severance and that the partition had been illegal.

And the land claim was ignored as well.

Winston Churchill had called Russia a riddle wrapped in a mystery inside an enigma, but he might just as well have been anticipating Thomas Locken and how the man had been able to purchase a property that should not have been for sale.

Or why having acquired it, Locken would have given it to me.

I hadn't asked for the school. The deed to the property was waiting for me with my severance package. I think it was his way of telling me that if I no longer wanted to engage with the world, I should go home.

So I did.

Not that Cradle River was home. Not that it had ever been home.

THE CROWS WAKE ME. Evidently, they've decided that I've slept long enough and should get back to work. They're particularly noisy and don't sound all that happy, as though something has disturbed their world.

A fox along the riverbank.

An owl caught out in daylight.

A politician with a plan to end poverty.

I sit on the edge of the bed and let the melancholy wash over me. Should I go out to the graveyard and pull up more crosses? Or should I just kill myself? Both have much to recommend them. Working among the graves might take my mind off the world. Suicide will take me out of it.

And then there's lunch.

As soon as I stand up, I realize that I'm hungry. But, as I imagine my normal lunch, as I see it on a plate in front of me, I find that I have little interest in hard-boiled eggs and toast, that I'd prefer something hot, something someone else has made.

The Piggy Bank.

Support local business. If Ada's daughter is making a go of the café, then everyone should do their part.

I'll do lunch.

I take my time in the bathroom. I shave, wet my hair so it doesn't stick up. I find a clean shirt and a jacket that does not have burn holes in it.

It's probably just the change in the weather, but by the time I get downstairs, I'm feeling hopeful. I'll have lunch, stop by Dino's to see if he has any grapes, surprise Swannie and pick up a small *gâteau basque* for the hell of it.

The grocery list is on the kitchen counter. The grocery bag is hanging on the doorknob.

I don't notice the girl until I turn to leave.

It's the girl from the graveyard. The girl I saw this morning when I was burning crosses. This is the first time that any of the dead have left the graveyard, the first time I've found a ghost in the school. I know it's a momentary apparition, a turn of imagination. I know that I'll look away or close my eyes or take a deep breath, and the girl will be gone.

But here she is. Sitting at the table. The cat on her lap.

"Hello," says the ghost. "Is there any peanut butter?"

18

The girl, sitting at my table with the cat on her lap, is not a ghost. She's Lala Stillday, Ada's granddaughter, Emma Still-day's child.

"Sometimes Mum-Mum makes me a cheese sandwich."

I can't believe the cat is sitting on her lap.

"One time, we had waffles with strawberries and whipped cream for lunch," Lala tells me, "but that was a special occasion."

And the beast is purring.

"After we eat, can we pull up more crosses and burn them?"

The cat and I need to have a heart-to-heart on the subject of loyalty.

"I know all about matches," says Lala, "but I'm not supposed to play with them."

The cat and I need to reach an understanding.

"This is a nice house," says Lala. "Some of the rooms have black-boards."

Shelter and food. These are not minor issues.

"Do you have children?"

THERE ARE PEOPLE in the Piggy I have never seen before. Someone has put sprigs of parsley in tiny vases on each table, along with tea candles.

Lala skips into the café and starts turning circles in front of the counter, her arms out, her head thrown back.

Florence is behind the counter. She's wearing an apron that says "Kiss My Barista."

"Good," she calls out to me. "You've met Lala. Would have mentioned it earlier, but I wanted you to get settled."

I've only been gone four days.

"Couldn't put Emma and Lala in one of the trailers, now could they? Mouldy single-wide's no place for a child."

Florence grinds a batch of beans. She packs the basket and lifts the lever.

"The old school's not ideal, but it's got room and it's clean. You won't even notice that they're there."

I wait for the rest of the explanation to show up.

"Don't look at me like that." Florence sets a macchiato on the counter. "Wasn't my idea."

Ada and Nutty.

"Besides, you're going to like having Lala around. Little girl like that brightens the world." Florence puts the tarot deck in front of me. "And a little brightening wouldn't hurt you one bit."

I shuffle the deck and cut it four times.

"Ace of Cups!" Florence slaps her hand on the card. "Look at that. Beginning of good things. Joy, love, beauty, health. Breakthrough in spiritual understanding."

The door to the kitchen opens and Lala is off, bouncing across the restaurant towards a woman who has to be her mother.

"Mum-Mum!"

Emma Stillday grabs Lala and lifts her high in the air. "What are you doing here, sweetie? You were supposed to stay home."

"It's okay, Mum-Mum," says Lala. "Pop-Up brought me."

Florence comes out from behind the counter. "Emma. This is Jeremiah Camp."

"Mr. Camp." Emma holds out a hand. "Sorry about the imposition."

"Don't worry," says Florence. "He don't bite. Man don't even talk."

"I really appreciate you helping us out until we can get settled."

Lala puts her hands on her hips. "Pop-Up doesn't talk?"

"Lala," says Emma. "Manners."

"Then I won't talk either."

Lala helps herself to a jar of crayons and some paper and takes over the small table near the kitchen. Florence makes her a hot chocolate, and Emma brings her daughter a sandwich.

I have the uneasy feeling that there's something I'm supposed to do. But I can't think of what it might be. So I just stand there and watch.

THE LUNCH SPECIAL is shepherd's pie with a small salad. I eat it at the counter, while Florence fills me in on what I've missed while I was gone.

"You see what Wegman's up to?" Florence makes a face. "Woman tried to make off with your pile of crosses."

The salad is fresh and crisp.

"But Roman beat her to it. He's got them stored in Nutty's trailer. Says he'll bring them out when it's time for the big bonfire."

The shepherd's pie is excellent. Between bites, I check the blackboard to see if there are any desserts.

"You missed the news, but there wasn't much to it. World's falling apart. Same as last week." Florence looks over at Lala. "Not right for a child to sit in a café all day. She should get out into the sunshine. Take her for a walk. Have some fun."

I stop eating.

"She could help you with the renovations at the school," says Florence. "Pull up some of the crosses."

A blind man could see where this is going.

"So, Pop-Up," says Florence. "How's it feel to be an uncle?"

Florence doesn't have to spell out the fact that Emma is tied up with work, or that Florence has to help her, or that Nutty's too old to look after an energetic girl, or that Ada can't do it on her own, or that I'm not doing anything anyway.

But she does nonetheless.

"It's only for today." Florence says this as though she expects me to believe it. "Tomorrow, Lala will be in school."

LALA STILLDAY IS A CONSTANT and inexhaustible stream of questions.

"Why don't you talk?"

"How old are you?"

"Can we go to the bakery?"

"What's the cat's name?"

"Do you like me?"

"What other things should we burn?"

THE GROCERY STORE has grapes. The large black variety. Dino Kiazzie and his son Javi are arranging melons in a basket. Dino sees me and hurries over.

"Midnight Beauty," he says. "Delicious. Very firm."

I check the origin information.

"From Chile." Dino picks two grapes off the bunch and hands me one. "This time of the year, it is what we can get."

He hands the second grape to Lala. "You must be the special little girl I've heard so much about."

"Lala Stillday," says Lala, "and I am no longer little."

"So smart," says Dino. "Much better to be smart than pretty."

"I'm also pretty," says Lala.

Dino claps his hands. "Javi," he shouts to his son, "what do we do with smart girls who are also pretty?"

Javi is in his early twenties. Coal black hair with soft eyes and long lashes. "We give them an apple."

Lala's face erupts in a smile, and she bounces about from one foot to the other.

"That's right, we give them an apple." Dino picks a Golden Delicious from the stack. "This is a special apple."

"It is?"

"Oh yes." Dino's eyebrows are thickets. His moustache is a pile of dry brush. "A long time ago, there was a famous lady named Hera, who had a grove of apple trees that was guarded by a fierce dragon."

"A real dragon?"

Javi holds his arms up over his head and screws his face into an impressive snarl. "An enormous dragon," he says. "It could eat a hippopotamus in one bite."

"One bite?"

"And the apples that grew in this grove," says Dino, "were all the colour of precious gold."

"Like this one," says Lala.

"Exactly like this one," says Dino, and he hands her the apple. "But what makes these apples special is that they have the power to heal."

"Like if you scraped your knee?"

"Better than that," says Javi. "They have the power to heal the spirit."

Dino nods and puts his hand over his heart.

Lala ponders this for a moment. "But you can still eat them?"

"Of course," says Dino. "Eating has always been a part of healing."

"That's why," says Javi, "they're called Golden Delicious."

"Can Pop-Up have one too?"

AT THE BAKERY, Swannie gives Lala a *sablé breton*.

"The shortbread," Swannie tells her. "Very much the butter."

I stand in front of the case and check the trays. All the brownies are gone.

"And what will you become," says Swannie, "when you have become grown?"

"A dragon," says Lala. "I'm going to be a dragon."

"*D'accord*," says Swannie. "This the world needs."

I don't see any point in trying to explain the intricacies of mythology to either of them.

"Will you be the fierce dragon?"

Swannie has changed into a long-sleeved shirt. You can't see the hair under her arms, but the area is dark with sweat.

"Not too fierce," says Lala. "Otherwise people won't like me."

"Ah," says Swannie. "And then you would be sad."

"Pop-Up is sad." Lala takes my hand. "That's why he doesn't talk."

As soon as we get back to the school, Lala takes me to one of the large classrooms. It's been converted into a bed-sitting room. The desks are long gone, but the blackboards are still up and functional. Lala has found some chalk and has started drawing stick figures and flowers on the old slate.

"That's Mum-Mum's bed," says Lala. "Sometimes I sleep with her. Like if there's a storm. Or my stomach hurts. Or Mum-Mum is feeling lonely."

Someone has brought in a dresser, a kitchen table, and a television.

"The television is old, and it doesn't work. Maybe you can fix it."

There's an air mattress in the corner covered in stuffed toys and books. It has a soft look to it, as though it's worn out and can't get up. Lala jumps on it and it makes a sharp hissing sound.

"My bed is broken," she says. "Maybe you can fix it, too."

Emma gets back to the school a little after four. Lala and I are sitting in the kitchen, sorting through a pile of books. We've been doing this for almost an hour. Lala chooses a book and reads it to me. And then I choose a book, and she reads it to me.

"I'm sorry," says Emma. "I thought I would be done sooner."

"Pop-Up doesn't mind," says Lala. "Do you?"

"Honey, Mr. Camp is a very busy man."

"And he's going to fix the television."

"Lala . . ."

"He's already fixed my bed."

I'd found an old tire-patch kit someone had left behind. The glue was still good. All that was needed after that was a decent set of lungs.

"And now," says Emma, "it's time to let Mr. Camp get some rest."

"Pizza," says Lala. "Pizza, pizza, pizza."

"Yes, honey," says Emma, "we're going out for pizza."

"With Roman?"

Emma stiffens. "Your father said he'd meet us there."

"Hooray!"

"We'll see." Emma takes a long breath. "We'll see."

LATER THAT EVENING, I hear Emma and Lala come into the school and go to their room. As soon as the cat hears the front door open, she's off the chair and down the stairs.

I don't mind. If I want reliable companionship, I can always get a goldfish.

19

The next few weeks fall into an easy and dependable routine. Emma goes to the café early, and I look after Lala. I introduce her to quinoa, Parmesan cheese, and cottage cheese.

She is not impressed.

"Pop-Up, you eat this every day?"

Lala's idea of breakfast is a bowl of sugar-flavoured cereal and sliced bananas.

"No wonder you're sad."

And I walk her to school. This is pleasant enough. Lala likes the crows, tries to mimic their calls.

"I can talk to crows." Lala hops around on one foot. "And they talk to me. They tell me things."

I try to imagine what secrets crows would share with a child, what lies they would tell.

"Can you talk to crows?"

TODAY, IKU TAKAHASHI and Koala appear on the path. As soon as Koala sees Lala, the dog begins dancing on its hind legs.

"Mr. Camp," says Takahashi. "And Lala-chan. Koala asks about you every day."

"What are those?"

Takahashi slips the binoculars off her neck. "These are binoculars."

"Binokers," says Lala, picking her way through the syllables.

"With these, you can see the world," says Takahashi. "With these, you can see the future."

"Really?" Lala holds the binoculars up to her eyes. "I can't see anything."

"You have to relax your eyes," says Takahashi. "Then everything will look larger."

Lala sways from side to side. "Is the future large?"

"These were my husband's binoculars. Very expensive. Very high quality."

Keizo Takahashi. Taught history at the high school. Heart attack. Sudden and complete.

"I can see something," says Lala, "but it's all blurry."

"He wanted to watch birds," says Takahashi. "He did not think about the future."

I have to get Lala to school. I'd look at my watch. If I had one.

"Would you like my binoculars?"

Lala puts the binoculars down. "Sure."

"Maybe Mr. Camp will buy them for you."

I hand the binoculars back to Mrs. Takahashi.

"Your niece has such nice manners." Mrs. Takahashi tightens up on Koala's leash. "My husband had nice manners, too."

I DROP LALA OFF at the school, walk over to the bakery, pick up a brownie, and get to the Piggy in plenty of time for a macchiato and the news.

Today the café is full, and I have to sit at the counter.

"Business gets any better," says Florence, "and I'll have to shut the place down."

I take the brownie out of the bag, so Florence can see it.

"This is the way it used to be when Reggie was alive." Florence takes a deep breath. "Who wants to work this hard?"

Roman comes out of the kitchen carrying plates of food.

"Had to hire someone," says Florence, by way of explanation. "Evidently, café hours and musician hours go well together."

Roman looks to be in good spirits. He smiles at the foursome sitting at the table as he sorts out the plates, even laughs at something that's said.

"Thinking I may have him play a little music on the weekends. Sort of a brunch-time concert. See how that goes."

Florence grinds the beans.

"And it gives him and Emma some time together. Don't know that it will work out. Not even sure if they're trying."

I wait as Florence fills the basket and tamps it down.

"How are you and your niece settling in?"

Florence has continued to experiment with the espresso blends. This one is black cherry with nutty undertones.

"You missed a bunch of days." Florence cuts the brownie, the division favouring her side. "So there's ground to be made up."

I sip my macchiato slowly. When I was in Rome, I watched people walk in off the street, order an espresso, and toss it back in one gulp. As though it were a nasty tonic that a doctor had prescribed.

"I feel sorry for Emma," says Florence. "She shouldn't be cooking. Woman has a law degree. She should be in a courtroom ripping the lungs out of some corporate maggot."

And they drank it in paper cups.

"She and Roman were together for a time. Didn't work out. That's why she moved to Winnipeg. New start. Evidently, lawyers can move about. Like plumbers and truck drivers. But she couldn't find any lawyering work in Winnipeg, so she started cooking. Discovered she was good at it."

I mean, really. A paper cup?

"So she's back. But because she was gone, now she has to come up with a bunch of law dues for the years she missed. Before they'll let her practise."

For me, life is too short to rush past the pleasures. Espresso should be experienced slowly, in a heated porcelain cup, with something sweet to complement and soften the bitterness.

"I figure soon as she gets the money for those dues, she'll go back to law." Florence holds her arms out. "And leave this paradise behind."

I finish the macchiato and set the cup to one side. I'm thinking of ordering another one when Roman comes over.

"Cuz," he says. "How's my girl?"

"Easy enough to find out yourself," says Florence.

"Have to be here early," says Roman. "Jeremiah don't mind."

Florence throws a towel over her shoulder. "You could pick her up after school."

"Got to practise today," says Roman. "Big gig coming up."

"Today's the only today the two of you going to have."

Florence grabs my cup and takes it to the sink. I lean away from Roman, so Florence can tell us apart.

"You understand, cuz." Roman hitches his pants, gives me a quick smile. "Man's got to make a living."

I HAD FORGOTTEN about the upcoming election. But when I get to the plaza, there it is. Election central. The Neighbours and their families have been replaced with canopy tents that are lined up along the perimeter of the square. Some of these are for candidates. Others are for issues that will be on the ballot.

I have little interest in politics and even less in people who can imagine themselves as politicians.

"Jerry."

Mayor Bob. With an enormous button on his lapel that says "Bob's the One."

"Just the man I wanted to see."

Mayor Bob grabs me by the shoulder and drags me over to a double tent with "Re-Elect Bob" signs stacked up like cordwood.

"Here you go."

Mayor Bob pins one of his buttons on my jacket. I feel like a goat that's been tagged for slaughter.

There's a large table with a scale model of a housing development. Cradle River Estates. Executive lots and luxury condos.

"Cradle River Estates is going to be a major focus of my election campaign."

It's the reserve. The trailers are gone, the old school is gone, the graveyard is gone, all replaced with concrete and steel, wood and brick. With pathways and playgrounds.

"Phase one." Mayor Bob waves a hand over the model. "Right here is going to be a shopping centre. Along with a medical complex."

The model makers have even named the streets in honour of what they're going to replace. "Ojibway Lane," "Iroquois Road," "Cayuga Crescent."

"This was going to be the new library." Mayor Bob taps one of the toy buildings with a finger. "But we decided to go with a sports bar instead."

It's Loomis's master plan for the old school and the graveyard, for the reserve. He had the model built a number of years back, and he shows it off at every opportunity.

"The library will be in phase three."

Miniature buildings glued to a board. Tiny strips of indoor-outdoor carpet marking out the lawns and green spaces. In the centre of the development is a circular park labelled "Loomis Commons."

"I'm counting on your vote."

I've heard about the project. But this is the first time I've seen the model.

"Vote early," says the mayor. "Vote often."

Two tents down, Maribelle Wegman is getting signatures on a petition.

"The crosses are a bee in her bonnet," says Mayor Bob. "Not sure I can support Maribelle on that one. Technically, the school and the graveyard are on private land. And everyone knows my views on the sanctity of private land."

Now that I'm in the plaza, I decide to check out the rest of the booths. The election isn't the only order of business. Beeswax candles. Raku pottery. A heavy-set man selling home water-filtration systems who assures me that I'm killing myself drinking town water. A double tent with a banner that says "For a Greater Gleaming."

A young woman with a clipboard rushes out of the tent. "It's a research project," she tells me, "to see what people want in a community. There are five questions. All you have to do is read them and indicate whether you agree or disagree. Yes or no."

And then she's off to find another participant.

The questions are crafted in a way to get the correct response.

Shouldn't members of a community share the same values?

Shouldn't communities be able to plan for and pursue a common destiny?

Shouldn't communities be able to expand as expansion is needed?

Shouldn't the health of a community be unobstructed by special interests?

Shouldn't everyone in a community pull their weight?

I answer no to each question, sign Bob's name to the survey, and drop his button in the trash can. I don't stop by the widow Wegman's booth. I expect I'll see her soon enough.

Swannie Gagnon has set up an outdoor display of pastries to take advantage of the increased foot traffic.

"*Ta petite fille*," Swannie tells me, "she is *charmante*."

I buy a small bag of *sablés bretons* for Lala.

"That one," says Swannie, "she make the stone happy."

I buy a *pain aux raisins* as well.

"Oh, *mon dieu*." Swannie throws her arms in the air, her eyes wide with astonishment. "The world, it is ending."

I ignore the mockery and Swannie's underarms, take my pastries, and walk away from the plaza, away from Wegman and Mayor Bob, the man with the water-filtration system, and the promise of a better Gleaming.

And I don't look back.

20

Nutty Moosonee is relaxing in her recliner, but she's not alone. Wes Stanford and another man are standing on the roof of her trailer. Wes has his hands on his hips, while the older man walks around in a circle.

"They heard my roof was in trouble," Nutty tells me, "so they came by."

Slick is perched on the garbage can. He's all puffed up, as though he's trying to impress the world.

"The one with the beard is Jimmy," Nutty tells me. "He's done roofing work before."

Slick has one eye shut, but the other one is open just a crack in case trouble comes along. He may be young, but he's no fool.

I pull up a chair and sit.

Wes and Jimmy climb down.

"No good news," says Wes.

"Trailer roofs," says Jimmy, "are generally made out of fibreglass or rubber. Don't much matter which, so long as she stays watertight."

"But this one ain't," says Wes.

"You got pinholes in the rubber membrane," says Jimmy. "Best you can do is roll a coat of roof cement over the whole thing and hold your breath."

"It's not cheap," says Wes.

"Couple hundred for the material," says Jimmy. "Then there's labour."

Wes shakes his head. "Don't know it's worth doing, seeing as the main problem here is the mould."

"It's what I got," says Nutty. "Mould and all."

"Good money chasing bad," says Wes. "Just so you know."

Slick opens both eyes and shakes himself awake. He stretches his neck and gives a sharp caw.

"We don't mind doing it for the cost of materials," says Jimmy. "You can't live like this."

Slick begins his dance on the garbage can. Nutty takes a peanut out of her pocket and tosses it to the bird.

"Be okay if we take a look at some of the trailers?" says Jimmy. "See how bad the mould problem is. Word is the mayor's still pushing the band council about renting the empties and sticking us in them."

"Right now, we got the old box factory," says Wes, "but that ain't going to last much longer."

"Sticking us in the trailers is cheaper than coming up with afford-able housing," says Jimmy.

Wes nods. "They don't want us in the park."

"As if we want to be there," says Jimmy.

Slick uses his beak to turn the nut around, as though he's check-ing it for quality and size. Then he puts it down on the garbage can lid and waits.

"Don't even think it's legal. Moving us onto treaty land. Rent or no rent." Wes wipes his hands on his pants. "Figure the mayor's just blowing smoke, making it look as though he cares. So he can get re-elected."

"You get that membrane cement," Jimmy tells Nutty, "and we'll put it on."

Wes and Jimmy head off into the trailers. Nutty throws another peanut to Slick.

"He's not satisfied with one," she tells me. "The other day, he tried to stuff three in his mouth."

Slick sets the nut next to the first one and taps his beak against the can.

"Picking up bad habits from somewhere," says Nutty. "Not naming any names, but you got to wonder if he's been talking to certain folks in town."

I put the *pain aux raisins* on the table next to Nutty.

"This from the bakery?" Nutty tears off a small piece. "Ada tried putting raisins in bannock once."

As soon as Slick sees the pastry, he begins cawing and dancing at the same time.

Nutty tears off a small piece and tosses it to him. "Babies can be greedy. But if you give them what they want, as they get older, they grow out of it."

Slick gobbles down the piece of pastry, grabs both nuts, and flies away.

"Or they don't," says Nutty. "Not much you can do about that. Easy to get lost. Easy to stop caring."

I tuck the blanket in around Nutty, bring her a bowl of yogurt and canned cherries.

"How's the graveyard going?" Nutty asks. "My sister is buried there. You got a couple of aunties and a bunch of cousins. Babies, all of them. We all got people in that place. Good someone is looking after them."

I haven't found any Camps yet, but there are still a great many more graves to go.

"And Roman could use a big brother. Hold on to him when he runs off in a bad direction."

I flash on Koala breaking her leash and plunging headlong into the river and over the falls. With Mrs. Takahashi rooted to the spot, watching the calamity through her binoculars.

"He's got one beautiful daughter," says Nutty, "and a woman who may still love him."

Roman needs to hold on to himself.

Nutty leans back and closes her eyes. "That's more than some people got."

ROMAN AND EMMA are sitting on the front porch. Emma waves when she sees me.

"Mr. Camp," she calls out. "I hope you don't mind."

"He doesn't mind," says Roman. "Besides, he doesn't really own the school. It's treaty land. Cradle River land. Ain't that right, cuz?"

"Mr. Camp is very gracious, letting us stay here."

"Can't buy and sell what's not yours. That's the law."

"So now you're a lawyer?" Emma looks at Roman in mock horror. "I'd stick to the high Cs if I were you."

LALA IS AT THE KITCHEN TABLE with a sandwich and a glass of water.

"Pop-Up!" She leaps off the chair and wraps her arms around my legs. "Where have you been?"

I pull up a chair and sit down. I'm hungry but I can't think of anything I want to eat.

"Pancakes was worried about you, too."

On cue, the cat appears, hurries to Lala, and jumps on her lap.

"I call her Pancakes," says Lala, "'cause I like pancakes."

Lala starts rubbing the cat's ears and the animal begins purring loudly enough to disturb the dead in the graveyard.

"Pancakes and I have been in every room in the whole place," says Lala. "Do you know how many there are?"

I've counted the rooms myself. More than once.

"Mum-Mum says I'm not supposed to go into your room, and that I'm not to touch any of your things."

The cat rolls over on her back, her paws in the air.

"Like that old lunch box on the windowsill."

I go to the refrigerator. Outside, I can hear voices. Roman is talking to someone, and neither one of them sounds happy. And then a woman's voice, rising above the rest, firm and unrelenting.

Maribelle Wegman is standing by a patrol car. Two officers in uniform are standing with her. Roman and Emma hold the high ground on the porch. I arrive just in time to stop World War III.

"There he is," says Wegman. "Arrest him."

The two policemen look somewhat embarrassed. The taller one puts out a hand in an attempt to defuse the situation.

"Let's stay calm," he says.

"He unlawfully crossed a crime-scene perimeter." The widow Wegman has blood in her voice. "And he burned city property and historical artifacts in direct defiance of a court order."

"How about it, Mr. Camp?" says the tall cop. "Did you do that?"

I'm not about to answer that question. And I don't have to. Emma is off the porch in a flash.

"I think we have a jurisdictional problem," she says.

Wegman jumps in before the cop can open his mouth. "And who are you?"

Emma takes a deep breath, finds a smile. "I'm the band's attorney."

"You're a lawyer?" says the tall cop.

"Damn right she is," says Roman.

Emma steps in front of Roman. "And from what I can see, you have no jurisdiction here."

Wegman turns to the shorter of the two cops. "Tell her."

"Tell her what?" says the cop.

Emma keeps her smile in place. "As I remember, the town ends at the old riverbed. Which means your jurisdiction ends there."

The cops look at one another.

"We might argue whether this is private property outside city jurisdiction or Cradle River First Nations land under treaty," Emma continues. "But in either case, you have no authority here."

Wegman is not about to give up. "There's a court order."

"Actually," says the shorter cop, "it was a motion passed at city council."

"And that's the law," says Wegman.

"On city property, perhaps," says Emma. "But not here."

Wegman looks at the two cops. "So, you're just going to let him burn the crosses? You're just going to allow him to desecrate a graveyard?"

"Not sure what we can do."

"The graveyard is a historical site," says Wegman. "It's part of our heritage."

"Maybe," says the taller cop, "you could work out a compromise."

"That," says Emma, "you will have to take up with Mr. Camp and/or the band council directly."

"This is a Christian country!"

"And if you come onto the property again without written authorization or a proper warrant, it will be considered trespass and you may be subject to criminal charges and civil suits."

The whole confrontation lasts about ten minutes, and then the two policemen and the widow Wegman get back in the car. Even at a distance, over the noise of the car's engine, you can hear Wegman continue to argue her case.

I feel motion behind me, and I turn to find Lala standing in the doorway. On the verge of tears. Emma sees her, too.

"It's okay, honey." Emma gathers her daughter in her arms. "Mum-Mum was just talking to some people who were lost."

Lala blinks away tears. "They were angry."

"No, honey, they weren't angry. They were just lost."

"Why were they lost?"

"Sometimes people get lost," says Emma. "Sometimes they don't watch where they're going. And when that happens, they get upset."

"I get upset sometimes."

"Yes, you do."

"When you want me to eat beets."

"Beets are good for you, honey."

"But I don't like them."

"Then," says Emma, "we won't have beets tonight."

EMMA TAKES LALA back in the house. Roman shakes a cigarette out of a pack and offers me one.

"Bet you don't drink either," he says.

Somehow, the day has disappeared. It's not evening yet, but the light has softened and the temperature has cooled.

"Emma and me used to be real tight." Roman takes a long drag, fills his lungs. "She's a good woman, but she's not easy."

In the house, I can hear Lala arguing with her mother about a bath.

"I love my daughter. No doubt about that."

The point of contention is Pancakes.

"I'm playing at the Bent Nail tonight." Roman drops the cigarette on the porch and steps on it. "If you like jazz."

I watch Roman walk off through the graveyard, touching the crosses as he goes. Then I sit on the steps and wait for the day to end and for the crows to come home.

21

I'm heating chili when Emma comes into the kitchen. She leans up against the counter and sighs.

"She wanted to bring the cat into the tub."

I try to look sympathetic.

"I hope you didn't mind me jumping in." Emma gets a glass from the cupboard. "Wegman's always rubbed me the wrong way."

I take bread out of the freezer and put two slices into the toaster.

"She's not going to give up." Emma fills the glass at the sink and heads down the hall. "But I guess you know that."

THE THREE COMMA CLUB.

Unlimited money. Unrestricted power. Your desires met. Your authority absolute. A careless narrative of imagined omnipotence.

I knew most of the people on the list, had sat down with them at business meetings, had talked with them at parties. And, except for the fact that they were all rich beyond belief, there was nothing notable about any of them.

Tall, short. Fat, skinny. Healthy, sick. Intelligent, stupid. Friendly, belligerent. Ambitious, lazy.

Ordinary. They were all one remove from ordinary.

I CAN HEAR LALA in the classroom, laughing. Her mother is reading her a story about a princess and a dragon. I catch parts of it. Mostly the sound effects. The dragon roaring, the princess roaring back, until they both tire and fall over giggling.

The chili is still on the stove in the pan. I dump it into a bowl and put the bowl in the refrigerator. I leave the bread in the toaster. In the classroom, Emma and Lala are singing a song I don't recognize.

Something about being happy and clapping your hands.

I turn off the light in the kitchen, grab my jacket, and am out the door.

THOMAS LOCKEN was several removes from ordinary. He understood the complexities and stratagems of wealth and power, but he was fascinated by the arcana and esoterica of human existence.

In particular, by questions that could not be answered.

Why do we dream?

What is music?

What is life?

What is the purpose of death?

He wasn't concerned that there were no definitive answers to such questions, wasn't troubled by the probability that any attempt would only create a shifting assortment of patterns.

Locken believed that seeing and understanding those patterns was answer enough.

ON FRIDAYS, the Bent Nail hosts wet T-shirt contests. On Saturday and Sunday afternoons, it's a sports bar. Monday is trivia night. Tuesday evening is karaoke and open mic. Wednesday is board games. Thursday is music.

All of this crammed into a dark, dingy, low-ceilinged space that smells like a holding pond at the back of a brewery.

There's a picture of Roman and his horn pasted to the front door of the Nail. Half of Roman's face is in shadow, so he looks aloof and mysterious. The handwritten caption says "One Night Only."

This is that night.

I have no idea when Roman will start playing, but I have no interest in waiting around in a beernut landfill, watching young men grow old, while a guy on the jukebox tells me why his woman left him, when why was never the question.

So I cross the street, walk into the park, and sit on a bench by the bandstand. The night has cooled, but it's still pleasant. I have nowhere to go, so here is as good a place as any.

I feel the shadow before I hear the voice.

"Cuz."

Roman, all in artist black. He looks good. Clear-eyed, clean shaven, hair slicked back and hanging on his shoulders.

"Guess if you're here, Emma's not going to make it." He sets his horn case on the grass. "I mean, she can't leave Lala alone."

There's a family coming out of the Plaza Hotel. Mother, father, two young sons. Dressed for a casual evening. A movie at the mall. A hockey game at the rink.

"She used to come to all my gigs." Roman lights a cigarette and blows the smoke into the air. "And then I screwed up."

I keep my eyes on the family.

"Your mum screwed up, too," says Roman. "Ada says she ran off and got pregnant."

The family moves off down the street. The older boy runs on ahead, gets as far as the corner before he stops and waits.

"She really kill herself," Roman asks, "or is that just Ada being a shit?"

The younger boy stays with his mother. The father lags behind, as though he's already given up.

Roman wets his lips. "Better head in. Don't want to keep the drunks waiting."

I smile and nod.

"You and me are a lot alike, you know." Roman picks up his case. "The difference is that I have to go in there, and you don't."

Roman crosses the street. The Bent Nail is aglow in neon. An Open sign in blue. A Moosehead Lager sign in green and red. I've never heard Roman on the horn, only heard the reports, reviews that compared him to Baker and Davis, to Farmer and Hubbard. Maybe he'll play "Almost Blue" or "Body and Soul." Or "They Can't Take That Away from Me."

There's nothing to stop me from slipping into the Nail. I could sit at the back, close my eyes, and let the music find me.

Instead, I stay on the bench. No stars tonight, and I can't see the moon. But there's heavy cloud cover, so it could be there. Just hidden and out of sight.

Like me.

22

The next morning, the three of us sit around the kitchen table.

"I'm late." Emma rinses her cup in the sink. "My phone died last night, so no alarm."

"Pop-Up wants to walk me to school." Lala taps her spoon on the side of the bowl. "But we have to go to the falls first."

"Mr. Camp isn't taking you to the falls, honey."

"My teacher said I had to go to the falls."

Emma's shoulders sag a little. "I don't think your teacher said you had to go to the falls."

"I have to draw a picture of the falls for show and tell."

"I don't want you going there without me."

"But you have to work, and Pop-Up doesn't work."

Emma is already in her coat. "I'll pick you up after school. Maybe we'll go to the falls then."

"You have to promise."

"We'll see."

Lala looks to me for support. I keep my head down over my quinoa and pretend to be invisible.

"That means no."

"No, it doesn't."

"Yes, it does."

"I have to go, honey."

Lala slams her spoon down and bits of cereal and milk fly off in all directions. Then she bangs her elbows on the table and sits back in the chair in a huff.

Emma stands in the kitchen doorway, the patience draining out of her face. "I love you."

"If you loved me, you'd let me go to the falls."

Emma smiles at me. "Thank you, Mr. Camp. You don't know how much I appreciate this."

"And I'm not going to school."

But Emma is gone, already out the door. Lala slumps in her chair.

"Do you have a mum-mum?" she asks.

I finish the quinoa and put the bowl in the sink.

"I'll bet she's nicer than mine."

THE CROWS ARE WAITING for us. As soon as they see Lala, they begin calling out.

"They're asking if we know any stories," says Lala. "They like stories."

They like peanuts and shiny things, as well. Freshly washed cars and garden wagons.

"I know a story about a dragon." Lala shuffles her feet, kicks up bits of gravel, throws up tufts of dust. "But I don't want to frighten them."

We follow the river path until we have to turn in towards the town. The sun feels good on my shoulders. We take our time, stopping to look at the mallards and mergansers as they work the river. When we get to the school, Lala gives me a quick hug.

"I love you, Pop-Up."

And then she skips off into the building.

SWANNIE GAGNON'S HAIR is bright blue with white stripes. She looks like a Greek flag.

"*Les couleurs du Québec*," she tells me, as she puts my brownie in a bag. "*Je me souviens.*"

Swannie hasn't forgotten her underarms. One is blue. One is white.

"It is the food colouring," she says. "I wash and poof, it is gone."

Swannie has made rhubarb Danishes today. I'm tempted but resist. A routine is only a routine if it's maintained.

"I am at the bar last night," says Swannie. "I hear your cousin play. 'La Vie en Rose.' So beautiful. I am in tears. Édith Piaf. Such a voice."

I hadn't gone into the bar. I sat on the bench and listened to the music as it filtered out of the building, the gabble of voices, the sound of Roman's horn trying to cut through the din.

I stayed in the park, until the cloud cover broke apart and the moon arrived to light up the night.

"The petition of the crosses?" Swannie makes a popping sound with her lips. "I do not sign it."

THE PIGGY IS NOT as busy as it has been. The Three Bears are at one table. Wapi has his tablet out and is poking at the screen. Louis and Enola are going through a folder of invoices. Florence and Emma are at the counter.

I set the brownie down and wait.

"Hear Swannie is making rhubarb Danishes," says Florence. "Don't suppose you happened to pick up one of them."

"I'm sorry about this morning," says Emma. "Sometimes she can be difficult."

"You ever had one of her rhubarbs?" Florence puts the beans in the grinder. "They're really good."

"Roman was at the Bent Nail last night," says Emma. "Did you go?"

I watch Florence make my macchiato.

"He asked me to come," says Emma, "but I've got too much on my plate."

The milk is thicker than usual and gives the espresso the texture of heavy cream.

"Lala takes up most of my free time." Emma pushes out of the chair, heads for the kitchen. "Roman had his chance."

Florence sets the cup in front of me. "Okay," she says. "News, blues, and comfortable shoes."

"Used to be a woman up north had a radio show." Louis closes the folder. "Used to start it off with 'Here Are the News.' She was pretty popular."

"Edith Josie," says Enola. "Up in Old Crow."

The brownie is particularly moist, the dark chocolate the perfect companion to the espresso.

"On the international front, Chinese authorities have opened fire on demonstrators in Hong Kong and Singapore, killing fourteen."

"You can bet they killed more than fourteen." Enola leans in against Wapi and the tablet. "Social media out of Hong Kong has the number closer to one hundred."

"While in Britain," Florence continues, "a new survey suggests that voters have lost all faith in their politicians."

"Not much of a revelation," says Louis.

"In Montana, authorities are looking for a gunman with a high-powered rifle who is shooting at eighteen-wheelers on the interstate."

Louis makes a rifle with his arm. "Cabs or trailers?"

"Doesn't say," says Florence. "While here at home, the premier is justifying the dismantling of wind turbines and electric car charging stations as an unnecessary burden on taxpayers."

"The Tao of government," says Enola. "Build something at public expense and then tear it down at public expense."

"Or," says Louis, "build something at public expense and then sell it at a discount to private enterprise."

"The 407," says Enola.

"Hydro One," says Louis.

"Canada Post," says Enola.

Louis shakes his head. "Only parts of Canada Post are privatized."

"Just a matter of time," says Enola. "Any profitable public company gets sold."

"Sold," says Wapi.

"While in Gleaming," says Florence, jumping in before the Three Bears can run away with the conversation, "Mayor Bob has introduced a new anti-loitering bylaw in council that would require any individual or organization wanting to use the plaza for functions or activities to obtain a use permit."

"This is about the Neighbours," says Emma. "It's nothing more than anti-homeless legislation."

"Mayor is citing public safety as the rationale," says Enola.

"Man's the poster boy for public safety." Louis swings his arm around the café as he makes shooting noises.

Florence reaches under the counter and comes up with the tarot deck.

"Good thoughts, good card," she says. "Today, I got one of the Major Arcana. Number eleven. Lust."

I shuffle the deck.

"It isn't really about *lust* lust. It's more about strength and creativity, control of inner beasts and overcoming old fears. Triumph of the spirit. That sort of thing."

I cut the deck and get The Lovers.

"Look at that," says Florence, as though she's found a loonie on the sidewalk. "Another of the Major Arcana. Number six. Relationships, attraction, union of opposites. Finding connections. Becoming conscious."

I finish my half of the brownie. Florence takes my cup and wipes down the counter.

"This got anything to do with your lady friend?"

I hadn't expected that Ash Locken would go unnoticed for long. Not with booking the top floor of the Plaza. Not with Oliver Flood and the hounds in tow.

"Hear she comes with her own army."

I slip the sixth trump back into the deck and slide it to Florence.

"Gleaming's not a backwater, but we don't see that many expensive people in town."

Florence waits. And I let her.

"So," she says, "you want another macchiato?"

I GO STRAIGHT BACK to the school. I don't waste time. I change quickly, get the wagon and the chisels, and go into the graveyard. I trowel a stone into place, sketch the name in pencil so I have some sort of guide.

Then I lean forward beneath the warming sun and begin chipping away.

23

Emma and Lala find me in the graveyard stacking river stones and pulling up crosses.

"I got four gold stars and a robin." Lala holds up a sheet of paper.

"It's a story she wrote," says Emma. "About dragons and crows."

"They save the princess from monsters," says Lala.

Emma rubs her daughter's head. "Would you mind if I tape it to the refrigerator?"

Lala picks up one of the crosses. "Can I have this?"

"It's not a toy, honey."

"I could use it as a sword and hit the monsters."

"It's not a good idea to hit anything."

"Helen hit Linda."

"What?"

"Linda pushed Helen's little sister, and Helen pushed Linda."

"At school?"

"Pushed her right over."

"And that's not the right thing to do, is it."

Lala turns around in a circle. "Linda started to cry, so we called her crybaby."

"Children." Emma sighs. "They're a blessing."

I STAY IN THE GRAVEYARD the rest of the day. The chiselling is slow, and I'm only able to do two stones before the light goes and I have to drag the wagon back to the school.

Emma and Lala are in the kitchen. Emma has made spaghetti with meat sauce, and Lala is sucking up each strand one at a time.

"Watch this," she calls out. "I'm a vacuum cleaner."

"Honey, that's no way to eat spaghetti."

"But it's fun."

"It'll make a mess of your clothes."

"Then you can wash them."

Emma holds up a plate. "Would you like some? We have plenty."

The knock on the front door is quick and hard, and whoever it is doesn't wait. The door opens and there are footsteps in the hallway. Lala is in mid-suck when Florence rumbles into the kitchen.

"Let's go," she says. "Nutty's in the hospital."

Emma puts the plate on the counter. "Hospital?"

"Ada took her in," says Florence.

"Is it serious?"

Florence's face is tight. "We should get there."

"Is Grummy sick?"

Emma turns to me. "Can I leave Lala with you?"

"I want to see Grummy!"

"A hospital won't be any fun," says Emma. "Mr. Camp might read you a story."

"I want to see the hospital!"

"We can take her," says Florence. "Do Nutty good to see Lala."

I float away from the table, try to slip casually out of the kitchen.

Florence blocks me with a hip. "And just where do you think you're going?"

FLORENCE'S SUBARU is roomier than it looks. I sit in the front seat. Emma and Lala sit in the back.

"So Nutty's been complaining about her chest for the last couple of days." Florence slides through several stop signs, tapping the brakes for show. "Ada and her were watching baseball at Ada's place when Nutty began having trouble breathing."

"Is Grummy going to die?"

"No, honey," says Emma. "Grummy is not going to die."

"Helen had a cat," says Lala, "and it died."

I wonder if this is the same Helen who hit Linda.

"She had a goldfish and it died, too."

THERE ARE NO PARKING SPOTS on the street, so Florence has to use the hospital parking lot.

"You believe this," she says as she takes the ticket from the machine. "They charge sick people for parking?"

There's a special five-dollar rate after 6:00.

"You got to be real greedy to do that."

"Even worse in the city," says Emma. "In Winnipeg, it would cost you twice as much."

"No wonder Jesus was born in a manger."

There's nothing close, and Florence has to park against the back fence.

"Maybe I should start renting out space at the Piggy. Put one of those taxi meters on the tables."

"Taxi meter?" says Lala.

"First half-hour free," says Florence. "Eat fast."

WE HAVE TO WANDER the hospital corridors until we find the reception desk. The place is warm enough, but the lights are the colour of ice. The smell doesn't help. I try to stay away from hospitals because of the smell.

"Nutty Moosonee," Florence tells the woman at the desk.

"Are you family?" asks the woman.

"You bet," says Florence. "I'm her daughter."

The woman doesn't look at all convinced.

"And this is her other daughter and her granddaughter."

"And him?"

"Baby brother," says Florence. "He's her baby brother."

THEY HAVE NUTTY on the third floor, in a room all by herself. Ada and Roman are sitting by her bed. Nutty looks small and shrunken. And out of place.

"Come here, Chipmunk," says Ada. "You can sit on Nooko's lap."

"How's she doing?" says Florence.

"But you guys got to find your own chairs," says Ada.

"I'm fine," says Nutty. "Just get me out of here."

"You're not fine," says Ada, "and there ain't no way in hell you're going back to that trailer."

"Nothing wrong with me," says Nutty.

"Not what the doctor said," says Ada.

"It's a respiratory infection," says Roman. "Her lungs sound like a blown transmission."

"I just got a cough."

"You probably got pneumonia," says Ada.

"I'm just hungry," says Nutty. "They won't feed me."

Ada shakes her head. "They don't want to give you anything until they do all the tests."

"They already got most of my blood."

Lala leans into Ada. "They have Grummy's blood?"

"No, honey," says Ada. "Grummy's just being funny."

"Don't see me laughing," says Nutty.

Florence and I search the hospital. We finally find a couple of chairs in an empty room. They're a sorry-looking pair. One has a bent leg. The other is missing the padding on the seat.

Ada and Roman have evidently spent the time we've been gone arguing about what to do with Nutty, because when we get back, they've almost come to blows.

"My auntie died of pneumonia," says Ada.

"She was ninety-four," says Roman, "and she was diabetic."

"I'm diabetic," says Ada. "You trying to tell me something?"

"I know a story about a really big dragon," says Lala.

"You guys were gone long enough," says Ada, turning her attention to Florence and me and the chairs. "That the best you could do?"

Florence hands the car keys to Emma. "Why don't you take everyone home. Ada and me will stick around and look after Nutty."

"I want to stay, too," says Lala.

"You have school tomorrow, honey."

"No, I don't," says Lala. "Tomorrow's Saturday. So there."

"You're right. It is Saturday," says Emma, "but you don't want to miss going to the bakery."

This stops Lala in her tracks. "But what if Grummy dies because I'm not here?"

"Not going to die," says Nutty. "So long as I get something to eat."

Lala goes to the bed and pats Nutty's arm. "I'll bring you a cookie."

"I'd like that," says Nutty. "That'll cure me for sure."

"What about me?" Roman grabs Lala and dumps her on his lap. "What about me?"

"Grown man," says Ada. "You can get your own cookie."

I HADN'T PAID much attention to where we parked in the lot, and finding the car in the dark is not easy.

"I think it was this aisle," says Emma.

"You guys forgot where you parked?" says Roman.

"I can find it," says Lala.

"Subaru," says Emma. "Look for a Subaru."

In the end, Florence's car is easy enough to find. First, it has a bumper sticker that says "Black Lives Matter." Second, standing next to the Forester is Oliver Flood.

Roman tenses. "What the hell."

"Good evening, Forecaster." The Tesla is blocking the row. Rover is driving. Spot is shotgun. "Have we caught you at a bad time?"

Roman turns to me. "Who are these guys?"

"Business." Flood waves a hand in a lazy arc. "Rather pressing, as it turns out."

Spot gets out and opens the back door. Rover stays behind the wheel.

Roman holds his ground. "You going with these guys?"

"That would be best," says Flood.

Emma touches my hand. "You go. It sounds important."

"Yeah, Mr. Important. You go ahead and go." Roman holds his hand out. "I'll drive everyone home."

Emma keeps the keys. "Who made you the designated driver?"

Lala squeezes in against her mother. "Can I drive?"

I'm in the back with Flood.

"The old woman," he says, "she a relative?"

Spot's cellphone goes off. He looks at the screen and then turns to Flood.

Flood nods. "Our ride has arrived," he says to me.

Rover glides along the edge of town on his way to the open field and the waiting helicopter.

"Did you know," says Flood, as the car slips through the night, "that those assholes at the hospital charge five dollars for parking?"

24

Ash Locken is waiting for me in the room with the windows and the view of the lake. It's dark. You can't really see the water, but you can enjoy the lights of the high-rises along the lakeshore.

If you're so inclined.

The panorama is of no interest to me, and so far as I can tell, it's of no interest to Locken either.

"How was the ride in?" she asks. "I hear there was wind."

The wind had buffeted the helicopter all the way to the city, had blown it sideways on final approach.

"I've asked Oliver to monitor Mrs. Moosonee's situation, so you don't have to worry about that."

There's food on the table. Enough to feed a family of eight, with leftovers. I help myself to a cracker and a piece of cheese that looks as though it's started to rust.

"As you might guess, the situation has changed since last we talked."

I normally don't drink coffee, but a little caffeine might help keep me alert.

"There have been two more deaths." Locken opens the laptop and turns the screen towards me. "Lady Amahie Zuma."

The video on the screen is of wreckage scattered over a dry, scrub brush landscape. In the far distance, antelope with long horns are turned towards the camera. Off to one side, an obstinacy of Cape buffalo forages for food.

"Her Gulfstream crashed on a flight from Cape Town to Amsterdam." Locken leans on the table. "The plane went down in the national park, on the border between Benin and Niger."

The antelope and the buffalo disappear. They're replaced by a mansion done up to look like a Mexican hacienda. Adobe. Red roof tiles. A large fountain in the middle of a high-walled courtyard.

"Carlos Boeme. His estate in River Oaks."

There's not much to see. People moving back and forth, standing around. Someone being carried out of the house on a gurney. An IV is attached to the metal rails. Medics on either side lift the body into the ambulance.

A Lamborghini Urus waits at the far end of the compound next to a Karlmann King with its tinfoil angles and $2-million price tag.

"Word out of Houston is that Boeme shot himself while cleaning a gun. Accident? Suicide? Maybe even murder. Take your pick."

Why anyone would bother paying that kind of money for a tricked-out Ford 550 is beyond me. But then, I don't own a car.

"So, now our list of twelve is down to three." Locken closes the laptop. "Any thoughts?"

I help myself to a miniature cheeseburger, take a bite. It's roast beef rather than hamburger.

"Do you like sex, Mr. Camp?"

I take another bite.

"I've never understood the appeal it seems to hold for a great many people. I suppose it's a combination of instinct and hormones."

I wonder how Nutty and Florence and Ada are going to manage in a hospital room without food or a baseball game to provide some distraction.

"But I'm told that sexual activity can improve cognitive function, that it boosts cell growth in the areas of the brain that control memory."

Emma and Roman are a different story. And Lala. The three of them? The possibility of a new beginning?

"So, if you think that sex would help you with your forecast, all you have to do is ask."

Locken puts a hand to her mouth. Tries to look embarrassed.

"I'm not offering, mind you. But if you're interested, it can certainly be arranged."

How might Emma explain Roman to Lala? How might Roman explain himself to his daughter?

"You have to allow that I have been more than a little indulgent with your eccentricities."

How does anyone explain themselves to another person?

"I'm not a patient person, Forecaster. The rich never are."

How do we explain ourselves to ourselves?

Locken stifles a yawn. "But it's late. I'm never at my best when I'm tired and cranky. And, we have the weekend."

Locken walks to the door and taps the keypad.

"You already know where everything is. Let's begin fresh in the morning."

I help myself to some grapes. They're quite good. Maybe I can get the name of the supplier and pass it on to Dino Kiazzie.

My room at the Lighthouse is as I left it. Bed, desk, computer, printer, television. I strip the blanket off, wrap it around me, and lie on the floor in the corner. It's uncomfortably hard. And unnecessary.

But it's a useful reminder that here, in this world, I am not a guest.

25

Ash Locken doesn't appear until midday. She finds me in my room at the computer watching a video on crows.

"I just talked with Mr. Flood." Locken helps herself to the edge of the bed. "Mrs. Moosonee will be going home later this afternoon."

The guy in the video has stuck a long pole in the ground with a small platform mounted to the top where the crows can land. Every day, he puts out pieces of hot dog, a treat that he swears crows love.

"She has a respiratory infection," says Locken. "It's not pneumonia, so that's good."

I'm not all that impressed with the video. Crows will eat almost anything. Peanuts, hot dogs, road kill, fast food wrappers, dog shit. They're the goats of the bird world.

"But the real culprit appears to be malnourishment. Seems she hasn't been eating all that well."

I watch as several crows land on the platform and pick their way through the hot dogs, looking for the biggest piece.

"Evidently, this is a problem as you get older."

I turn off the video. The guy doesn't understand crows at all. He thinks they want to be friends with humans. He thinks they like him.

LUNCH IS SERVED in the main room with the view of the lake. Today, it's a catered meal rather than an ostentatious buffet.

Locken nurses a glass of iced tea. "I hope you like chicken."

Oddly enough, I find I have a yen for hot dogs.

"Did you sleep well?"

With Dijon mustard and a smear of ketchup on a toasted whole-wheat bun. Shredded lettuce and diced tomatoes.

"We've had a situation come up overnight." Locken gestures with one hand and a young Asian man comes out of nowhere and hurries into the room. "I'll let Dr. Bak bring you up to date."

Bak looks as though someone has nudged him with a cattle prod. His whole body is buzzing as he comes to attention.

"Dr. Joo-Won Bak. Senior research administrator. Biotech oversight."

He snaps the introduction off in crisp, military fashion. I half expect him to finish it with a salute.

"Dr. Bak is the head of a team that monitors new developments in the fields of genetics and bioengineering."

Now that he has dispensed with the formalities, Bak seems unsure of what to do next.

"This is Mr. Jeremiah Camp," says Locken. "You can tell him everything you've told me."

"It is highly sensitive," says Bak. "Are you sure this is wise?"

Locken's nod is barely perceptible.

"Yes, of course. Sorry." Bak tries to find somewhere to put his hands. "We have been monitoring a number of companies that are doing research and development in the reprogramming of murine skin cells."

Bak waits to see if I have been able to follow anything he's just said.

"There are three major stem cell types that comprise early-stage embryos. In the past, we've had to extract these from umbilical cords, but in the last five years, we've discovered ways to reprogram skin cells, to turn them into stem cells."

"I don't understand it either," says Locken.

"What this means," says Bak, "is that these PSCs—"

"English," says Locken. "For the non-geniuses in the room."

"Yes, yes, of course. Pluripotent stem cells. Think of them as a blank piece of paper on which you can draw any part of the human body. Anything from brain cells to a heart or a pancreas. And these new cells, these new organs, will be identical in every way to the original."

"Spare parts," says Locken. "Without the danger of rejection."

"We have every hope that PSCs will allow us to create entire organisms."

"Test-tube babies," says Locken. "Without the need for the sticky reality of copulation."

"Right now, several of the cutting-edge research facilities are trying to create a mouse from these cells," says Bak, his body beginning to buzz again. "Larger organisms will come later."

"Lions and tigers and bears." Locken smiles at me. "Oh my."

"We could repopulate extinct species."

"Golden toads on Bay Street. A troop of dodos strolling Parliament Hill. A flock of pterodactyls soaring above Alberta." Locken leans forward on the table. "But we can't do any of this just yet."

Bak takes a step backwards, as though he's been hit.

"Yes. No," he says, "but we are very close."

"Tell Mr. Camp about last night." Locken looks at Bak and waits.

"Yes, yes," says Bak. "Last night, the research facility at R&R Laboratories in Rome was destroyed. It appears to have been a gas explosion. This is a major disaster. R&R has been a leader in PSC research."

"Giuliana Rocca," says Locken. "Her father, Roberto Rocca, was the head of R&R until his death eight years ago, when his daughter took over."

Bak stands still as a statue.

"Thank you, Dr. Bak. Please let me know as soon as there is any additional information."

Bak can't move fast enough.

"He's a brilliant researcher," says Locken, as Bak disappears through the door. "A bit nervous when it comes to women and authority."

I take a grape from the fruit plate. It's as good as the ones from the night before.

"We don't yet know who was in the R&R facility at the time of the mishap," says Locken, "but since Rocca's name is on the list, you can see the concerns this raises. And if she was killed, then the only two individuals on the list who are still alive are Bernard Dassault in Paris and Kommer Heineken in Amsterdam."

Locken takes a bite of her omelette and pushes the plate away. "What do you know about billionaires?"

I try the balls of cantaloupe.

"In general, there are two kinds. Antediluvian and neoteric. A fancy way of saying old money and new. Antediluvian billionaires did not create their wealth. They inherited it. They come from families who have had wealth down through the ages. The neoteric variety are the ones who make their money themselves. One or two generations. Maybe they invent something or are wizards at investments, or they create companies that create companies and piggyback their way to wealth through acquisitions and takeovers."

"But you know all this." Locken helps herself to the coffee. "Here's a curious thing. The names on the list are all antediluvian billionaires. Including my father."

The sun coming in through the windows is bright and warm, and my eyes begin to droop.

"And they all seem to have some sort of attachment to Ankh Technologies, as though they were members of a clandestine board of directors or partners in a large enterprise."

I suppress a yawn. It's barely noon, and I'm ready for a nap.

"Let's say that Dr. Brown is correct, that we're dealing with someone who doesn't like billionaires. Not that I blame them. We are among the biggest assholes in the world. But why would you bother? What difference would our deaths make? Others will just step in to take our places. The Lernaean Hydra. Cut off one head and more heads appear.

"And the logistics are staggering. How do you go about killing twelve well-protected individuals and make the deaths appear to be natural or accidental? It's possible, I suppose, but incredibly difficult."

175

Locken goes quiet for a moment.

"Oliver will meet you when you get home tomorrow," says Locken. "He's taken care of everything. If you need anything else, just ask him."

Locken reaches out and touches my hand.

"You're not a prisoner, you know. Tonight, you might want to sleep in the bed."

I SPEND THE AFTERNOON and evening in my room, going over all the information that Locken's research team has compiled. Some of it interesting. Most of it white noise.

Fabrice Gloor took the money from his great-grandfather's successful watch manufacturing business and moved into robotics and artificial intelligence. Divorced twice. Currently married to a woman younger than his oldest daughter. Numerous citations for insider trading. No convictions, no fines. Rumoured to have a temper and an alcohol problem. A sports-car aficionado.

Overweight, type 2 diabetes, balding, thought that he looked like Jean-Luc Picard.

Jonathan Weston, oldest son of William Weston, inherited S.K.I.N., a cosmetic conglomerate with a focus on anti-aging technologies and therapies. Single, never married, possibly bisexual. Reclusive.

A Georgian townhome in the Mayfair area of London that he seldom left. Regular visits to a plastic surgeon. Fresh-cut flowers delivered to his residence every day. Two of the company's products, Crème de la Sol and Belle Pelle, took S.K.I.N. to the top of the market. Subject of an investigation by the FDA over the presence of pesticides found in the company's facial products and hair dyes. Currently embroiled in a chemical-dumping scandal in Thailand.

Also played the piano.

WHAT I HAVE OF MY MOTHER, what I know of my mother, is in her Lone Ranger lunch box. A green stone, two photographs, a letter from Family and Children's Services, a child's chain with a St. Christopher medal, and a handful of road maps tied up with a ribbon.

My mother died before I had the chance to ask her the questions I might have asked. I like to imagine that the answers would have made a difference then. I like to imagine that they would make a difference now.

AMANDA CHO SUCCEEDED her father as head of a generic pharmaceutical empire. Widow. Two sons, one daughter. A long-running history of patent infringement along with numerous prosecutions for the sale of out-of-date drugs to Third World markets. An obsession with shoes and designer clothes. Owned several islands in Micronesia. Subject of an FBI investigation into her role in a campaign-financing scheme that funnelled illegal contributions to the Republican Party.

Long love affair with dogs. Owned three chows that she dyed to look like giant pandas.

ONE OF THE PHOTOGRAPHS is of my mother as a young woman standing next to a motorcycle. I'm nowhere to be seen, so I've always assumed that the picture predates my arrival. I can only see part of the motorcycle. A Harley, perhaps. Or a Norton. Or an Indian.

I've tried to figure out the make and the year, but the bike is out of focus and there's not enough for a positive identification. I assume that it was my father's motorcycle, and I assume that it was my father who took the picture. There is nothing in the image itself or on the back of the photograph to support either of these conclusions.

Except for my mother. In the photo, she is radiant and alive. And she is smiling.

GUNTHER VOGEL'S INTERESTS were in genetics and deep-ocean organisms. An avid blue-water sailor. Married, two sons. Vogel had financial interests in several soccer teams and was a major stock-holder in Hexagon Management, an international sports agency. A business reputation for ruthlessness and arrogance. Several of his companies had been heavily fined for their part in the destruction of a coral reef off the coast of Australia.

Under indictment for tax fraud in Switzerland.

IN THE SECOND PHOTOGRAPH, my mother is not smiling. Here, she looks different. Her hair is shorter, and she is thinner. She's in a room with other people. A party. She has a cigarette in one hand and a drink of some sort in the other. She looks to be talking to someone just beyond the frame. The flash from the camera has caught her in the middle of an emotion.

Delight or anger.

I've looked at this photograph countless times, but it's impossible to tell.

She's older in this photograph. Again, I am not in the picture, but I imagine that I'm close by. Perhaps in a spare bedroom away from the noise, tucked up in a pile of coats on a bed. Or at a neighbour's house, stashed away for the night.

The only thing I know for sure is that this is the last photograph I have of my mother and her life.

ARJUN CHAR BUILT a telecom juggernaut out of the family fortune that his father and grandfather had amassed, a success that was wholly due to the management team he had assembled to run the business. Char was more playboy than entrepreneur. Fast cars, elaborate parties, celebrities, drugs. Numerous arrests for driving while intoxicated. Several lawsuits for sexual harassment and rape, complete with non-disclosure agreements. One conviction for drug possession, which was stayed. Under investigation for his role in a network of phone-scamming centres in India and Ukraine.

Rumoured to be HIV-positive.

Oleg Baranov. Married with three daughters. Family fortune in oil. He had used his wealth and influence to branch off into alternative energy sources such as wind, solar, tidal surge, and algae biofuels, while at the same time doubling down on older technologies, using his money and power to influence policy on fracking and exploration in the Arctic. A moderate man, his one obsession was with movies. He tried to buy MGM and United Artists, and when that failed, he formed his own studio, where he made B movies, spy-vs-spy adventures with muscular men and half-naked women. He had even cast himself in several of the early features.

At the time of his death, he had been involved in a sexual-assault suit brought by several of the actresses who had worked with him on his films.

THE OTHER ITEMS in the lunch box are less important. The St. Christopher medal came with me, was part of my dowry, and was passed along from one foster home to another. The letter is just an official acknowledgement of my having been safely tucked into a social services system that cared for me as one would care for a folder in a file drawer.

The stone is something I imagine my mother picked up by a lake. In the water, it would have been bright green and glowing. Out of the water and dry, it is faded and dull. I have no idea why she would have kept it.

I keep it because she did.

AS WITH HIS FATHER and grandfather, Carlos Boeme had started out in oil but moved quickly into the international arms industry, buying surplus military equipment and selling to anyone who could afford it. Several of his companies were indicted for selling restricted technologies to embargoed or sanctioned regimes. Boeme himself was a heavy contributor to the NRA and had close ties to the Heartland Institute and Americans for Prosperity.

His daughter worked for Greenpeace. His son died of an overdose his first year at university.

AFTER BOEME, I take a full break. Food, coffee, something with sugar. Then I lie down, try to imagine that I'm in a cabin in the mountains, somewhere near Penticton. Mind over matter. It doesn't work. When I open my eyes, I'm still in the Locken tower, rummaging through the lives of dead people.

LADY AMAHIE ZUMA was a major player in Africa's and South America's energy extraction industries. Most of her companies were legitimate businesses. But there were several cases before the courts in Peru involving illegal gold-mining practices and the human trafficking of young men and women as cheap labour and sex workers.

Over the years, her foundation had been a regular contributor to UNICEF and World Relief.

THE BUNDLE OF ROAD MAPS is the curiosity. There are ten in all. One for each of the provinces. I've opened them in turn to see if there are any clues as to where she might have gone, where she might have wanted to go.

Of course, if the motorcycle in the first picture did belong to my father, the maps might have been his. I like the idea of my mother and my father sailing across the whole of Canada on a motorcycle, going nowhere and everywhere fast and free.

It is a romantic notion that more properly belongs in a paperback.

ROBERTO ROCCA HAD STARTED R&R Laboratories in and around Naples, but when his daughter took over, Giuliana Rocca moved the headquarters to Rome and added toxic waste disposal to the company's portfolio. Long rumoured to be a major polluter and in partnership with the Mafia, the company was embarrassed by the release of a video that showed toxic waste being dumped into the ocean. Additional videos surfaced of R&R burying unprocessed garbage and waste in fields near Casapesenna and Castel Volturno. Public outrage, but no action taken by the Italian government.

Giuliana had homes in Cannes and Napa Valley, as well as an estate outside Rome, where she kept peacocks and Lady Amherst's pheasants.

BERNARD DASSAULT. Real estate magnate. Dassault Holdings is the world's leader in office towers, convention centres, and bridges, with interests in concrete and steel. Multiple citations for the use of substandard materials in construction projects, especially in Third World countries.

An avid golfer with multiple club memberships around the world, Dassault's main aspiration is to play in the Pebble Beach Pro-Am.

His handicap is low enough, and he certainly has the money and position to wrangle an invite to the annual tournament.

But he is known to cheat. A virtue in business, a felony in golf.

AT ONE TIME, the tin lunch box had a matching Thermos. But it's long gone. As well, the image on the front has faded. The Lone Ranger still gallops across the prairies on his horse, but parts of the scene have flaked off or rusted away so that now pieces of Silver's face are missing and the ranger is minus his left arm.

There are dents all around. The metal folding handle catches, and the latch won't close completely. Still, the box is the perfect size for the pieces of my mother's life.

DUTCH EAST SHIPPING, or DES. Privately owned by the Heineken family with a long history in oil tankers and cargo ships. In the last fifteen years, Kommer Heineken moved DES into the lucrative field of luxury cruises, building a fleet of smaller, more opulent ships that could go places the larger liners could not. Heineken himself has been the subject of media scrutiny for his public views of immigrants and immigration, and for his support of white nationalism.

In addition to a world-class wine cellar, he also has a fine collection of vinyl records and a selection of vintage turntables.

TWELVE BILLIONAIRES. Activities included the Frieze Art Fair in London, the Fort Lauderdale International Boat Show, the Snow Polo World Cup St. Moritz, Paris Fashion Week, and the Dubai World Cup.

Twelve billionaires. Stocks, gold, real estate, fine art, rare coins. Swiss and offshore bank accounts, trusts, and tax havens.

Twelve billionaires. Twelve out of 2,473 worldwide. Predominantly male. All from wealthy families. All with inherited fortunes.

I give up a little after midnight. There's the chance that a good night's sleep will bring with it renewed energy and clarity. But when I wake up the next morning, the world looks just as tired as it had when I closed my eyes.

26

As promised, Oliver Flood is waiting for me when the Sikorsky touches down in the field. He looks happy to see me, has a smile on his face, which is somewhat unnerving. Even Spot and Rover appear pleased to have the band back together again.

"Welcome home," says Flood. "We've missed you."

Definitely unnerving.

"Have you missed us?"

Flood stays talkative all the way to town.

"Mrs. Moosonee has a nasty respiratory infection, probably caused by the mould in her trailer. But she's eating well and recovering nicely. She's a sweet old woman. Knows how to tell a story. It's a lost art, you know."

I try to ignore Flood.

"And that Lala is full of the dickens. She's going to give you a run for your money. What is it she calls you? Pop-Up? Makes me laugh whenever I say it."

I debate whether to go home or stop in at the café first.

"Ms. Locken asked me to make sure you have everything you need to facilitate the forecast. I've had to make most of the decisions on my own, but if there is something that I forgot, please let me know."

I decide to get out at the plaza.

Spot pulls the car up against the curb. Rover opens my door. Flood leans forward in the back seat.

"I'm serious," he says. "Anything you need, just let me know."

THE PLAZA IS BUSY. Good weather has the effect of bringing people out into the world. Wes Stanford and the Neighbours are camped out in the far corner. Several other families are scattered about on the blankets. There's even a small group of musicians in the band-stand, playing show tunes.

I look for Roman, but he's not there.

I find a bench. The sun is warm, no wind. I close my eyes, try to relax and enjoy the moment. Blue skies, happy voices, nothing to do, nowhere to go. Twelve names on a list. I try to flush it out of my mind, but there it remains.

Twelve names on a list.

"Jerry."

Bob Loomis. Blocking out the sun.

"Haven't seen you around."

Thirteen names on a list.

"Having a little fundraiser at the club tonight, and I'm hoping you can join us."

Mayor Bob is dressed in a three-piece suit. He has a big "Bob's the One" button on his lapel. The button is attached to a blue ribbon that hangs halfway down the jacket.

As though he's been awarded first prize at a livestock show.

"Food, dancing. Bring a friend, if you like. Couple of big announcements." Mayor Bob looks over his shoulder at the Neighbours. "Time we get serious about public safety."

The mayor crosses the street. He stops in front of the bakery. He stands there admiring his reflection in the window and checking for anyone who might be watching. Then he slips into the hotel, smooth as water down a drain.

It's too soon to hope that Emma and Lala have found a place of their own. Not that they've been a problem. They've been quiet and inconspicuous. Still, I miss the complete seclusion and isolation of an empty building.

If I go back to the old school right now, Emma might still be at work and Lala might still be in school.

And then I remember. It's Sunday.

THE CROSSES STAND STIFFLY above the graves. The stones lie silently on the ground. There is no cordon of police tape around the graveyard, no notices of city bylaws and warnings of trespass.

I search the trees for the crows, but they're off somewhere else. I want to give them Mayor Bob's address. In case they can't find his place on their own.

Three of the stones have been stacked on each other. A group of eight has been arranged to look like a bird. I don't have to guess which little girl's imagination has been at work here.

The school looks quiet enough, dark and inviting, as though it's happy to see me. I can feel the tension drain out of me, can feel my shoulders drop and settle. I take a long, deep breath, open the front door, and step inside.

Emma and Lala are in the kitchen. So are Nutty and Ada and Roman. Along with Jake Somosi, Gordon James, and Benjamin Hunt.

"About time," says Ada.

As soon as she sees me, Lala is out of the chair with a squeal.

"Pop-Up, Pop-Up, Pop-Up," she shouts, and dances in place.

"The man of the hour," says Emma. "This is all very generous, but you should have asked me first."

Lala has a cellphone in one hand.

"I can take pictures," she says.

"She's a little young to have a cellphone," says Ada.

"No, I'm not."

"Yes, you are, honey," says Emma.

"It's my phone," says Lala.

"But you don't get to use it all the time."

"Linda and Helen have cellphones, and they use them more than all the time."

Emma looks at me, a pained expression on her face.

"Television and the internet are another matter," says Ada. "Baseball really comes to life on that big screen."

I have no idea what they're talking about, and I'm afraid to ask.

"I can take pictures of Pop-Up and the graveyard," says Lala. "For show and tell."

"Roman was going to move my bed over, so I could look after Nutty," says Ada. "But that guy of yours just bought everything new."

Oliver Flood.

"Pretty generous, cuz," says Roman. "Looking after Nutty like this."

FLOOD HAS INSTALLED a satellite system for television and internet. He has set up a television in Emma's room and one in the classroom across the hall where Ada and Nutty are staying. He's also bought beds for everyone, along with dressers and tables, a couple of easy chairs, and a recliner for Nutty that works by remote control.

He has given Lala a cellphone and blamed it on me.

I add another name to the list.

"We couldn't take Nutty back to her trailer," says Roman. "And then that guy from the parking lot shows up. Says you arranged all this, and that we were to bring her here."

I can feel my shoulders start to creep up my neck.

"Nutty's getting better already."

"That big-screen television is something else," says Ada. "Didn't know what I was missing."

Roman waves a drumstick around in a circle. "I invited the boys over to practise. Your guy said it would be okay if we used the big room at the end of the hall."

"We'll try to keep it down," says Jake.

"The Clay Pigeons ride again," says Gordon.

"Roman says you were thinking about sitting in," says Benjamin. "You know how to sing?"

I head towards the staircase and my room.

Roman calls after me, "Your guy said you wouldn't mind."

THERE'S A BRAND-NEW laptop on my desk. Next to the laptop are Keizo Takahashi's binoculars tied up with a bow. Along with a note that says "Welcome Home." Not that the school feels like home anymore. Not that it ever felt like home.

Even with the door to my room closed and the lights out, I can hear the television in Nutty's room. A baseball game of some sort. Every so often, Ada's voice explodes, full of enthusiasms. I catch snatches of an argument between Lala and her mother. Over everything else is the sound of the drummers at the other end of the school, hard into a round dance.

At seven thirty, I give up and get dressed. My only suit, blue shirt, red-flecked tie. I have to shave and wet my hair so that it stays close to my head. The end result is not encouraging but falls short of a disaster.

I slip down the stairs, making as little noise as possible, and as I step out into the night, I realize that, in spite of my best efforts, I am now functionally homeless.

THE CLUBHOUSE at the Gleaming Golf and Country Club is an *hommage* to the clubhouse at Augusta National. Right down to its ornamental cupola.

I'm sure there is someone somewhere who cares.

During my time at Locken, I attended more than my fair share of social events, affairs where I had been required to walk the room, smiling, shaking hands, talking with strangers. They were nothing more than displays of wealth and power, the one-percent's version of butt sniffing.

I'm under no illusions. I know there's little pleasure to be found in this place. But having lost my sanctuary, the choices are a night in the park on a bench or the anonymity of a large crowd with free food.

I get as far as the entrance to the great room before I'm tackled by an older woman with a "Bob's the One" button.

"You don't have a name tag." The woman's name tag says Doris. "And everyone needs to have a name tag."

A band is setting up in the far corner of the room. The Jeff Bird Trio. Keyboard, double bass, horn. I write my name on a peel-off label, and Doris sticks it to my lapel.

"Elaine is taking donations for the campaign," says Doris. "And there's a silent auction that you don't want to miss."

I pat my tag. To make sure it doesn't fall off.

"And of course, you have to see the model." Doris bubbles away. "It's all very exciting."

I locate the food table with little difficulty. Cheese, fruit, spring rolls, sliders, hummus, crackers. It's not a real meal, but it will do.

"Jerry!"

Mayor Bob pushes through the assembly with all the grace of a snowplow.

"Eat up," he says. "Don't want to be taking any of this home."

I keep the plate between myself and the mayor and imagine that I'm someplace else. A zoo, perhaps. Or an animal fair.

"You remember the Cradle River Estates project?"

Now the song is in my head.

Loomis guides me through the crowd to the scale model. Cradle River Estates is looking somewhat the worse for wear. The shopping centre is tilting to one side and several of the street-name stickers have begun to lift.

I went to the animal fair. The birds and the beasts were there.

"We just got these in." Mayor Bob hands me a brochure, "Cradle River Estates. Your Future Now." It's a full-colour artistic rendering of what the development will look like when it's finished.

The big baboon by the light of the moon was combing his auburn hair.

"Natural materials and earth tones," says the big baboon. "Man and the land in harmony with each other."

The brochures stink of ink.

"Best of all, the brochures didn't cost taxpayers a cent." The mayor lowers his voice, as though he's sharing a secret. "Foundation came along and picked up the costs. What do you think about that?"

I don't know why I thought coming to Mayor Bob's party was a good idea.

"Couple of the folks are here tonight," says Loomis. "You should meet them."

Clearly, I was wrong. I would have been better off on a bench.

"Wonderful party, mayor."

Ash Locken and Oliver Flood materialize out of the crowd. Locken is looking splendid in a midnight-blue cocktail dress with a sequined bodice. Flood is in a dark wool suit that reminds me of coffins.

"And here they are," says Mayor Bob.

"Here we are," says Ash.

Flood is trying not to laugh.

"This is Jeremiah Camp," says the mayor, "one of our prominent citizens."

It's too much for Flood, and he has to turn away.

"Pleased to meet you, Mr. Camp," says Locken. "I hope you like the brochure."

"He loves it," says the mayor. "Everybody loves it."

Flood takes my plate. Locken takes my arm.

"Perhaps Mr. Camp could show me the veranda. I understand it's quite the view in the moonlight."

Locken doesn't wait for an answer. She leaves the mayor to Flood and steers me to the French doors.

"You would think that by now, I'd be used to this kind of thing," she says, as we clear the room and step into the night. "But I'm not."

The moon isn't up yet. No light. No view.

"The mayor tells me you can see the eighteenth green from here. I guess I'll just have to take his word for it."

There are tables on the veranda. With umbrellas that have been shut for the evening.

"I was hoping that you'd come."

There are lounge chairs as well.

"I imagine you're wondering what we're doing here." Locken waits for a moment. "The brochure? The Ankh Foundation?"

Locken leaves my side and walks to the edge of the veranda.

"No point in wasting a perfectly good corporation, and Oliver thought you might need an object lesson."

Locken extends her hands. One holds air. The other holds a brochure.

"Heaven," she says. "Or Hell."

Now that my eyes have adjusted, I can just make out the green with its little flag.

"I never understood golf." Locken smiles. "My father, on the other hand, loved it, wanted desperately to be a member at Augusta. But the membership there is limited to around three hundred individuals, and the only time there's an opening is when someone dies."

Locken stands in the dark, her arms wrapped around herself to ward off the chill.

"Then you have to be asked to join. You can't just apply. And he was never asked."

I walk to where Locken is waiting, take my jacket off, and put it over her bare shoulders.

"My hero."

Inside, Maribelle Wegman is making a toast to Mayor Bob and his re-election, against a chant of "Bob's the One," and Mayor Bob follows it with a toast to the Cradle River Estates project and Gleaming's new prosperity.

"Bernard Dassault is dead."

I wait.

"In Paris. An apparent stroke."

Oliver Flood appears in the doorway, nods, and steps back inside. Locken slips my jacket off and hands it to me.

"The forecast," she says, and starts back into the clubhouse. "When you have the time. We don't want the mayor's master plan to become a reality."

Inside, the trio is playing "Chances Are," and several couples are dancing. I stand by the windows and wait for the moon to come up.

So I can find my way home and not get lost.

27

The next morning, everyone is in the kitchen. Emma has cooked pancakes, and there are still some left.

"Pop-Up!"

Ada waves a fork at me. "Emma said you were going to walk Lala to school."

"That's right, Nooko," says Lala. "Pop-Up always walks me to school."

I have my quinoa in the refrigerator, but it will keep.

"You wouldn't believe what Ada and me saw on television last night," says Nutty.

"There's this woman," says Ada, "and a bunch of guys."

"And she gets a date with each one," says Nutty.

"I like dates," says Lala.

"Not that kind of date, Chipmunk," says Ada.

"And after she goes out with each of them," says Nutty, "she has to choose one to marry."

"Can we get some dates?" says Lala.

The pancakes are excellent. I'm sorry that there aren't more.

"I don't think it will last," says Nutty. "Those guys are all stuck on themselves."

"Sure," says Ada. "All they got in common is the sex."

"I know what sex is," says Lala.

Ada and Nutty stop laughing and try to look serious.

"Isn't it time for you to go to school?" says Ada.

"Linda says her big brother has a magazine full of sex." Lala jumps off her chair and grabs her lunch. "She says if me and Helen give her a loonie, she'll let us see the sex."

Ada gives Emma a hard look. "You need to talk to your daughter."

Emma puts the pan in the sink. "Leave it alone, Mum."

Ada shrugs. "You don't want her making mistakes."

Lala slips into her jacket. "If I had a loonie, I'd buy dates."

LALA IS WORKING her phone as soon as we get out the door. She takes pictures of the graveyard, of the squirrels, of the clouds in the sky. She takes a number of pictures of me.

"Stop right there," she yells. "Don't move. Hold your arms out. Lift your foot up as though you're really walking. Smile."

She takes a picture of Mrs. Takahashi and Koala.

"Aren't you a little young for a cellphone?" says Takahashi.

"I can do videos, too," says Lala.

Takahashi smiles at me. "Your Mr. Flood was very kind," she says. "He told me how much you wanted Keizo's binoculars."

I don't try to explain Oliver Flood to Mrs. Takahashi.

"I gave him a good price." Takahashi shakes the leash and Koala hops to her feet. "Maybe you will be able to see what Keizo saw."

THE CROWS FOLLOW US along the river path, and Lala takes pictures of them as they dance from tree to tree.

"Maybe I'll make a movie," she says, "about crows."

Before the earthquake changed the course of the Cradle River and drained the right channel, there was a bridge that joined the reserve and the town. After the river went dry, the bridge fell into disrepair, and now, all that remains of the structure are the skeletal pilings, sticking out of the ground like broken teeth.

When we get to the old riverbed, Lala runs down and stands between the pilings, so I can take her picture with the phone.

The crows settle in a tree close to the bank and wait. Black holes cut into the sky.

"Mum-Mum says I have to give you my phone." Lala runs up the far bank, and then she runs back down. "But that's not fair, 'cause Linda gets to keep hers."

I try to imagine a classroom filled with cellphone-wielding children.

"You should take a bunch of pictures while I'm in school," says Lala. "That way, I can see what you do all day."

FLORENCE SEES ME as soon as I come into the Piggy. She throws up her arms in mock horror.

"I had nothing to do with it."

I think, *Monuments of Injured Innocence*. But I keep my mouth shut, set the brownie on the counter.

"I voted against it," says Florence. "But Ada don't have enough room at her trailer for the both of them, and there's the problem of the mould."

Emma comes out of the kitchen. I take Lala's phone out of my pocket and hand it to her.

Emma shakes her head. "I can't believe she gave it up. The girl sleeps with the thing."

"Whereas you have lots of room." Florence dumps beans into the grinder. "And then that friend of yours came along, and that pretty much did it."

"But you didn't have to pay my law society dues as well," says Emma. "You've done so much already."

Florence lifts the lever. I watch the cup start to fill.

"Thank you." Emma wipes her hands on the apron. "I'll reimburse you as soon as I can."

"Emma's going to open her own business right here in Gleaming." Florence froths the milk, angling the pitcher to one side. "Cradle River Legal. Pretty good name, eh?"

Florence sets the macchiato in front of me, along with the tarot deck. "Caffeine for the party animal."

The macchiato is hot and bitter. The brownie helps to soften the taste.

"Heard you were at the mayor's big party last night." Emma pulls up a stool and sits. "Cradle River Estates? You got to love the arrogance."

I take a second sip, another bite of brownie.

"He wants to throw us out *and* use our name for his subdivision?" Emma holds up a brochure and tears it in half. "Man can build all the models he wants. Print enough of these things to reach the moon. And Cradle River will still be treaty land."

"Emma gets done with him," says Florence, "old Bob won't know what hit him."

"That's what I want to talk to you about." Emma looks to Florence for support. "I'm going to need temporary office space. Just until I can find something more permanent."

"Ada says there's an extra room at the end of the school," says Florence. "Has an outside door."

"I'll split my day," says Emma. "Work here during the morning and early afternoons. Do the legal stuff in the evening. Just till I get established."

I nurse my coffee while Florence tells me the news. Murder, mayhem, scandal, another school shooting, this time in Ohio. Emma goes back to the kitchen to check on the soup.

"Figure as soon as she gets the business up and running, I'll go back to normal." Florence wipes down the counter. "Running a real restaurant with real customers is too much work. Had my fill of that when Reggie was alive. And if I stay open much longer, Mayor Bob is going to want me to buy a business licence."

There's a sign on the wall that says "We Reserve the Right to Refuse Service to Anyone."

"Worse, he might drop in and order a latte." Florence frowns at the thought. "No one wants to see that."

I shuffle the tarot and cut the cards. Some guy hanging upside down, one leg crossed over the over.

"Major Arcana," says Florence. "The Hanged Man. Learning to see in a new way. Necessity to break old habits. Brink of an awakening."

The guy's arms are outstretched and there are nails driven into the palms of his hands.

"Card looks worse than it is."

So now the school is home to a mother and her child, two older women, and a law office. As well as a practice room for the drum team. The next thing I know, the crows will be on the front porch, looking to move in.

"Almost forgot," says Florence. "Wes Stanford got himself arrested. Along with his wife and a bunch of the Neighbours."

There's a ring of froth around the inside of the cup. I scrape at it with my spoon, but it's dry and crusty.

"They were in the plaza, minding their own business," says Florence. "Going to be Emma's first big case."

I wet my finger and poke at the bits of brownie left on the counter.

"Another one of the mayor's public safety initiatives." Florence wets a towel. "You got to have a fixed address or you're a vagrant."

Florence takes my cup. Wipes down the counter.

"Course, having a fixed address don't mean you got a home," she says. "Having a fixed address don't mean you got people who care for you."

I think about having a second macchiato, but then I remember that the brownie is all gone, and now there's nothing left to cut the bitter taste.

28

Nutty is waiting for me in the graveyard. Someone has brought out two chairs from the school. Nutty is sitting on one. Slick is perched on the back of the other.

"I'd rather sit on the ground," she says, "but it's pretty hard getting down, and it's real hard getting up."

Slick plumps his feathers, rocks back and forth.

"He's waiting for a peanut."

Slick hops across the top of the chair in one direction, and then he hops back in the other.

"But I don't have one." Nutty slumps in the chair like a sack of laundry. She's pale, and her eyes are cloudy. "So he'll have to settle for company and conversation."

Slick stretches his wings and begins clucking to himself.

"Had Roman bring the chairs out," says Nutty. "A little sun is good medicine."

I sit on the ground, settle in against one of the crosses.

"Ada wants me in bed. She catches me out here, she'll have a fit."

It hasn't rained, but the earth feels moist and soft.

"There was a time when there was a bridge over the river. Before the big quake. Before that bad winter." Nutty shifts in the chair. "Now the river and the bridge are gone. Mayor and the town get their way, we'll be gone, too."

Nutty's right about the sun. I can feel my body begin to relax, my eyes begin to droop.

"Pretty strange being back in the school, I can tell you that." Nutty sticks her cane in the ground and pushes up. "Pretty strange."

The wind comes out of nowhere and rattles the branches of the trees. Slick's head snaps up. He crouches down and then explodes into the air, cawing as he goes. I watch the crow as he gains altitude and disappears over the river.

"Must have heard something he don't like."

I help Nutty back to the school. She moves slowly, using the cane to pick her way through the graveyard, but we get back to the room before Ada shows up. The television is on. The sound is turned off.

"Ada likes to watch that *Murder, She Wrote*," says Nutty. "Likes the idea of a woman detective. Even if that Mrs. Fletcher is White."

Flood has been extravagant. In addition to satellite service and a fifty-five-inch television, he's arranged for Netflix and a Super Sports package.

"Baseball and *Murder, She Wrote* on a big screen." Nutty eases into the recliner, works the remote until the footrest comes up and catches her legs. "You may never get rid of Ada."

I go to the kitchen and rummage in the refrigerator. There's orange juice and apples, a package of cheese and a bag of cookies. I put orange juice in a glass and four of the cookies on a plate.

Nutty is still in the chair. She has the chair remote in one hand and the television remote in the other.

"There's this button you can push," she says. "So you can see what everyone is saying."

"It's called *closed caption*." Ada stands in the doorway with shopping bags in each hand. "And you can record programs so you don't miss them, and so you can fast-forward through the commercials."

On the television, Mrs. Fletcher is explaining how she doesn't want to get in the way of a police investigation.

"Ada's already recorded a couple dozen programs," says Nutty.

Ada sets the bags down. "Sure, but a lot of them are for Lala. Educational stuff. That girl is so smart. She already knows most of her times tables."

Nutty helps herself to a cookie. "I always had trouble with the eights."

"You're not supposed to eat a lot of sugar," says Ada. "You need protein to help with the blood."

"I like cookies."

Ada picks up the bags. "I got a bunch of vegetables. Broccoli, carrots, green beans. And some tomatoes."

"Thought you were going to get pizza."

"This stuff is healthier."

I stay with Nutty while Ada goes to the kitchen to put the groceries away. As soon as she's gone, Nutty takes another cookie.

"You know what the Catholics gave us to eat?" Nutty slips the cookie under her pillow. "Breakfast was grey mush. Sometimes we'd get a couple of pieces of stale bread with some jam. Most of the time, we had this soup for lunch. They'd boil up whatever they could get was cheap. Dinner was more bread and jam and fried potatoes."

Nutty closes her eyes and bows her head.

"We were always hungry."

I can hear Ada rummaging in the refrigerator, hear her opening and closing the cupboard doors.

"Hope you're not eating any more of them cookies," she shouts to us from the kitchen.

Nutty nods. "It's why Ada is fat and got diabetes."

I can smell onions cooking and some kind of meat. On the big screen, Mrs. Fletcher is pretending that she has no interest in a double homicide that involves one of her nieces. Along with the onions and the meat, I can smell fried potatoes. And suddenly I'm hungry.

"Grummy!"

Lala comes sprinting down the hall, rushes into the room, and gives Nutty a big hug.

"Pop-Up!"

Nutty takes the cookie from under the pillow and holds it out.

"I'm not supposed to have sweets until I eat my dinner."

"Cookies aren't sweets," says Nutty. "Cookies are appetizers."

"What's an appetizer?"

Emma appears in the doorway. "It's something you eat before the meal."

"It is?"

"But cookies aren't appetizers."

"They're not?"

Emma gives her daughter a pat. "Go see if you can help Nooko."

"If cookies aren't appetizers," says Lala, "what are they?"

ADA BRINGS IN A BIG POT and sets it on the coffee table. Lala follows behind her with bowls and spoons.

"Reserve stew," says Ada.

Emma looks in the pot. "Potatoes and onions and meat."

"Got some red peppers in it as well," says Ada. "There's warm bread, too."

Nutty sniffs the air, smiles. "Sure don't smell like the slop they used to feed us."

Ada purses her lips. "You want seconds, you're going to have to do a whole lot better than that."

WE EAT THE STEW while we watch a movie on the television. It's a cartoon about a bunch of animals who are trying to save their forest from being destroyed by an evil developer.

"Well, that's a little close to home," says Ada.

"This is nice," says Nutty. "Family is all here."

"Roman's not here," says Lala.

"We'll save him some stew," says Nutty, "in case he shows up."

"Maybe we will," says Ada, "and maybe we won't."

Lala hops over to Nutty. "Can I have my appetizer now?"

I LEAVE BEFORE the movie is over. I go upstairs and lie down on my bed. The binoculars are on the desk next to the laptop. I haven't bothered to look through them. Maybe tomorrow I'll watch the crows, see if I can learn anything.

And I haven't opened the computer. I don't want to. But Ash Locken has been pretty clear about my options, and the fact that I don't have any. I could catch a bus or a plane to somewhere else, but she would find me, and we would dance this dance all over again.

I try to sleep, but I can hear the television, can hear Ada and Nutty arguing about the details of some long-forgotten offence, can hear Lala counting through the sevens and eights of the times table.

I always had trouble with eight times seven.

Lala gets it right the first time.

Later, the television is turned off. Ada and Nutty go to their respective corners. Emma and Lala give up math for bed.

And when the old school is finally quiet, I crawl into bed, pull the covers around me, roll against the wall. Eight times seven is fifty-six. Eight times nine is seventy-two.

Two plus two equals four.

You'd think knowing this might change the way we imagine our place in the universe.

But, of course, it doesn't.

29

There are nights when I can't sleep, when I find myself wide awake. Nights when everything slows down, when nothing moves quickly, not even sound.

Tonight is such a night. I lie in my bed and listen to the usual creaks and groans of the old timbers in the school as they cool and shrink. As they shift into a more comfortable position.

Someone is snoring. I don't know who. It's not me.

A little after one, I give up on sleep and get out of bed. When I turn the laptop on, I'm greeted with an on-screen message.

GOOD MORNING, MR. PHELPS,

YOUR MISSION, IF YOU DECIDE TO ACCEPT IT, IS TO DISCOVER WHY BILLIONAIRES ARE DYING. AS ALWAYS, SHOULD YOU OR ANY OF YOUR I.M. FORCE BE CAUGHT OR KILLED, THE SECRETARY WILL DISAVOW ANY KNOWLEDGE OF YOUR ACTIONS.

Funny.

Ash Locken is too young to remember the *Mission: Impossible* television series. Flood, on the other hand, is not.

There is a series of folders on the computer, one for each of the names on the list. Archival materials, newspaper articles, television interviews, the transcripts of judiciary hearings. Most of this information is familiar, but I read through it all again, in case I've missed something.

False dawn begins to light the sky as I begin my forecast. No rush. I like to let my ideas sit awhile and relax, give them a chance to catch their breath, make sure that, after they've rested, they still make sense.

I'M IN THE KITCHEN, eating breakfast, when Emma and Lala show up. Lala is pouting, and Emma is trying to ignore her daughter.

"I can't go to school," says Lala, "because I'm sick."

"You're not sick, honey," says Emma. "You're just anxious."

"Linda said I was an Indian."

"You are an Indian, honey. Cradle River First Nations."

"That's good, right?"

"Yes, honey, that's good."

"Linda said it was bad."

Emma makes Lala a bowl of cereal. "How about I slice some banana. That will make you feel better."

"Will Pop-Up take me to school?"

Emma looks at me.

"I want him to tell stupid Linda that Indians are good."

"Linda's not stupid, honey," says Emma. "She's just prejudiced."

Lala finishes her breakfast, goes back to the room to get her jacket.

"Some of the kids at school are picking on her," says Emma. "I may have to talk to the principal before it gets out of hand."

Emma makes a bologna sandwich and puts it in a bag, along with an apple and a box of juice.

"I don't want bologna."

"You like bologna."

"I like peanut butter and jelly."

"You can't take peanut butter to school."

"But I like it."

"There are children who might be allergic to peanuts," Emma tells her daughter.

"Then I won't give them any of my sandwich."

Emma turns to me. "I have to stop by city hall after work," she says. "Is there any chance you could pick her up this afternoon? I'd ask Roman, but sometimes he forgets."

Lala is back with the cat in her arms. "I'm taking Pancakes to school with me," she announces. "If Linda is mean, Pancakes will scratch her."

"You can't take Pancakes to school," says Emma, "but maybe you could take Little Bear."

"Little Bear is a toy," says Lala. "Linda won't be frightened if I bring a toy."

"You don't want to frighten Linda," says Emma.

"Yes, I do," says Lala.

Emma puts the lunch in Lala's Batman backpack and gives her daughter a hug. "Mum-Mum will miss you."

"Then why don't you stay home?"

"Mum-Mum has to work."

"If you stayed home," says Lala, "we could help Pop-Up with the crosses."

"And you have to go to school, so you can get smart."

"I'm smart already," says Lala. "Is there a cookie in my lunch?"

"There's an apple and a box of juice."

"Linda's not smart, and she gets a cookie."

TODAY, IT'S FOGGY on the river trail, and it feels as though Lala and I are on the coast. Everything is grey and hazy and soft. People on bicycles and joggers come out of nowhere and disappear quickly and silently.

We run into Mrs. Takahashi. She doesn't have Koala with her.

Lala stops. "Where's Koala?"

"Koala," says Mrs. Takahashi, "is at the doctor."

"Koala is sick?"

"No, Lala-chan," says Takahashi. "Koala is getting fixed."

Lala frowns. "Koala is broken?"

Mrs. Takahashi looks at me, but I'm going to leave it to her to try to explain spaying to a child.

"Keizo also bought a camera," Takahashi tells me. "Very expensive. Very nice. It goes with the binoculars."

"Pop-Up fixed my bed," says Lala. "'Cause it was leaking."

"He wanted to look at birds," says Takahashi. "And then he wanted to take their picture. Maybe you can explain this to me."

"But then Pop-Up bought me a new bed."

Mrs. Takahashi pats Lala's head. "I will tell Koala that Lala-chan misses her."

AT THE SCHOOL, I wait until Lala remembers to give me her phone.

"Linda keeps her phone." Lala holds the phone against her chest, in case I see the logic. "And she gets a cookie in her lunch."

SWANNIE HAS A FULL TRAY of chocolate brownies. I resist pointing out that some are larger than others. There's a bulletin board next to the cash register where people can post notices of services and things for sale. Someone has tacked a Cradle River Estates brochure to the board.

Swannie catches me looking at it.

"You see," she says, "the school, she is gone." Swannie taps the brochure and gets powdered sugar on Loomis Commons. "The graveyard? Poof. All the trailers? Poof. And where will you go?"

Swannie's hair is back to normal. "Where will the people go?"

Sometimes, it doesn't help to think about something too hard. Sometimes, if you ignore it, it will come to you.

Swannie puts my brownie in a bag. "Poof, poof," she says. "Poof."

THE PIGGY IS FULL. Emma is busy moving from table to table. The Three Bears are at the counter.

"Standing room only." Louis waves me over. "We got here early, and it was like this."

"We may have to go somewhere else for coffee," says Enola.

"But Wapi likes the hot chocolate," says Louis.

"Chocolate," say Wapi.

"Keep the coffee," says Louis. "Lose the people."

Florence comes out of the kitchen looking as though she is being chased by something large and dangerous.

"I'm going to need most of that brownie," she says. "Never knew success could be such a failure."

I take the brownie out and set it on top of the bag. Florence heats a cup and hands me a knife.

"Hear you and your girlfriend were at the country club the other night," says Louis.

"That estate thing is so much noise," says Enola. "No way it's going to happen."

"That's what they said about Adolf Hitler and Donald Trump," says Louis.

"News, blues, and comfortable shoes." Florence sets the macchiato in front of me. "In China, several scientists have been convicted of genetically editing babies."

Florence has to raise her voice to cut through the clatter of happy patrons.

"The head guy was sentenced to three years in jail and fined almost half a million dollars."

"Whereas you get the Nobel Prize for genetically modifying a tomato," says Enola.

"That's because we value ripe tomatoes more than we do people," says Louis.

"In New York City, a man has been arrested for throwing the

pages of books off the top of the viewing platform at the Hudson Yards building."

"*Fahrenheit 451*," says Enola. "Redux."

"Among the books that were destroyed for their pages," Florence continues, "were *The Prophet*, *The Fountainhead*, *To Kill a Mockingbird*, and the Bible. He's been charged with public mischief and held over for psychiatric evaluation."

"We should send him the Indian Act," says Louis.

"Did he dislike the books," asks Enola, "or was it random?"

"Did he throw the pages off the building," asks Louis, "or did he cut them up into confetti first?"

"Confetti," says Wapi.

"Doesn't say," says Florence. "And here at home, the spring festival is just around the corner."

"Roman and the Clay Pigeons are going to sing," says Louis.

"I sing," says Wapi.

"You bet," says Louis, "but more than that, you're my number one helper."

"Number one," says Wapi.

Louis starts in on a list of the jobs that have to be done now that winter is in the rear-view mirror.

"All the generators have to be serviced and filled. Couple of the trailers need their electrical services replaced. Water lines have to be flushed."

I stay for the first round of repairs and replacements, but when Louis moves into the world of local politics, the Gleaming town council, and federal treaties, I step away from the counter and slip out the door.

THE FOG HASN'T LIFTED. If anything, it's thicker now and seems content to have settled in for the day. Fog dampens sound, but I still hear the door bang open and shut behind me.

"We need to talk."

Florence catches me at the cedars.

"That woman don't belong here."

Ash Locken.

"Expensive people like her show up in a town like this and you can bet they got trouble in their carry-on."

Florence pauses to see if I want to fill in any blanks.

"Trouble with strings attached. Her and Mr. Sunshine."

Oliver Flood.

"New television. New furniture. Cellphones." Florence sets her hands on her hips. "Nothing's free. And I'm guessing you the one paying the bill."

The fog is cool and damp. With any luck, it will stay around. Florence is about to take another run at me when the door to the café opens and Emma sticks her head out.

"We need four lattes at table six."

Florence and I stand in the cedars. Waiting for the other to make the first move.

"You really think you get to hide away in an old schoolhouse all by your lonesome?" Florence turns back to the Piggy. "Get to spend your life sitting in a graveyard, chipping at stone?"

It's only after Florence has gone back into the restaurant that I remember what I like best about fog. It comes out of nowhere, doesn't make a sound, and as it forms, the rest of the world disappears.

30

The musicians are in the bandstand. Sometimes, they cover popular songs, but today, it's improvisation.

The crows are there as well. In force. About fifty birds are clustered on the roof of the bandstand. I don't think they've come for the music, but with crows, you never know.

"Jerry!" Mayor Bob trots across the grass. "What do you think?"

This is not a question he wants me to answer.

"The new bylaw?" Loomis holds his arms out in an attempt to encompass the plaza. "The anti-vagrancy legislation?"

The Neighbours are nowhere to be seen.

The musicians launch into a piece that sounds like enamelware falling down an elevator shaft, and the crows join in, cawing and screeching.

The mayor shakes his head. "I like it better when they play show tunes."

The birds begin dancing. They bob their heads, hop into the air, spread their wings, and shit on the roof. The overall effect is unexpected.

"May have to do something about the crows as well," says Mayor Bob. "They're as bad as pigeons."

The musicians quickly fall in line with the crows, and in a blink, everyone is hopping about and cawing and flapping their arms.

"I'm the future." Mayor Bob puts his hands together, as though he's praying. "And you know what they say."

Swannie Gagnon comes out of the bakery to see what all the racket is about. Dino Kiazzie stops arranging oranges in the display at the front of his store. Maidie Matthews stands next to a barbecue that's on clearance, her fingers keeping time on the metal hood.

The mayor brings his fingertips to his nose. "You can't stop the future."

I'm tempted to offer him a pair of binoculars at a good price.

"The future is here to stay. Plain as the nose on your face."

And then as quickly as it has started, the concert stops. The musicians put their instruments down, and the crows rise up and vanish into the sky.

"But you don't care about the future, do you? Hell, you don't care about much of anything." Loomis rocks back on his heels. "Is that why you don't talk? Because you don't give a shit?"

The mayor hands me another business card. He's written a figure on the back and underlined it.

"Take the money and run. Go someplace where nobody knows you, someplace where you're not in the way."

He scoops a handful of "Bob's the One" buttons out of his pocket and starts across the plaza towards the bandstand and the musicians.

"And don't forget to vote."

WHEN I GET BACK to the school, the place is empty. There's a note on the kitchen table from Ada.

"Took Nutty to get her lungs checked," it says. "You're out of eggs and fruit."

I open the refrigerator. We're out of tomatoes as well. And cookies. There's bread and cheese, so I make myself a sandwich. Butter, mustard, a piece of lettuce. I'll go shopping when I get Lala.

I take the food up to my room and set the plate next to the laptop. I already know what I'll tell Locken, already know what my forecast will say. That's the easy part.

What comes in the aftermath will be more difficult.

As for Mayor Bob, he's probably right. About my caring. After all, I didn't come back to Cradle River on my own. I came back because Thomas Locken had given me the school and the property, and because I couldn't think of anywhere else to go.

Sure, the reserve was my mother's home. And yes, I was born here. But then we left. And in all those years, we never came back.

So here is not mine. And yet here I am.

There's no good reason not to sell the school to the mayor. Pack my bags and head west. The Horatio Alger solution to ambition. Not that I'm interested in ambition. Not that I have any other place in mind. The coast perhaps. Maybe an island.

How far west could I go? There's twice as much water as land on the planet, so the odds of drowning are excellent.

The forecast is done. Finished. I could look at it one last time. To make sure I haven't missed any patterns.

Or I could watch the crows.

They're never in a rush. They'll sit in trees for hours, test the wind for smells, listen for sounds. They'll watch the clouds, contemplate the quality of light. And when they've considered all the possibilities, all the patterns, then and only then do they act.

This is how crows forecast, and for the most part, they're better at it than humans. When they see trouble, they don't ignore it and rationalize a happy ending. When they see an easy passage, they don't speculate on the possible calamities that might be around the corner. If they see something they don't recognize, they don't pretend that they do.

But then crows don't understand human nature. They're smart and they're cautious, but they would never be able to comprehend our fancy for deceit, deception, and self-destruction.

A murder of crows. Quite disingenuous. Considering the source.

I read the forecast over one last time.

31

I'm waiting outside the school when Lala comes tripping out. She's with two other girls, and they're laughing as they come down the steps.

"Pop-Up!" She rushes over. "Where's Mum-Mum?"

I give Lala her cellphone. Emma has sent her a text message.

"Mum-Mum has to work late," Lala announces, "so you have to take care of me."

The other two girls keep their distance. I wonder if one of them is the dreaded Linda.

"This means you have to do everything I tell you to do."

I check the sky. No sign of rain.

"The first thing we have to do is pull up more crosses."

It's a short walk from the school to the plaza. Lala is all energy and motion. She skips and jumps, runs on ahead and runs back, talking all the time.

"But before we do that, we have to get ice cream. Otherwise, we'll be hungry."

219

Dino has fresh grapes and they look good. Dino takes Lala through the produce section, shows her the vegetables, tells her where they're from.

"The avocados are from California," he says. "The cantaloupes are from Mexico." Dino holds up a bag of dates. "These come in from Turkey."

I get the dates. Along with tomatoes and apples, a bunch of bananas, a sandwich ham, as well as two bags of cookies. I pick up another loaf of bread, eggs, and a block of butter.

Dino gives Lala a tiny box of raisins.

"Did you know that the ancient Nemeans gave raisins as prizes to the winners of sporting events?"

"Like baseball?"

"Sure," says Dino, "like baseball."

I try to imagine Mike Trout hitting home runs or Mookie Betts shagging fly balls for a bag of dried grapes.

"I'm going to save Pop-Up some raisins for when he has to lift the stones."

Dino looks at me, a sad smile on his face. "The things we do for our children."

I pick up some hot dogs, and Lala comes out of the freezer with a carton of ice cream. I'm surprised that it's vanilla. I would have supposed that little girls would like something with colour, strawberry or chocolate or rocky road. Neapolitan would have been my guess.

"Vanilla's the best," she tells me, "'cause you can put chocolate syrup on it."

So we get a can of chocolate syrup as well.

"No harm in spoiling a child," Dino tells me. "I spoil my grand-kids all the time."

I don't plan on stopping at the bakery, but Swannie sees us coming.

"A bad day for the business." She hands Lala a small bag. "Today, I make the lemon tarts too many."

"Look." Lala holds the bag open so I can see. "Lemon goes with ice cream."

"*D'accord*," says Swannie, "this is widely known."

"That's a funny word," says Lala.

"*D'accord*," says Swannie, "this is French." Swannie fixes me with a glare. "This one will learn French, yes?"

If we spend any more time in the plaza, Eddie Ott is going to rush out of the Bent Nail, offer Lala a beer, along with a pair of tickets to the next hockey game, and Maidie Matthews is going to give her a rake.

"And you must get a dog. *D'accord?*"

ALL THE WAY BACK to the school, a dog is all Lala talks about.

"If we had a dog, Pancakes would have someone to play with when I'm at school."

If Pancakes didn't rip the throat out of the puppy first.

Lala starts spinning around. "And we could take the dog for walks."

And pick up dog poop in plastic sacks.

"If we had a dog, Pancakes wouldn't get into trouble. When Pan-cakes started to do something wrong, the dog would tell her, 'No!'"

Lala stops moving.

"Pancakes didn't mean to go into your room. I think she got lost."

I wait.

"And she didn't mean to knock that box off the windowsill."

My mother's lunch box.

"I put everything back on the desk." Lala holds her hands at her sides. "Pancakes says she's sorry."

I try to imagine a penitent Pancakes.

"I know I wasn't supposed to be in your room," says Lala, "but Pancakes wouldn't come when I called her. So I had to go and get her."

When we arrive at the old riverbed, Lala runs down the bank and stands in the middle of the dry channel.

"If we had a dog," Lala shouts at me, "you wouldn't be so sad."

WES STANFORD AND AUTUMN DARE are standing by the front porch of the school. Along with the guy who was on Nutty's roof, whose name I've forgotten.

"Hope you don't mind," says Wes.

"Emma got us out on OR," says Autumn. "Told us to meet her here."

Wes nods. "She's going to help us with the town."

"Nothing but harassment," says Autumn. "You'd think they had better things to do."

Jimmy, the guy's name is Jimmy.

"You got a nice place here, Mr. Camp," says Jimmy. "1920s?"

"We have ice cream," says Lala. "And a lemon tart."

"Then you better get that ice cream into the freezer," says Autumn.

"If it melts," says Lala, "I'll use a straw."

NUTTY AND ADA are in the kitchen drinking tea. As soon as Ada sees the lemon tart, she gets a knife and cuts it into three pieces.

"What about Pop-Up?"

"Nutty's sick," says Ada. "But she's too stubborn to admit it."

"I'm just tired," says Nutty.

"That's 'cause you're sick."

Lala helps me put the groceries away. She puts the ice cream in the freezer at the front where it will be easy to retrieve, and she sets the syrup in plain sight on the counter.

Ada eats her piece of lemon tart in one bite. "They want to do more tests."

"I can help Grummy with tests," says Lala. "I get gold stars on my tests."

"Don't need no tests," says Nutty. "Nothing wrong with me."

Ada points her fork at me. "We're going to have to stay here a little longer," she says. "Until Nutty's better."

"That's the big-screen television talking," says Nutty. "And that cable service."

"Can't put a sick old woman in a mouldy trailer."

"Who you calling old?"

Through the window, I see Emma coming up the path, striding out, swinging her arms, as though she's on her way to a military exercise.

"Come on," says Ada, "finish that tart. There's a game on in a couple of minutes."

"All you think about is your baseball," says Nutty.

"Watching television is relaxing," says Ada. "And relaxing will help you get better."

By the time I get back outside, Emma and the Neighbours are in the middle of a heated discussion.

"How can they do this?" says Autumn. "It's not right."

"And that's why we're going to fight them," says Emma.

"We can't pay you," says Wes. "We can't even afford rent."

"That's the first problem," says Emma. "We have to get you guys a fixed address. A legal residence."

"How we going to do that?" says Jimmy.

"Mayor shut down the shelter last year," says Wes. "Said it was attracting 'undesirables.'"

"A homeless shelter that doesn't want the homeless," says Autumn. "Go figure."

"And the old box plant sure as hell ain't an address we can use," says Wes.

"How many people we talking about?" asks Emma.

"Eight families," says Autumn. "Twenty-two, twenty-three people."

"Any serious issues?"

Autumn tenses. "Like what?"

Emma doesn't back off. She plows right ahead. "Drugs, alcohol, mental health, domestic abuse."

The world goes silent.

"Come on," says Emma. "I need to know what I'm dealing with."

Wes shoves his hands in his pockets. "Some," he says.

"Okay," says Emma. "We'll need to sort that out. And how many of you get Ontario Works?"

Emma and the Neighbours spend the next twenty minutes going over the new bylaw and the ways in which it might be challenged. Emma is in her element. She doesn't waste time on anger and outrage. She lays out the situation in clear and concise terms.

"So, if we can get the bylaw struck down," says Autumn, "they'll stop harassing us?"

"No promises," says Emma. "But we're going to try."

"What about the legal address?" says Wes. "How you going to manage that?"

I don't see it coming until Emma turns to me with her gentle smile. "That dormitory room on the second floor," she says. "How many people do you think it will hold?"

32

Even with the door to my room shut and locked and the lights turned off, I can hear people in the school.

Everywhere.

My school. My quiet place. My refuge from the world.

Suddenly, I'm captive at a rock concert in the Rogers Centre. I can hear Ada in the kitchen arguing with Nutty. I can hear Lala trying to convince her mother that ice cream with chocolate syrup is a perfectly good snack before dinner.

An appetizer.

Now that she has the word, she wields it like a sword.

My mother's lunch box is on the desk. The stone, the photographs, the letter, the medal, and the bundle of maps are lined up, side by side. Either Pancakes is a very neat cat or she's had help. The box itself has a new dent in one corner, and now the latch won't close at all.

In the old dormitory next to my room, Wes and Autumn and Jimmy try to figure out the sleeping arrangements for a crash of adults and a cackle of children.

Temporary, temporary, temporary.

I keep repeating this to myself, in case there is magic in the word. I use my new laptop to search the internet for noise-cancelling headphones. Just in case. There's a well-reviewed pair for under five hundred dollars.

THE REST OF THE EVENING is given over to the sounds of community. Ada and Nutty watching *Murder, She Wrote* reruns, Emma reading stories to Lala and singing songs in a vain attempt to get her daughter to bed. The Neighbours arriving in force, clumping up and down the stairs like a herd of elephants on the gallop.

Pancakes arrives at my door, scratches frantically, wanting to get in, but she's already made her bed, and there's only enough air and darkness in the room for me.

I try to press the dent out of the lunch box with my thumb and am somewhat successful. The lid sits slightly sideways, but now the latch catches. I arrange the memorabilia in the box as it was and set it back on the windowsill.

Pancakes makes several more entreaties for sanctuary, thrusting a paw under the door and trying to pull herself through, making all sorts of promises she has no intention of keeping, pleading at decibels well above the legal limit.

Just after midnight, I attach the forecast to an email and send it on its way. Then I crawl into bed, huddle against the wall, and wait for the world to end.

EVIDENTLY, CHILDREN DON'T sleep in.

At six the next morning, the school is on the move. The floor in my room shakes as the Neighbours empty out of the dormitory and onto the first floor. I take my time getting dressed, listening the while for a break in the clamour.

I never realized just how quiet the school was until it wasn't, didn't realize how content I was with an empty building and an empty life.

I get downstairs to find Lala and Ada and Nutty in the kitchen.

"You missed all the fun," says Nutty. "Forgot what a treat children are."

"Was a regular circus," says Ada.

"Dogs!" Lala shouts. "They have dogs!"

And on cue, three dogs wander in from the porch and begin barking. Lala begins patting the dogs, calming them down.

"This is Shadow and this is Diesel and this is Malibu." Lala dances around the dogs. "Malibu is going to have babies, and I get to keep one."

"That's not what your mother said," says Ada.

"I'll call my puppy Waffles," says Lala. "That way, it won't matter if it's a boy dog or a girl dog."

"Your mother said that there's no room for a dog."

"But I'll have to get a rope, so Waffles doesn't run away."

"Emma's gone to work," says Nutty. "The Neighbours were going to take Lala to school with their kids, but she said that that was your job."

I can't tell one dog from the other, and I've already forgotten their names. The large black one flops down on the floor and begins licking himself, while the small brown pooch, who looks like a scrub brush, starts scratching. I can hear the fleas exploding off its back.

"We have to go now, Pop-Up." Lala slides into her backpack. "Or I won't get my gold star."

I look at the pile of half-eaten pieces of toast on the table.

"You can get breakfast at the Piggy," Ada tells me. "And you better pick up more bread and peanut butter."

"The grapes are gone as well," says Nutty.

ALL LALA CAN TALK ABOUT are the dogs.

"Malibu can do tricks, which means she's smart, and that means her puppies will be smart."

By now, Ash Locken will have received my forecast.

"Shadow is really strong," says Lala. "He looks after the other two."

Which means the fallout is on the horizon.

"Diesel is the silly one. He makes me laugh."

Which means it should not be long in arriving.

"But he's not too smart."

Mrs. Takahashi comes around the bend in the trail. Koala is with her. The dog has a plastic cone on its head.

"Mr. Camp." Iku has a camera hanging around her neck. I recognize the brand. "How are you enjoying the binoculars?"

As soon as Lala sees the labradoodle, she bolts and sprints up the path. By the time I get there, Koala is on her back and Lala is giving her a tummy rub.

"Careful," says Mrs. Takahashi. "She's still healing."

"What happened to her?"

"She had an operation," says Mrs. Takahashi. "That's why she must wear the hood. So she doesn't lick herself."

"An operation?"

"A dog operation," says Mrs. Takahashi.

"We have dogs," Lala announces. "Three dogs."

"Three dogs?" Mrs. Takahashi is equal parts surprise and concern. "What kind?"

"A big one and two small ones," says Lala.

Takahashi turns the focus ring on the camera. "This was Keizo's camera. It takes excellent pictures."

"I can take pictures with my phone."

Takahashi brings the camera up to her eye. "These dogs," she says, "are they purebreds?"

Lala looks to me for the right answer.

"Do they have papers?"

"On the back porch," says Lala, "but mostly they go outside."

I GET LALA TO SCHOOL on time. In spite of stopping for Koala, Mrs. Takahashi, and her camera. But today, Lala is determined not to give up her cellphone.

"I'm not a baby," she says. "I won't use it during class."

I wait.

"Linda has a cellphone, and she doesn't use it during class."

I wait some more.

"So I should be able to keep my cellphone."

I have a building full of people, most of whom I don't know, as well as three dogs. I'm not about to get between a mother and her daughter over a cellphone.

"Today could be a test," says Lala. And she skips into the school with the phone. Before I have a chance to object.

Even if I wanted to.

I PICK UP A BROWNIE, but I don't go to the Piggy right away. I wander out past the Petro-Can to the old Bambridge & Moore building. The plywood fence around the property is covered in graffiti, and there are gaps in the wood where the sheets have been torn off and replaced with wire mesh. The building has been deserted for years, has stood abandoned while the elements have begun to work their magic.

But today, there is activity. A long-arm excavator with its ugly metal beak has been moved to within striking distance of the two-storey building, along with several wheel loaders that wait at the ready. Someone has set up a construction trailer on the property.

A sign on the side of the trailer reads "Future Home of the Gleaming Community Centre."

As I stand at the fence and watch, a pickup pulls in and several men get out. One of them is Bob Loomis. He's resplendent in Carhartts, Red Wings, and a Skullgard. He has a long paper tube in one hand that he waves around, as though he's leading a marching band. All in all, he's an arresting figure. The stiff new coveralls, the just-out-of-the-box work boots, the bright white hard hat.

He certainly looks to be having a good time.

So this is where the Neighbours have been staying. A roof over their heads. A place out of the wind and rain. It isn't much. But it's what they had.

THE CAFÉ IS REASONABLY QUIET. The only people left are the Three Bears. They are at their usual table, bent over Wapi's tablet.

"About time." Florence comes out of the kitchen. "You missed everyone."

I put the brownie on the counter.

"Almost missed the news," says Florence. "Lucky for you, I was busy with paying customers."

Enola waves me over. "You should try this."

"Very sketchy," says Louis.

"No, no," says Enola. "Here, have a go."

"It's a website that predicts how you're going to die," says Louis. "You answer a bunch of questions, and then a mainframe somewhere in the Ukraine comes up with a completely fallacious scenario."

Enola whacks her father on the shoulder. "It said you were going to die in your bed."

"Very sketchy," says Louis.

Florence taps a spoon against the side of the espresso machine to get everyone's attention. "News, blues, and comfortable shoes."

"Shoes," says Wapi.

"On the international scene, U.S. forces in Turkey have shot down an Aeroflot plane on its way to Greece with 210 passengers on board. A spokesperson in Adana says that the incident is under investigation."

"We hardly pay any attention to how we live," says Louis, "but we're willing to consult a computer as to how we'll die?"

"In Vancouver, a Heiltsuk man and his twelve-year-old granddaughter were arrested at a Bank of Montreal branch when he tried to open an account for her."

"There's also a site that can tell you if you will be successful," says Enola.

"Bank officials called the police because of the large amount of the cheque, and because he was Native."

"And another one that can predict whom you will marry."

"I added the 'because he was Native' part," says Florence. "Both the man and his granddaughter were arrested and handcuffed, but later released, with bank officials blaming the incident on 'mitigating circumstances.'"

"My daughter did the marriage one," says Louis, "and the prediction was that she would marry a rich woman."

"Which was an error," says Enola, "since I'm not gay."

"Not what the computer says," says Louis.

"The fact that the man had been a customer at that particular branch for over six years," says Florence, "didn't seem to matter."

"You know, all those things are just scams," says Louis. "Data mining. They want your email address, your phone number, your social insurance number."

"We get calls at the office all the time," says Enola. "Clean our ducts, threats from 'Revenue Canada,' alerts that our credit cards have been compromised."

"We used to get letters from Nubian princesses," says Louis, "who just happen to have millions of dollars they want to share with someone like you."

"The new capitalism," says Enola.

"Meet the new boss," says Louis.

"Same as the old boss," says Enola.

"While here at home," says Florence, ignoring the interruptions, "the annual Gleaming Spring Festival is right around the corner."

Louis sits up straight. "Don't get me started."

"Mayor can't find any money to help with the water and hydro," says Enola, "but he's got enough to hire a drum and dancers from Curve Lake to play at the festival."

"Thought Roman and the Clay Pigeons were going to do that," says Florence.

"They are," says Enola. "There's even talk of Harold and Ester's boy, Marlon, coming down from the Cape with his hoops."

Wapi begins working his tablet.

"Rumour is," says Enola, "that the Curve Lake drum is going to do an honour song for his worshipness."

"Maybe we should make him an honorary chief," says Louis. "Give him an Indian name."

"Wasn't there a radio show that gave away authentic Indian names?"

"There was," says Louis, "but CBC cancelled it."

Florence disappears into the kitchen. I sit on the stool and drink my macchiato. Wapi finds a video on hoop dancing, and the Three Bears huddle around the tablet as the sound of the drum and the voices of the singers fill the café.

I leave my half of the brownie on the counter. There are days when all the caffeine and sweetness in the world are not enough.

33

I haven't worked in the graveyard for a while, and it takes some time to find the rhythm. I go to work on the stone for William Benson. It's a long name for the stone, and I have to draw *William* on one line and *Benson* on the other. There is a moment when I'm tempted to shorten the name and save myself some work. Maybe his friends called him Willie or Will or Bill.

But then I remind myself that I'm in no rush. I have all the time in the world. And if I dig around a bit, I can always find a larger stone.

I NEVER KNEW WHY my mother left the reserve, never understood why she died. One day she was there, and the next she wasn't.

Foster-care roulette until I was eighteen. Smart enough to get a scholarship. Dumb enough to think that the world owed me something.

And in all those years, I never came back to Cradle River. Part of me believed that, in some way, the reserve was responsible for my mother's leaving, that the reserve was responsible for her death. By the time I was an adult, there was nothing left in my memory to anchor me to the place.

And then Thomas Locken bought the old school and the grave-yard and gave the property to me.

He would have known my history. Locken loved to keep track of that sort of information. If he knew where a person came from, if he knew their biography, he felt he could predict how they would conduct themselves in business and in their personal affairs.

Maybe he gave me the school in an effort to connect me to my past. Maybe he didn't think the adage "you can't go home again" would apply. Maybe he just liked the irony and wanted to see what I would do with it.

I've just finished the first *L* in *William* when Oliver Flood walks out of the trees and into the sunshine. I half expect that he will turn to dust the moment the light hits him.

But he doesn't.

"Do you know the epitaph on Mary Oliver's gravestone?"

I erase the second *L* and redraw it.

"'Tell me, what is it you plan to do with your one wild and pre-cious life?'" Flood takes off his hat and runs a handkerchief around the sweatband. "I met her once. At a reading in Provincetown."

I put my goggles on and strike the chisel with the mallet. Pieces of stone and dust fly into the air like tiny birds. The sound of the steel on stone echoes in the quiet afternoon.

"I'm impressed," says Flood. "All these crosses, all these stones."

I move the chisel along the length of the letter, striking each time I shift position. I imagine that I'm keeping time with a song.

"And when you're done, what will you have accomplished?"

I set the chisel to one side. It's clear that ignoring Flood will not drive him away.

"I hear you have a full house."

Flood takes a plastic key card out of his pocket and drops it on the ground.

"We've reserved a room for you at the Plaza. Away from the madding crowd. Someplace where we can talk in private. Tonight. If you can find the time."

Flood stares into the trees.

"You got a lot of crows," he says. "They're god's spies, you know. Supposed to be a symbol of bad luck."

I brush off the stone, check the chisel marks.

"Though how yours could get any worse is beyond me."

Flood walks through the graveyard in a circle. When he gets back to where I am sitting on the ground, he stops.

"Course, crows are also nature's survivors," he says, "so I suppose that's cause for optimism."

The edge of the *L* is uneven. I pick up the chisel and begin to straighten the line, and when I stop again and look up, Flood is gone.

I'M PULLING UP another cross when Lala arrives back from school, running ahead of her mother.

"Pop-Up!"

My arm aches and I can't feel the fingers in my chisel hand.

"Can I try?"

"Leave Mr. Camp alone while he's working."

"I can draw," says Lala. "I can draw my name."

Lala opens her backpack and takes out a pencil. She sits down next to one of the river rocks and writes her name on the stone.

"See."

"Come on, honey," says Emma. "I think there's some hot chocolate."

Lala heads for the school at a run. "And toast?" she shouts over her shoulder.

"Thank you, Mr. Camp." Emma follows her daughter. "You don't know how much Lala enjoys your walking her to school."

Toast.

Damn. That's what I've forgotten. Groceries. I put the chisel and the mallet to one side, slip the key card into a pocket. I stand up and brush off my pants.

I don't need a list. We need everything.

DINO'S HAS GOOD RED GRAPES. The cantaloupes look serviceable. The bananas are a little on the green side, but they'll ripen up quickly. Hamburger, a large box of spaghetti, and bread, along with butter and cereal and milk. Everything barely fits into two large shopping bags, which weigh as much as buckets of water.

Halfway home, I realize that I don't have nearly enough to feed everyone at the school. To do that, I'd need a functioning truck.

The light is beginning to drop. When I get back to the cemetery, I put the bags down for the moment, find my eraser, and scrub Lala's name off the stone.

I'm not a superstitious man, but I see no point in taking a chance.

NUTTY AND ADA AND LALA are at the kitchen table. I put the bags of groceries on the counter.

"About time," says Ada. "You get cookies?"

I put everything away. I'm not sure why I bother. It'll be gone by tomorrow.

"Emma's making up a batch of chili at the café," says Nutty. "She's going to feed the Neighbours there."

"'Cause this kitchen ain't got enough room," says Ada.

"That's not nice," says Nutty. "Jeremiah is doing the best he can."

"What happened to my toast?" says Lala. "I have to have toast with my chocolate."

A LITTLE AFTER SEVEN, Emma and the Neighbours return.

"I would have brought you some chili," Emma tells me, "but there was barely enough as it was."

Wes and Autumn introduce me to their kids.

"This is Zorina," says Autumn, "our oldest."

"Zoe," says Zorina.

"Zoe's my best friend," says Lala. "She's nicer than Linda."

"And these are the twins, Nicholas and Nicodemus." Wes pats the head of each boy in turn.

"Nick," says Nicholas.

"Nico," says Nicodemus.

"We'll try to be as quiet as we can," says Autumn, "but you know kids."

There's standing room only in the kitchen. I retreat to the porch with the dogs.

"Watch out for Diesel," Wes warns me. "He tends to be nervous around strangers."

He's not the only one.

One of the Neighbours comes up with a guitar that needs to be tuned, and someone starts singing "Hotel California." I check my pocket to make sure the key card that Flood gave me is still there.

Then I pick my way past the dogs and slip out the back door.

34

I walk to the middle of the graveyard before I stop and turn back to the school. The windows are alive with light, and I can hear the guitar and the jangle of voices trying to keep time and tune. The night is colder than I thought it would be, but I'm not about to go back and get a heavier jacket.

Emma and Lala. Nutty and Ada. Wes and Autumn and Jimmy and the rest of the Neighbours.

The dogs.

I may never go back.

I wouldn't have asked for a room at the hotel, certainly wouldn't have spent money on it, but given the circumstances, I'm not unhappy that I have a place to go, where I can close the door and lock out the world.

Of course, that's what the school was supposed to be, and look what happened to that plan.

"Sounds like they're having a good time."

Roman Moosonee. Standing at the edge of the graveyard in the shadow of the trees.

"They kick you out?"

I can't tell if Roman is drunk or sad. Or both.

"Every asshole with a guitar plays that song."

I didn't leave the school so I could have a heart-to-heart with Roman.

"Looks like you and me are the same," says Roman. "Nobody wants us, and we don't fucking well need anyone."

In the school, the village people have started in on "Blowin' in the Wind," the guitar and the voices in different keys.

Roman smiles and shakes his head. "Whatever gets you through the night," he says.

I turn away and start to town.

"What do you think?" Roman leans against the tree. "If I stay here long enough, you think she'll find me?"

THE BANDSTAND IS ALIVE. Someone has set up a modest sound system. Big band tunes. People dancing. There's a sandwich board in the park that says "Moonlight Cabaret."

I look, and if there is a moon, I can't see it.

I recognize Eddie Ott and his wife and Maidie Matthews and her husband. Dino Kiazzie is there, and so is Swannie Gagnon. Bob Loomis is standing at the stairs to the bandstand, shaking hands and passing out buttons.

I'm already in the lobby before I realize that I don't know my room number. I take the card out, but there's no help there. It's just a piece of white plastic.

"Top floor."

I hadn't sensed Oliver Flood's presence, but there he is, standing at my side.

"You have the River Suite." Flood leads the way to the elevators. "Penthouse view."

Spot and Rover are waiting for us. Spot steps forward and I feel my body tense, but Flood waves him off.

"Mr. Camp is our guest," says Flood, and Spot and Rover have a quick smile between themselves, as though this is an inside joke.

THE SUITE IS SPACIOUS and has a view of the river.

"Get settled and join me at the bar," says Flood. "We have much to discuss."

I have little interest in joining Oliver Flood at the bar. My interest is in ordering room service and locking the door.

Flood stops at the door. "And in case you've not heard, Kommer Heineken is dead."

THE BAR AT THE PLAZA HOTEL is a relic of the 1920s. It reminds me a bit of the Owl Bar in Baltimore. Or Chumley's in Greenwich Village. Southport Lanes in Chicago. Dark wood. Mahogany leather. Tarnished brass. The stylish spaces in the world that absorb light and sound.

Flood is sitting at a corner table, looking like a character from an old gangster movie.

"Do you want something to eat?" Flood arranges his cellphone so that it's parallel to his napkin. "The special is prime rib with Yorkshire pudding."

I find the most expensive single malt on the bar menu and order a double shot.

"I have no idea why they call it Yorkshire pudding," says Flood. "It's just a big dinner roll."

I'm not going to drink the whisky. I'm not a drinker. But the glass gives me something I can move around on the table. As I listen to what Flood has to say.

"So, now the circle is complete." In the dull light of the bar, Flood suddenly looks grey and spent. "Twelve people on a list. All of them dead. Remarkable, don't you think?"

I swirl the amber liquor around in the glass. Curious that something so pleasant a colour should taste so awful.

"I saw what you sent Ms. Locken." Flood takes a long, deep breath. As though he's about to dive underwater. "Quite astute, and mostly correct. I'm intrigued as to how you came to your conclusions."

Whisky gets its colour from the charred white-oak barrels in which it's stored.

"The two questions at this point are what are we to do with your forecast? And what are we to do with you?"

And because alcohol is a solvent, it leaches pigment from the wood. The longer the whisky is in the barrel, the darker the colour.

"I will say that Ms. Locken and I are divided on the answer."

But over time, barrels lose their ability to colour, so many manufacturers add a small amount of spirit caramel, or E150 as it's known in the business, to the mix.

"Ms. Locken sees you as a potential asset, while I fear that you will become a liability. The former is problematic at best. The latter, unacceptable."

In general, whisky is made from five different grains. Corn, oats, wheat, barley, and rye.

"What to do?" Flood rearranges the napkin and the phone. "What to do?"

No one knows who invented the distillation process for the making of whisky. Historically, the Scots or the Irish get the credit.

"She hopes to further engage your skills, while I would prefer to kill you."

But it's quite possible that the Vikings brought the process with them on their travels to the west coast of Scotland, or that seventh-century Irish monks carried it back with them from their travels to the Mediterranean.

"I thought I would ask you for your opinion."

The phone on the table vibrates. Flood glances at the screen. I amuse myself, swirl the whisky around in the glass, let the glow from the candle set off the highlights.

Flood pushes the chair back and stands up. "We are summoned."

I leave the glass where it is.

Flood stares at me in disbelief. "You're not going to drink that?"

There must be a time-honoured language of signs common to saloons. Flood gestures to the bartender, and the man gestures back. For a moment, I think they intend to put the drink in a carry-out bag.

Flood makes a gun with his fingers and aims it at my head. "Come along, Forecaster," he says, "before I change my mind."

35

Ash Locken is waiting for us in the suite. She looks comfortable in the wingback chair.

Flood points his chin at me. "He ordered a double twenty-five-year-old Macallan and didn't drink it."

Locken crosses her legs at the ankles. "Oh my," she says. "Perhaps you should go and rescue the wee beastie while Mr. Camp and I talk."

"Then can I kill him?"

"Talk first," says Locken. "Then we'll see."

I'm reasonably sure that there won't be any shooting. At least not tonight. At least not in the hotel.

"I imagine that Oliver has told you about Kommer Heineken."

I sit on the sofa.

"Fentanyl," says Locken. "It seems our Mr. Heineken was a closeted drug enthusiast."

I wonder if Flood is really off to retrieve the glass, or if he plans to sit in the gloom of the bar by himself and enjoy my expensive Scotch.

"You don't care, do you? About the world, about people." Locken's face softens. "You truly don't care."

Maybe I'll join Flood. Order another double and leave it on the table to rot.

"My father cared. He cared about money, about power, about privilege. Because in the world he helped to create, these were the things that mattered. And he was obsessed with knowing. It didn't really matter what it was he wanted to know. For him, knowing was a religion. And what he wanted to know most of all was why we die. Or more to the point, why it is we can't live forever."

Or maybe I would drink it. Knock it back in one gulp, like a gunfighter in a Western bar. Bang the glass on the table and order another.

"In a 1963 commencement address to the graduates of American University, John F. Kennedy said, 'Our most basic common link is that we all inhabit this small planet. We all breathe the same air. We all cherish our children's future. And we are all mortal.'"

Sooner or later, some fast gun with a clever name—the Alberta Kid, Wild Billy James, Buffalo Sam—would stroll into the saloon and challenge me to a gunfight.

"My father hated that notion, the shared reality of mortality. Rather than seeing death as a quality of humanity, he saw it as the ultimate impediment. Why shouldn't we be immortal? Immortality had the potential to improve the human race. With immortality we could create stable and just societies. With immortality, we could go to the stars. With immortality we could be gods."

And when the clock above the bar struck high noon, I'd push through the swinging doors, walk to the middle of the street, and hope I was the faster draw.

"You created the list, didn't you. My father asked you to identify like-minded individuals. Individuals who shared his interest in immortality, individuals who had the means and the temper to pursue such a goal, no matter the cost. Twelve names. The Ankh corporation. Not a corporation really, more an exclusive club, come together for a single and what my father saw as a noble purpose."

In most westerns, shootouts generally end with the hero victorious. But there are exceptions. *Butch Cassidy and the Sundance Kid*. *Hombre. The Shootist.*

"But noble purposes require noble people. And immortality is not necessarily a noble purpose. You recognized that, didn't you? You said as much to my father. I imagine you warned him of the implications. He didn't see that immortality could just as easily create monsters. But you did, didn't you?"

Sheriff Jeremiah Camp and the outlaw Oliver Flood. With a guest appearance by Ash Locken, as the dance-hall girl with a heart of gold.

"Who would get to be immortal? That's easy. The rich and the powerful, of course. They would be the only ones who could afford immortality, because such a condition would be a commodity. It would be the *ultimate* commodity."

Or I could climb up to the bell tower in the church with my Winchester 1873 and bushwhack everyone as they came out into the street.

"Of course, immortality is useless without eternal youth. The Cumaean Sibyl should be object lesson enough."

The Cumaean Sibyl. A priestess who presided over the Apollonian oracle at Cumae. Apollo offered her eternal life for her virginity. But she failed to ask him for eternal youth, and though she didn't die, she did shrivel up until there was nothing left of her but her voice.

"Or Methuselah. But there you have the same problem."

Methuselah. Biblical patriarch. Supposedly lived to be 969. Though there is a great deal of controversy as to how years were figured in early human history. "As old as Methuselah" is a phrase that isn't used anymore, in part because nobody wants to be as decrepit as the phrase suggests.

"Or the Cherokee Nunnehi."

Race of immortal spirit people. They're not humans, but they are supposedly friendly to humans. And, at times, helpful. In Cherokee, the name means "traveller." Depending on who's telling the story, the Nunnehi can be little people, supernatural beings, or visitors from outer space.

"This is what the Ankh corporation hoped to achieve. Eternal life. Eternal youth."

Tithonus. Mattathias. The Wandering Jew. Sir Galahad. Ashwathama.

"In *Moby-Dick*, Starbuck, the *Pequod*'s first mate, suggests that vengeance on a dumb beast could be seen as blasphemy, and Ahab tells him that he has little concern with blasphemy, that he'd strike the sun if it offended him. That was my father, Mr. Camp. Willing to risk everything, to strike through the mask of humanity in the belief that there was something behind it."

Walter Donovan and Dr. Elsa Schneider. Ponce de León and the Fountain of Youth.

"Have you ever wondered whether immortal and immoral are simply sides of the same coin? Eternal delight? Existential despair? Which do you think, Forecaster?"

And all the other unnamed, unimagined monsters that would arise from such an enterprise.

"Of course, we have no way of knowing. So all we can do is guess. And if we can guess, we can act."

Locken shifts in the chair.

"My father acted. He formed Ankh, concentrated all his energy and money on the solution to one problem. He recruited eleven other like-minded people to his cause, even though he understood that, long before we achieved immortality, the problems of the increased longevity we would acquire along the way would destroy the planet."

I stand up, walk to the window. The river is down there somewhere, running deep in its channel.

Locken joins me at the window. "And now they are dead. These destroyers of worlds."

If the moon were up and full, I might be able to see the water.

"But that's not the issue, is it? You realized something else, didn't you? In the process of putting the list together, you realized the larger danger. You saw the greater monster."

OLIVER FLOOD is at the same table, my glass of single malt in front of him, untouched.

"'Home is the hunter,'" he says as I sit down, "'home from the hill.'"

A licensed rendition of Robert Louis Stevenson's "Requiem."

"So now you know." Flood gestures to the bartender. "The logistics were fascinating. Perhaps, one day, I'll share them with you."

Flood sits back and his jacket falls open. Given what I know of the man, I half expect to see a pistol in a shoulder holster and not a pair of red paisley suspenders.

"I can't imagine living forever." Flood rubs his hands together as though he's cold. "Life is fun, but I don't think that another two hundred years will improve on what I have right now. After a while, you'd run out of new experiences, and the stuff you used to do for the pleasure of it would begin to lose its magic."

A bottle of the Macallan 25 appears on the table.

"In the meantime," says Flood, "while we wait, I thought we might consider drinking ourselves into oblivion."

LOCKEN IS GONE when I get back to the suite. I lie on the bed and listen to the sounds of the town at night. Cars going by. Voices on the street. At points, I can hear music coming from the Bent Nail, and I wonder if Roman has been held over.

I think about going back to the school, but there's no room for me there. So I try to make the best of a good situation. I turn on the television. I take a bath. I try to order room service, but I've waited too long, and now the kitchen is closed. I raid the mini-bar, helping myself to a bag of peanuts, a package of chocolate chip cookies, and a can of soda. All at outrageous prices, all courtesy of the Locken Group.

The bed is comfortable enough, the sheets luxurious enough, the pillows soft enough. And I sleep well enough.

But in the morning, when I wake, it's not to the hum of the town coming to life. It's to the clatter of crows and the wail of a world on fire.

36

It's not crows.

It's sirens. By the time I get to the lobby, the whole town is in motion. Fire trucks. Ambulances. Police cars.

Dino and Swannie are on the sidewalk.

Dino waves at me. "Fire," he yells, pointing in the direction of the reserve.

I can see smoke rising above the trees to the west of town. The reserve? The school? A pile of crosses?

There is a moment when I consider going back into the Plaza and ordering room-service breakfast and turning the television to the Weather Network to see if I need to wear a light jacket.

If it's the reserve, there's nothing I can do. If it's the school, there's nothing I can do. The crosses can burn for all I care.

So, doing nothing makes sense.

Dino is at my side, his hands in motion. "You should go and see. God forbid it's the school."

The smoke is no help. It comes out of the trees in a shapeless cloud that is caught in the breeze and blown across the river. The source of the fire could be anything anywhere.

"Or the reserve," says Dino. "God forbid it's the reserve."

IT'S THE RESERVE. By the time I get there, the fire is under control. But the double-wide that had been the council office is a pile of ash and melted aluminum. The only thing that has survived is the steel underframe and the wheels.

The fire department is spraying water on the adjacent trailers to make sure they don't go up as well.

Florence and Nutty are standing off to one side with Ada and Emma and the rest of the families. Louis Bear is talking with his hands, trying to keep the peace.

Roman catches me. "Now they're trying to burn us out."

Bob Loomis and Maribelle Wegman pull up in Bob's BMW. They're followed by the van from the local TV station. Bob waits until the camera is up and running before he steps out of the car.

"You smell gasoline?" says Roman.

Wegman fixes the mayor's tie, pats his hair in place.

"This is that asshole's fault," says Roman.

The firefighters have stopped spraying and are beginning to pull at the wreckage with axes and long poles.

"City cut off our electrical, so we had to use generators." Louis is talking to one of the reporters. "And they cut off our water, so we couldn't fight the fire. All we could do was sit around and watch it burn."

Mayor Bob is in front of the camera now, his back to Louis and the ruin. He strikes a considered pose, one hand on his hip. He's put on his white hard hat, so there won't be any mistake about who is in charge.

"Public safety," he tells the reporter. "This is a matter of public safety."

"Fucker," says Roman under his breath. "He's going to wash his hands and blame it on us."

"I've long been concerned about public-safety issues on the reserve." Mayor Bob turns and looks at the remains of the trailer. "We were just lucky there were no casualties."

"We?" shouts Roman. "Who the fuck are 'we'?"

The news crew is quick. They leave the mayor standing by his car and collapse on Roman. Someone sticks a microphone in Roman's face.

"Are you saying this was arson?"

Roman looks back at the wreckage. "What do you think? City's been trying to take our land for years. They want to get rid of us. What do you think?"

"Are you accusing the city of setting fire to that trailer?"

"You smell gasoline?" Roman sniffs the air. "You smell gasoline?"

Actually, you can smell gasoline. It's faint, and it's buried in the stench of burned wood, scorched aluminum, and melted rubber. But it's there.

"Will you be bringing suit against the city?" A woman with a CBC jacket moves in closer to Roman. "Are you the spokesperson for the band?"

"You're damn right," says Roman, and he stalks off, leaving the news crew behind.

Ada steps forward. "Louis Bear is the chief. Talk to him."

The mayor strides forward and positions himself firmly in front of the camera. "People are angry. And for good reason. We're all angry."

"Is the city responsible for this disaster?"

"Public safety," says the mayor. "It's a major plank in my re-election platform."

NUTTY AND FLORENCE and Ada walk over to where I'm standing.

"You didn't come home last night," says Nutty. "Me and Ada were worried."

Nutty doesn't look all that good. Her eyes have a yellow tint, and her skin is grey. She's more stooped now, as though someone has strapped weights to her arms.

"Jeremiah has himself a suite at the Plaza," says Florence.

"That about his girlfriend?" says Ada. "What is it with Native guys and blondes?"

I don't spend any time wondering how Florence knows about my room at the Plaza. It's a small town.

"Man almost seemed concerned," says Ada. "They must teach that in mayor school."

"You might think about stopping by Dino's," says Nutty. "We need more bread and fruit."

"And eggs," says Ada. "Better get a couple dozen eggs and a bunch of bacon."

LOUIS IS STANDING at the edge of the fire looking at what's left of the double-wide.

"Hell of a mess." Louis pulls his pants up onto his belly. "Band papers, financials, health records. Had a lot of photos as well. The trophy for the old-timers' hockey game."

The water has turned the ash into a grey paste that sticks to everything it touches.

"We got a lot of the old records in boxes in a storage locker, but all the newer stuff is gone," Louis tells me. "Been wanting to sign up for one of those off-site backup services, but we could never afford it."

The firefighters are poking at a large slump of metal that had once been a filing cabinet.

"All our information was on hard drives." Louis hitches his pants again, points to a pile of ash and debris. "Computers used to be right about there."

The wind shifts and blows the smoke back into my face. I never liked the smell of burning rubber, and I don't like it now.

"Firefighters got here in record time. Probably saved a bunch of the trailers as well. Real decent of them. They didn't have to come on the reserve, you know. But they did."

Mayor Bob has finished his interview. I haven't been paying attention to what's been said, but I'm sure Florence will fill me in tomorrow when I stop by for morning coffee.

"Going to need a place for council business," says Louis. "You got any extra rooms at the school?"

LALA AND EMMA find me back in the graveyard, working on Morris Paul's stone. I've finished the *M* and have started work on the *O*.

Lala comes skipping through the crosses. "There was a fire," she shouts. "A big fire."

"They're saying it might be arson," says Emma.

"What's arson?"

"Good thing it was a Saturday," says Emma, "and not a workday."

"What's arson?"

"Roman thinks the mayor is responsible," says Emma, "but that's just the anger talking."

"Is arson bad?"

"I won't be at the café come Monday," says Emma. "I got a contract with a company that wants me to do a feasibility study on low-income housing. They're thinking of doing something here in Gleaming."

"Can we go and see the fire?"

"It's not the thing I normally do," says Emma, "but it's a way to get started. With any luck, Lala and me will be out of your hair by the end of the month."

"I don't want to be out of Pop-Up's hair."

Emma glances at the sky. "Big storm's supposed to come in tonight. Heavy rain."

"If there's lightning," says Lala, "can we go upstairs and watch?"

"Come on, honey," says Emma. "Let's get some hot chocolate."

"We could use the binokers. We could watch the lightning with the binokers."

I pick up the chisel and the mallet. With any luck, I'll finish Morris Paul's name before it gets dark.

Lala takes her mother's hand, and the two of them head for the school.

"Bananas," Emma calls back over her shoulder. "We're out of bananas."

37

The sky has darkened and the temperature has dropped. I'm in Dino's when the first tentative raindrops hit the awning.

"Big storm," says Dino. "May have to close early."

I hand Dino the list. He hands the list to Javi.

"Mr. Camp is a good man," Dino tells his son. "A patron. So generous."

I put a bunch of red grapes in a separate bag to take back to the hotel.

"Javi will deliver the food. Anything else you need, you tell Javi." Dino puts an extra apple in for Lala. "When I see the smoke and the firemen and the trucks, I think it's the school."

I grab a banana and a package of cheese as well. In case I get hungry later on.

Dino shows me the total. "Such luck," he says. "A weekday and there would have been more people in the office."

I can still smell the burning rubber from the tires and the stink of water and ash.

"Javi went to see."

Javi nods solemnly. "There was nothing left."

We stand together under the awning. The rain slows for the moment.

"Nothing like a hard rain," says Dino. "A hard rain cleans everything."

MY KEY CARD STILL WORKS. Which is good news and bad news. It means I still have the room at my disposal. But it also means that I haven't seen the last of Ash Locken and Oliver Flood.

The rain picks up, quick and heavy. I wonder how crows and ducks and foxes survive storms. Where they go when the weather turns on them.

I stand and listen to the storm batter the roof and rattle the windows. Then I step into the room and lock the door behind me.

THE NEXT MORNING, the rain is still coming down. I take my time in the bathroom. The irony of standing under a shower in the middle of a downpour is not lost on me.

The towels at the Plaza are large and fluffy. I wrap myself up in one that is the size of an overcoat and go back to bed. I lie there in the dark and listen to the weather outside get on with its business.

Nothing to do with me.

The room is dark and warm and silent. I settle into a familiar daydream where I'm safe at last, where no one knows where I am, where I can stay hidden forever and never be found.

And then the phone rings.

ASH LOCKEN IS WAITING for me in the hotel dining room. One corner of the room is awash in steam tables. A man in a white uniform and a chef's hat stands over a roast with a knife.

"Brunch," Locken tells me. "But we can also order à la carte."

The wind has teamed up with the rain, and the two of them have driven everything and everyone off the street.

"I'm glad you could join me for breakfast."

Disingenuous. Saying no had not been an option.

"Oliver will be joining us later."

A young man comes by. Coffee pot in one hand, juice pitcher in the other.

Locken stops him with a hand. "Do you have espresso?"

"No, ma'am. But the coffee is excellent."

"Just water, then," says Locken. "No ice."

"We have Voss and San Pellegrino."

"No Finé or Veen?" Locken smiles. "No Acqua di Cristallo Tributo a Modigliani?"

The man shifts from one foot to the other.

"I can be such a bitch," says Locken. "We'll have the Château Gleaming."

"Tap?"

"Please."

The waiter heads into the kitchen to tell the rest of the staff about the crazy woman at the table by the window. Then he'll look up Acqua di Cristallo Tributo a Modigliani on his cellphone.

There are small jars of jam on the table. Locken picks up one.

"Apricot," she says. "That's something you don't usually see. Strawberry, raspberry, blueberry, marmalade. They're common enough."

If I had a favourite jam, it would be rhubarb.

"My mother was a gardener. She was especially fond of fruit trees, and her favourite was the apricot. I don't know how many times she told me that if you wanted good apricots, you had to grow them yourself."

But all in all, most jams have too little flavour and far too much sugar.

"And in order to have a healthy and productive tree, you have to prune it constantly and judiciously. Cut the wrong branch at the wrong time, she would tell me, and you could traumatize the tree, even kill it. Prune too much or too little and you might not get any fruit. And then there were the diseases—bacterial canker, eutypa, phytophthora—and the insects—aphids, mealy bugs, mites, caterpillars. Always a concern. But if you were careful and you trimmed away just the dead wood, watched for any sign of diseases or insects, saw to it that the tree got just the right amount of water, you could look forward to a fine crop of fruit."

Locken puts her fork to one side and settles in the chair.

"And then there's my father. His obsession was with longevity, immortality. And to that end, he asked you to create a list of like-minded individuals, individuals who could afford the costs of such a venture, individuals who would allow nothing to get in the way of their shared goal."

Locken doesn't lower her voice or turn towards the wall. There are people all around us, but that's the beauty of restaurants. Each table tends to be its own little island, its own little world.

Unto itself.

"But you saw what my father could not, didn't you. The issue

261

wasn't immortality. The issue was the small group of men and women, individuals and families with such vast resources and privilege that they imagined themselves to be separate from society, invulnerable and invincible. The issue was individuals who were determined to reshape the world with no regard for the well-being of the rest of humanity or for the health of the planet, with no regard for the concept of balance."

The old couple at a table against the wall with their books. The young couple with two small children who are already squirming in their seats.

Locken arranges her napkin on her lap. "We exist at the sufferance of others."

The businessman at a table by himself, reading the news on his iPad.

"Of course, there are good billionaires as well as bad billionaires," says Locken. "At least, I like to believe that this is true."

The four older women, for whom Sunday brunch is a religion.

"And then again," says Locken. "Then again."

Oliver Flood appears at the maître d' station. Crisply dressed, as though he's just been taken out of the box. It doesn't appear as though the weather has dared to touch him. He sits down next to me without a word. Hems me in, in case I'm thinking about an escape.

"Think of us as an orchard." Locken folds her hands together. "In need of a little pruning."

Flood signals the server. "Everything is in place. We've already made arrangements to replace the double-wide that was lost in the fire. Not with a trailer, but with a permanent structure."

Flood hands me one of the Cradle River Estates brochures that the mayor passed out at the party.

"We'll be meeting with the band council early this week to put the full proposal on the table."

Locken nods. "And Ms. Stillday?"

"We'll request that she be lead council and the band's liaison with Ankh." Flood orders coffee, juice, and an omelette.

Now that I look closely, I can see that the plan in the brochure doesn't quite match Loomis's scale model.

"The mayor's plan was decent," says Flood, "but we were able to add a few improvements."

Locken turns back to me. "You see, we keep our bargains."

Flood smiles. "Of course, his worship isn't going to be pleased."

"Ah, yes," says Locken. "No Loomis Commons."

"May I tell him?" asks Flood.

"No," says Locken. "I think we'll leave that pleasure to Ms. Stillday."

Flood turns to me. "A quiet time in a nice hotel suite," he says, "and you still look as though you've been run over by community."

I LEAVE LOCKEN AND FLOOD to enjoy their breakfast. There's a fancy umbrella stand by the front door. Courtesy umbrellas with the Plaza's logo. I help myself to one of them and step out into the day.

Dino is wrong about rain. It just gets things wet.

38

Florence doesn't waste any time.

"You're late," she tells me as I come in the door. "You still sleeping at that hotel?"

I put the brownie on the counter. I take the sausage roll out of the bag.

"Hear brunch at the Plaza is staggering, but word is you passed it up."

The sausage roll is delicious.

"You stop talking is one thing," says Florence. "You stop eating and we start to worry."

I finish the roll in three bites.

"Ada thinks your acting funny is 'cause of your girlfriend."

The Three Bears are huddled in a corner with Wapi in the middle. Louis is grim-faced. Enola has an arm around her cousin. Both of Wapi's hands are bandaged to the elbow.

Florence cuts the brownie and takes the larger half to the table and sets it in front of Wapi.

"It wasn't his fault," Louis shouts to me from the table. "He didn't know."

Florence comes back to the counter, grinds the beans, packs the basket. "Hell of a thing. The boy loses his parents, almost dies himself, and now this."

I watch the dark brown liquid leak into the cup and wait for the rest of the story.

"He just wanted to help," says Enola. "Just wants to be like everyone else."

There's an art to frothing. Use the steam wand to pull the milk up the sides of the metal pitcher.

Florence pats the bottom of the pitcher as she works the milk. "Generator at the council office ran out of fuel."

If you do it wrong, all you wind up with is scalded milk and air. If you do it correctly, you get milk as thick as soft butter.

"Wapi tried to fill it." Florence pours the milk into the cup. "But the generator was still hot. Spilled some of the gasoline, and you know the rest."

"I could have made the same mistake," says Louis.

"Word is the mayor's thinking of charging Wapi with arson." Florence puts the macchiato in front of me. "You have to wonder who has the developmental problems."

"Anyone come for my cousin," says Enola, "and they come through me."

"No one's coming for Wapi." Louis ruffles his nephew's hair. "Everything is going to be fine."

"And Nutty's back in the hospital." Florence eats the rest of the brownie without offering me any. "Ada says she started breathing funny in the middle of the night."

"Wasn't his fault," says Enola.

Florence wipes the brownie crumbs off the counter. "Emma and Ada and me are going to see her soon as Emma's done in the kitchen."

I would have liked to have had a bite of the brownie.

"Ada's looking after Lala right now," says Florence. "But we need someone to step up while we're at the hospital."

Wapi holds up his hands and smiles. "Brownie," he shouts.

Florence gives Wapi a thumbs-up. Then she turns back to me.

"And you got elected."

Emma emerges from the kitchen. "All done," she says.

The Three Bears are on their feet. Wapi holds his hands out in front of him. He looks a bit like a kangaroo.

"We're going to take Wapi home," says Enola. "He can't play on his iPad, so he gets bored."

"We don't have cable," says Louis. "You think Ada would mind if Wapi watched hers?"

"You'll have to stay with him," says Florence.

"Yeah," says Enola, "we can do that."

I WALK BACK to the school with Florence and Emma. Louis and Enola and Wapi follow along behind.

"Are you going to pull up all the crosses?" Louis asks me.

"Are you really going to burn them?" says Enola.

Wapi runs off ahead of us, and then he runs back. "I help," he says.

ADA AND LALA are in the classroom that Ada and Nutty are using for a bedroom.

"Pop-Up!" shouts Lala. "You came back."

"Course he came back," says Ada. "He thinks he owns the place."

Wapi runs over to the big-screen television. "Cartoons," he says.

"We got lots of cartoons," says Ada. "You know how to work the remote?"

"Remote," says Wapi.

"Why don't we get something to eat first," says Enola.

"Pizza," says Wapi. "Pizza, pizza, pizza."

The Three Bears disappear into the kitchen. Ada and Emma and Florence get in Ada's car and head to the hospital.

"Come on, Pop-Up," says Lala. "We can pull up crosses."

I don't bother changing. I just grab the mallet and chisel and my gloves. The storm has moved along, but it's left a slate-grey sky and a crisp chill in the air, as though winter is planning a return engagement.

I squat down beside a river stone. Lala sits beside me.

"Nooko says you don't like people," says Lala.

I turn the stone over to see which side is the flatter. Then I take out my pencil and begin laying out the name.

"But you like me, right?"

Mary Camp. A woman I never met. Never saw. Not so much as a story. A name on a list kept by an obsessive priest.

Lala sees him first.

"Roman!"

"Hi, sweet stuff."

"I'm not sweet stuff."

"Sure you are, sweetie pie."

"I'm not sweetie pie."

I set the chisel on the edge of the *M*.

Roman looks at the name I've sketched on the stone. "Mary Camp," he says. "She would have been one of my aunties."

Dead at twelve. Hinch's map shows not only the location of each grave, but the dates as well.

"Yours, too, cousin."

"Then she's my auntie, too," says Lala.

"Great-auntie," says Roman. "I'm thinking of getting some ice cream."

"Ice cream!"

I slide the chisel down the stone. I don't know what arrangements Emma has made with Roman or if she has made any at all.

Lala tugs on my shirt. "Can I go?"

"Sure, you can go," says Roman. "Jeremiah's not your dad. I am."

"Can I have vanilla?"

Roman looks back at the school. "Where's Emma? How come she left her with you?"

"Mum-Mum had to go to the hospital. Grummy's sick again."

Roman stiffens. "Nutty?"

"Is she going to die?"

"Nutty's too tough to die," says Roman. "Let's go get that ice cream."

"Can Pop-Up come?"

Roman shakes his head. "He has work to do."

Across the river, a flock of crows has appeared in the overcast sky, black on black.

Lala jams a hand in her pocket and comes up with a fistful of peanuts. "If Slick comes looking for me," she says, "you'll have to give him peanuts."

I put the nuts next to the stone.

"Otherwise, he'll be grumpy."

I don't know how Emma will feel about Lala going off with Roman. Maybe she's okay with it. Maybe she's not.

The crows have taken over the trees on the far bank. They're too far away for me to see if Slick is in the hover.

Nutty is in the hospital. Florence and Ada and Emma are there, too. If the Neighbours are still around, I don't hear them. Lala is off with her father. And for the first time in a while, I'm alone.

I set the chisel on the inside edge of the *M* and strike down hard.

39

I finish the *M* and the *A* and the *R* before I give up and call it a day. My left hand, the hand that holds the chisel, is aching and swollen, and I now have a cut on my cheek where a chip from the stone caught me.

Mary Camp does not appear to me. Nor do any of the other children in the graveyard. Perhaps there are too many people at the school now, with no room for the dead among the living.

The crows have not come to this side of the river. I pick up the peanuts and fling them among the crosses where the birds can find them at their leisure.

I could return to the school, go upstairs to my room, and have a nap, but now I find that I'm a stranger to the place. And it to me. If there had ever been a bond with the building, it is gone. And all that I have left as consolation and comfort, if in fact I have anything, is the cemetery.

And the graves.

If I'm being honest, I have to admit that I enjoy feeling sorry for myself. So much so that I stretch out on the cold ground next to a cross, my face to the sky, and pretend that I'm dead.

I keep my eyes open, in case the crows try to sneak up on me. In case I look like roadkill to a passing corvid.

I'm surprised how different the world looks. Being flat on my back. The tops of trees, clusters of clouds, an open sky. It is a view that changes but remains much the same.

A simple and peaceable panorama. A natural world of sights and sounds. Nowhere are there market equities, hedge funds, venture capital, real assets. Not a corporation to be seen.

Odd ducks, corporations. They trace back to England and the royal charters granted to well-placed individuals and consortiums by the monarchy. The Locken Group is just the newest manifestation of an older concept.

Make money at any cost.

And then in 1886, in *Santa Clara County v. Southern Pacific Railroad*, the U.S. Supreme Court held that corporations were persons and entitled to protection under the Fourteenth Amendment's Equal Protection Clause.

Of course, corporations aren't, in fact, persons, but the ruling created a cynical and clever legal dodge that helped to increase and legitimize corporate power in the marketplace and in society.

THERE ARE SEVERAL PROBLEMS with lying on my back in the middle of a graveyard. It's not all that comfortable. And it's cold. And then there are the explanations I will have to concoct should someone come along and find me.

THE STORY OF HOW corporations became persons is more interesting than a simple court case, and there are two parts to it.

The first part featured the lead lawyer for the Southern Pacific, a Roscoe Conkling. In the 1860s, when Conkling was a congressman, he sat on the committee that drafted the Fourteenth Amendment. When the Southern Pacific arrived on his doorstep, Conkling swore that the drafters of the amendment had changed the wording, replacing *citizens* with the word *persons* so that the law would cover corporations.

CROWS, FOR INSTANCE. I can't see any from my vantage point, but they are a curious species, could come along at any moment with their trilogy of concerns.

Can we steal it? Can we eat it? Can we shit on it?

Not all that different from humans.

If the crows find me first, I'll simply tell them the truth. That I'm lying on the ground because, at this moment, I can't think of anything else to do.

CONKLING'S ASSERTION WAS a lie. The framers of the Fourteenth Amendment had had no such intention in mind. And, as it turns out, the decision in the *Santa Clara* case *did not* decide that corporations were persons. Evidently, the court clerk, a J.C. Bancroft Davis, who wrote the summary, added it in.

After the fact.

His own opinion.

That corporations were protected by the Fourteenth Amendment.

And because no one noticed or no one cared, the notion became the law of the land.

THOMAS LOCKEN LIKED to tell this story. And on each October 30 and December 29, Locken would invite select members of his corporate team to his office to raise a glass to the two men who had made corporations virtually untouchable.

And to sing "Happy Birthday" to the memory of Conkling and Davis.

I'M STILL ON MY BACK, watching the clouds, humming "Happy Birthday," when Oliver Flood arrives.

He stands over me and blocks out the light. So much for the trees and the clouds and the sky. So much for the peaceable panorama.

"When you're done playing dead," says Flood, "we'd like a word."

Flood has employed the royal *we* to denote a superior, such as a king or a pope or a god of some stripe, speaking to an inferior, such as me, as well as the rest of the world. William de Longchamp is generally credited with the introduction of the concept in the late-twelfth century.

I'd share this historical footnote with Flood if I thought he would care.

"Shall we help you up?"

I could also mention that Margaret Thatcher, when she was prime minister, used the royal plural to announce that she had become a grandmother, and that the affectation had not gone over well with the press.

But no one likes a pedant.

I get to my feet, brush myself off. I'm stiffer than I would have supposed, and I have to take several moments to get all the parts working correctly and in unison.

"Do you enjoy walking?" says Flood. "I know I do. There's a large park with a lake near where I live. Forty minutes at a brisk pace before breakfast. Does wonders for energy and cognition."

The crows are in the sky. They fly low, strafe the river, cawing as they go.

"Let's walk to the falls," says Flood. "I've heard so much about them. According to Tripadvisor and Expedia, it's the number one thing to see in this part of the world."

Flood walks along the river path bent forward at the waist, his hands clasped behind his back, as though he's practising for a scene in *Downton Abbey*. I walk along beside him, because I have nothing better to do.

Flood talks as he walks. "In the coming weeks, the press will break a series of stories suggesting that the deaths of our billionaires were not natural or accidental, but rather the work of a terrorist organization to be named later. We're still trying to come up with a catchy designation, something alliterative perhaps.

"There will be confusion and indignation, calls for a joint task force or a blue-ribbon panel of some sort, and we shall have to endure the drove of talking donkeys on Fox and CNN, and the cackle of conspiracy hyenas on the internet. Amazing how easy it is to create a stampede."

The crows swing around and come storming into the trees. They know entertainment when they see it.

"In three months, it will be old news, forgotten completely in nine. I plan to take some time off. Valencia is lovely this time of year. Or Prague. Perhaps even Vancouver."

Flood didn't come to the graveyard to fill me in on his vacation plans.

"Ms. Locken is of the opinion that the existence of billionaires is the sure sign of a failed social/economic system, and she believes that taking out the expensive trash could make a difference, that we are redeemable. I don't share this view, but I respect her passion and conviction, and I do what I can to help. Still, you can see our dilemma. We can't have anything that links her to the dispatching of rich folks, because then it would be difficult for her to continue on with the dispatching."

We come to the bend in the trail, and now I can feel the first faint tremors of the falls under my feet.

"From what I've seen, we don't win these wars." Flood glances up into the trees. "The war on drugs? Lost. The war on poverty? Lost. The war on guns? Lost. The war on racism? Also lost.

"And now Ms. Locken is waging a war on power and privilege, and what I need to know is whether you will help, hinder, or stand to the side and watch."

I wonder if Flood can feel the sensations as well.

"I've been instructed *not* to kill you," he says, "so there's no need for you to hedge your answer."

We walk the rest of the way in silence, Flood leading the way. When we get to the viewpoint, Flood goes to the railing and leans out into the spray.

"Broken Bough Falls." Flood's voice softens. "Did you know that the version of 'Rock-a-bye Baby,' the version every mother knows, first appeared in a mid-eighteenth-century publication."

The wind shifts, and the spray dances away from Flood.

"So, this is the famous Cradle River," he says. "Where the water falls into a pool and disappears."

The crows have followed us. They sit in the trees, waiting to see if anyone is going to jump.

"Do you think rivers are metaphors for life?"

I should have gone with Roman and Lala for ice cream. Or to the hospital with the women.

"We've kept your room at the Plaza," says Flood. "So at least you have somewhere to hide."

The crows are restless. If there's no murder and mayhem in the immediate future, then they have better things to do.

"So what about it, Forecaster?" Flood spreads his arms and leans out over the railing. "Do you think we're redeemable?"

I wait to see if Flood will take to the air and fly away.

"The world's going to hell, and you think you can sit in a grave-yard with a hammer and a chisel? The dead don't give a shit."

Or if he'll lose his balance and be washed over the falls.

"Fact is, we all have to make choices." Flood steps back from the railing. "Whether we want to or not."

40

Flood doesn't kill me.

He doesn't fly away, and he doesn't go over the falls.

The crows stick around until it's clear that the possibility for slaughter has passed. I can hear the disappointment in their voices as they explode into the air.

Flood and I walk back together. Two old friends out for a stroll. When we get to the bend, Flood stops. From here, you can turn away from the river and head into town. Or you can stay the path until you get to the graveyard and the school.

"I'm sure you have already concluded that you weren't the only forecaster we engaged." Flood stops, turns to me. "Lorna Collins in London. José Sandolo in Mexico City. Jia Yang in Beijing. Ernst Becker in Berlin. None of them was able to see what you saw."

Billionaires killing billionaires.

"How did you know?" says Flood. "How did you figure it out? What gave it away?"

I could tell Flood that it was the only explanation that made sense. Who else would kill them? Who else knew them well enough to get inside their defences? Who else had the resources and the will to stage such an elaborate and global slaughter?

Who else would know the extent of the damage such people inflict on society, on the planet?

Who else possessed the ego and the conceit to believe that they were called to such a task?

Who else had the list?

A gardener in a garden. Indeed.

"Ms. Locken likes you." Flood turns towards the town. "Damned if I know why."

ROMAN AND LALA are on the front porch. Lala has the remains of an ice cream cone that she is sharing with Pancakes.

"Pancakes likes ice cream," she explains. "Just like me."

"Nutty's not too good," says Roman.

"Grummy is sick," says Lala. "She has a cold."

"They're going to keep her in the hospital. Pneumonia."

Pancakes the cat stops licking and begins chewing on the cone. Roman takes out a handkerchief and wipes his daughter's face.

"Can we watch the baseball game?" Lala drops the remains of the cone on the ground for the cat. "Nooko told me to watch the game, so I could tell her what happened."

"No, she didn't."

"Did so."

"How about I teach you to play the horn, sweet pea?"

"I'm not sweet pea."

"Okay, honey bun."

"I'm not honey bun." Lala leans in against her father. "If we don't watch the game, Nooko will be sad."

THE WALK TO THE HOSPITAL doesn't take as long as I expected. The place is just as cold and frightening, the smells sharp and disturbing. I remember the floor and the room, but when I get there, someone else is in the bed.

My mistake.

There's no reason that they would have put Nutty in the same room, the same bed. Hospitals aren't hotels, where you can request a room with a view. You go where they stick you.

I check each floor, glance in the rooms that are open. No Nutty. I could ask, but I don't. There's the chance that she has died. She's old. She's sick. As I look, I try to imagine what she would say if I were to offer her immortality. And youth.

Rise up and go forth.

Would she say no? Would I say no? Unimaginable wealth and power? Would we say no to that as well?

So, Locken had used my list as a blueprint for gardening. Snip here, snap there. But societies are not trees. And there's no way to predict what will happen, what will change. If anything. What new patterns might emerge.

And yet she had stepped forward and cut away. As though she knew what she was doing.

I don't find Nutty. I don't find Ada or Emma either, for that matter. I wander the corridors, drift among the sick and the dying, until I find my way out into the night and back to my room at the Plaza.

41

I stay in my hotel room for the rest of the week. Most of the time, I lie on the bed, under the covers. I know the world has run on ahead without me. The school and the graveyard. Florence and the Piggy. Swannie and her brownies. Lala and Emma.

Nutty.

I don't care where it's going. Just so long as it's not coming here.

Morning, afternoon, evening. Morning, afternoon, evening. The fox on the bank. The duck in the river.

And then morning comes around again, and I hear the drum.

I get out of bed, go to the window. From my vantage point, I can see part of the plaza, and the part that I can see is awash in people. The festival. After all this, a festival? If I had any nascent ideas of leaving the room, they are now gone.

"Pop-Up!"

I stay by the window and pretend to be deaf as well as dumb.

"Pop-Up. It's me."

Which isn't exactly true.

When I open the door, I find Ada and Emma and Nutty and Florence standing in the hallway as well. Along with Wapi. His hands are still bandaged. Takahashi's binoculars hang around his neck. Lala rushes past me and into the suite.

"How many houses do you own, Pop-Up?"

Suddenly, my sanctuary is filled with people.

"Pretty fancy," says Ada. "So this is how the rich live."

"You have to come to the park with us." Lala bounces from the sofa to the chair and back again. "I'm getting my face painted."

"Closed the café," says Florence. "Too much of a success."

Wapi holds the binoculars to his eyes and sweeps the room.

"Nooko gave your binoculars to Wapi," Lala tells me.

"You weren't using them," says Ada.

"Wapi can see all sorts of things that no one else can see." Lala stands in front of the binoculars and makes a face. "He can see everything in the world."

"World," says Wapi.

"I've got legal work now," says Emma, "so I've had to stop working at the Piggy."

"Restaurant's no place for a lawyer anyway," says Ada.

"Which is why we came by," says Emma.

Ada orders room service for everyone. Coffee, fruit, eggs, bacon, toast. Locken won't mind, and I don't care.

"Do they have pancakes?" says Lala. "Grummy likes pancakes."

"Maybe one or two," says Nutty.

"What do you know about the Ankh Foundation?" asks Emma.

"Your girlfriend runs it," says Ada, "so don't be playing dumb."

"Nothing wrong with having a girlfriend," says Nutty.

"Sit down, you old fool," says Ada. "You just got out of the hospital."

It takes a while, but I get everybody sorted out on chairs and sofas. I wind up perched on the edge of a coffee table.

"Couple of lawyers met with the band council," says Emma. "They want to fund a demonstration project on sustainable communities."

"They want to build a new council office," says Ada, "and replace all the trailers with modular homes."

"Out of the blue," says Emma. "Has to make you wonder."

And then the women sit back and wait to see what I have to say. They're still waiting when the food arrives.

Flood has been busy. In addition to the new council office and the modular homes, the Ankh Foundation has offered to dig a well and set up a solar-power system for the reserve. Replace the septic system.

"As well as a satellite system and a wireless hub," says Ada.

"So I can use my cellphone," says Lala.

"These eggs are pretty good," says Nutty. "Not as good as Emma's, but pretty good."

Florence holds up the menu. "Have you seen these prices?"

"The foundation is sort of a dream come true," says Emma. "We still can't figure out what happened."

"Too good to be true," says Ada.

"Okay," says Florence as she helps herself to a whack of bacon, "news, blues, and comfortable shoes."

I lean back against the wall and pretend to be invisible.

"On the international scene, a terrorist group calling itself the Gardeners is taking credit for the deaths of several billionaires whose deaths were thought to be accidental. Intelligence services in several countries have formed a task force to deal with what they are calling a threat to the world economy."

"The Gardeners?" Ada slides a couple pancakes onto her plate. "There's a name that's sure to strike fear in the hearts of rich people."

"Good gardening is important," says Nutty.

"While in the land just south of us," says Florence, "Texas has admitted to losing over four thousand children who were removed from their families by immigration officials."

"That's more than careless," says Emma.

"A spokeswoman for ICE says that the children are not really missing, that they have just been misplaced."

Lala is on her feet and runs from one end of the suite to the other. "Can I have some coffee?"

"And in local news," says Florence, "the Spring Festival is on today in the plaza, featuring the Clay Pigeons on the big drum."

"Ada and me are going to dance," says Nutty.

"No, we're not," says Ada.

"Shawl," says Nutty. "It's spring. I feel like dancing."

"Can I dance?" says Lala. "I'm a good dancer."

I sneak some grapes, a piece of cheese, and a slice of toast. My hope is that once the food runs out, they'll forget about me and leave.

"And," says Florence, holding up a hand, "in more local news, the mayor's office has come under investigation over the improper letting of contracts."

"As in kickbacks," says Emma. "Appears the mayor was less than transparent in how the bids for the new community centre were handled."

"Bob's the one," says Ada.

I try one of the pastries. It looks as if it's lemon. But it's not.

"Can we go to the festival now?" Lala hops to the door on one foot. "You guys are boring."

EVERYTHING IN THE PLAZA is in motion. Musicians occupy the bandstand. Vendors ring the perimeter of the park. Earrings made out of spoons. Handcrafted cutting boards. Painted birdhouses. Wine cork key-chains. Two women have set a slackline between the bandstand and a lamp standard and are rope walking to "I Will Survive."

The Three Bears are here as well. Louis has his hand drums on display, along with Enola's beadwork.

The Clay Pigeons have set up the big drum in the middle of the park, next to the firepit. The fire is going, and the Pigeons are relaxing. The musicians in the bandstand are finishing up a piece that sounds like car alarms wrapped in tinfoil.

"Jerry."

All these people, and nowhere to hide.

"Just the man I want to see."

Mayor Bob is dressed in a bright blue golf shirt and a pair of tan walking shorts.

"What's all this bullshit about the reserve?" The mayor shakes his head. "New council office? New houses?"

I turn towards the drum. Roman sees me and waves me over.

Loomis grabs my arm. "Lipstick on a pig. You need to get everyone on board. Cradle River Estates is going to happen. It's a reality. It's the future."

I shrug him off, begin drifting away, as though the wind has picked me up and is carrying me along. The mayor follows.

"I didn't build a fucking model for nothing."

Loomis slows down as we get close to the drum.

"Didn't get brochures printed up for my own amusement," he calls out after me.

THE FIRE IN THE PIT is going pretty well. There's a stack of firewood off to one side, and it's only when I get close that I realize what Roman and the boys are burning.

Crosses.

The crosses that Roman rescued from Wegman. The crosses that he hid in Nutty's trailer.

"Cuz." Roman stands up and brings me to the drum. "You know the boys?"

I know Jake and Gordon and Benjamin. The other guys are strangers.

"Curve Lake drum," says Roman. "This is Narcisse and Leroy, Martin and Smiley."

I shake hands with each man in turn.

"This is Jeremiah Camp," says Roman. "He's a little weird."

"Weird," says Wapi, and he looks at each man through the binoculars.

"But he's family?" says Narcisse. "Right?"

"Yeah," says Roman, and he hits the drum with his drumstick. "That's the rumour."

I sit in the circle, keep my mouth shut, hold the beat. In between songs, Roman throws another cross on the fire.

"More where that came from," he tells the boys.

When Roman puts a cross on the fire, he puts it in flat. I'm tempted to stand them up in the pit, hammer them into the ground, so there's no mistake as to what's going up in flames.

I don't see Maribelle Wegman, but she might be closer than I think.

Roman smiles and turns his face up to the sun. "You guys know the Mighty Mouse song?"

WHEN THE BOYS BREAK to get something to eat, Roman stays behind.

"Someone has to sit with the drum," he tells me. "Maybe you can get Emma to bring me something."

I wander over to where Louis and Enola have their table. Louis sees me coming and holds up a drumstick.

"This is for you, Jeremiah," he says. "Don't know how you did it."

"Is that blonde really your girlfriend?" asks Enola.

"Man doesn't kiss and tell," says Louis. "Am I right?"

Enola makes a face. "You actually kissed her?"

The stick is a handsome thing, cedar and deer hide. I tap it against my hand, try to imagine that my palm is a drum.

"Now all you got to do," says Louis, "is learn to sing."

"We're going to Europe," says Enola.

"That's right," says Louis. "Got an invite to go to someplace in Germany. Bad something or other. Going to do a drum workshop. Enola is going to show folks how to bead."

Enola nods. "You ever been to Germany?"

"And we're taking Wapi," says Louis. "Give the boy a chance to see the world."

Wapi holds the binoculars up so I can see the lenses. "World," he says.

I MAKE A CIRCUIT of the plaza, stop at a display of raku pottery and check out a guy who works in metal. He has a cut-out of two crows arguing. I think about putting it in the kitchen window of the school to annoy the real crows, but then I remember the story of the farmer.

Lala and Emma catch me just as I decide to go back to the hotel. Lala has a drum in one hand and a drumstick in the other.

"Uncle Lou-Lou gave me a drum," she says. "Daddy's going to teach me to sing."

"I've found a place in town to rent," says Emma. "Plan is to move at the end of the month."

"I don't want to move."

"Children don't like change," says Emma. "They get over it quickly enough. They just don't like it at the time."

"I won't get over it."

"You want to get some pizza?"

"I want to stay with Pop-Up."

"And some ice cream?"

"A double scoop?"

"Maybe."

"That means no," says Lala.

"It's never a good idea to bribe children," says Emma. "At least that's what the books say."

Roman and the drum start up again. A fast song, full of energy and hope.

"We were supposed to get Daddy food," says Lala. "Now he's going to be hungry."

Emma sighs.

"Ice cream," says Lala. "Daddy likes ice cream."

"I don't think Roman wants ice cream for lunch."

"We could get him some vanilla," says Lala, "and if he doesn't eat it, I will."

I stand at the edge of the plaza and wait. Other men, faces I don't know, have joined the drum, and now the circle is whole and complete, no room for someone who can't sing. No room for someone who doesn't belong.

Lala gives her drum a whack. "And then I'll play my drum and sing."

I'm considering what my options might be when I notice the crows. They're on the wing, cawing and wheeling against the clouds. I watch them as they make several passes over the festivities, peel off and head out towards the Petro-Can and the old box plant.

And because I can't think of what else to do, I leave the plaza behind and tag along with the birds.

42

The next morning, Swannie Gagnon takes her time getting me a brownie.

"You are *mal*?" she says.

I want to explain the difference between dishevelled and sick, but I'm stiff and cranky and not in the mood to discuss the consequences of bad choices. I had not planned to spend the night at the old box plant, but having arrived there, through no fault of my own, I had stayed.

It had started off as an adventure. Sneak into the building through the plywood and the wire. Skirt the heavy equipment. Find my way to the second floor.

Which had the best view.

The remains of the Neighbours were still apparent. Several mattresses. Large pieces of cardboard stacked on one another. The remains of a cook fire. A makeshift clothesline.

Swannie puts the brownie in a bag.

"You have the dirt," she says, touching the side of her face. "Here."

There hadn't been a toilet or a sink or a mirror, and after spending the night in a deserted building, I have no idea what I look like. I had combed my hair with my fingers and wiped my face with my handkerchief, brushed off my pants and jacket. I didn't think I looked that bad.

"You sleep in a barn?" says Swannie. "With the animals? Yes?"

I can stop off at the hotel and clean up or I can go to the Piggy as is. The chance of getting any sympathy from Florence is negligible. She's not going to see my overnight as anything more than conceit. And she would be correct.

I didn't do it to be in solidarity with the homeless.

The Piggy has a closed sign in the window, but the door is open, and I can smell coffee. Ada and Nutty are at their table. The Three Bears are in their corner. Florence is behind the counter.

"That better be my brownie."

The world is back to normal.

"Our hero," says Ada. "Where's your girlfriend?"

"What happened to you?" says Louis.

"He slept at the old box plant," says Enola.

"Man has an entire school and a suite at the Plaza," says Ada, "and he sleeps in that dump?"

"It's kinda cool," says Enola. "Wapi and me snuck in there once. The view from the second floor is pretty good."

"View," says Wapi.

"Maybe he's auditioning to be one of those martyrs," says Ada. "The kind that crazy priest used to go on about."

"Saints," says Nutty. "There was that one guy who was hacked to death by children."

"Mohawks do that?"

"Not that one," says Nutty. "That one happened in Italy."

"Mohawks *did* kill a bunch of them," says Ada. "Probably got tired of all that holier-than-thou yap-yap."

"Yap-yap," says Wapi.

"Don't think sleeping on a cold concrete floor for a night is going to get you canonized," says Enola.

"Maybe Jeremiah was on a vision quest," says Louis. "I saw this movie about a guy who goes into the wilderness with nothing but a knife."

"That's *Survival*, Dad," says Enola. "It's a reality show."

Florence grinds the beans, while I nibble at my part of the brownie.

"Don't know how you did it," says Florence. "Getting that foundation to step in. But I'm impressed."

I watch her pack the basket and lift the lever.

"Who'd you have to kill?"

"Kill," says Wapi.

I sit on the stool and wait for my macchiato to arrive. After that, I'll worry about what to do for the rest of the day.

"Just so you know," says Ada, "Emma's using the school as an address for the Neighbours. So they can sign up for social services."

Florence froths the milk and dribbles it into the cup, makes a little heart pattern in the crema, sets the tarot in front of me. I shuffle the cards, cut the deck several times, and turn over the Fool.

"Well, would you look at that," says Florence. "That was Reggie's favourite card. New beginnings, setting off on a journey, joy of adventure, readiness to take a risk."

The Fool doesn't make any more sense than the rest of the cards. Some guy with a beard and horns, three flowers at his crotch, birds and butterflies, an alligator at his feet.

One foot off a cliff.

"Course, Reggie couldn't afford to move around like he wanted to," says Florence, "but he spent a hell of a lot of time dreaming about going."

"Going and sex," says Ada. "Sometimes, that's all men think about."

"Thought it was coming and sex," says Enola.

Ada turns beet red.

"Don't look at me," says Louis. "She's your niece."

"Sex." Wapi uses the binoculars to look at his feet.

"He sleeps with those things," says Enola. "Just so you know."

Florence straightens the deck and puts it away. "So, what's it going to be?" she says. "Stay or go?"

THE FESTIVAL IN THE PLAZA is up and running for a second day. There's a juggler tossing apples into the air and a guy on a didgeridoo blowing long, mournful tones and snapping off animal barks. Emma and Roman and Lala are on a blanket against the bandstand.

Emma waves me over.

"Pop-Up," shouts Lala, "watch me do a cartwheel."

"She's just learning," says Emma.

Lala gets to the top of the skill when her lead arm collapses and she goes down in a heap.

"Ta-da," she shouts, leaping to her feet and jumping into a finish pose.

"Not bad," says Roman. "Don't think I could do that."

"Course you can't do that, Daddy," says Lala. "You're too old."

Lala tries the cartwheel again with the same result. She gets up and slowly cartwheels her way across the park.

"You hear about the mayor?" says Roman. "Looks like he's got his ass in a vise."

"And Maribelle Wegman has flown to Florida," says Emma. "Extended vacation is the word. Did you know those two were having an affair?"

"What's with this foundation?" asks Roman.

"Not sure," says Emma. "But for the time being, I'm willing to leave good news alone."

Lala reappears with another girl in tow.

"This is Helen," says Lala. "And she can do cartwheels."

"I'm the best in the world," says Helen, and she snaps off several cartwheels in a row.

"She's going to the Olympics," says Lala.

"Right now, I'm too young," says Helen.

Lala and Helen return to cartwheeling, scattering people as they go.

"I can't even remember when I had that much energy," says Emma. "I get tired just watching her."

Lala is sweaty. There's a strand of hair hanging in her face. I push it to one side.

"Are you coming back to the school?" says Emma. "I feel as though we've kicked you out of your home."

"Not his home," says Roman. "Place belongs to us. Part of the land claim."

"Roman."

"It's true." Roman stretches out on his side. "Don't mind you being there, cuz, but I'm guessing you were never going to stay anyway."

"As far as I'm concerned, Mr. Camp," says Emma, "you can stay as long as you like."

"He's got to finish the graveyard," says Roman. "Before he goes."

I DON'T RETURN to the hotel. I'm done with that. And I don't go back to the school. I go to the only place where I know I won't be disturbed, the only place where no one is going to come looking for me.

The only place where I might be safe.

43

Nutty's trailer isn't all that bad. It smells and it's damp and the bed is lumpy, but the toilet and the sink work, and staying here saves me from another night on the cold floor of a deserted factory, or the indifferent luxury of a penthouse suite.

Even better, I have the place to myself. No Neighbours, no dogs, no Ada. No Nutty, no Emma, no Roman, no Florence.

No Lala.

When I get to the no Lala part, I pause.

THE NEXT MORNING, Slick is on the roof, waiting. As soon as he sees me, he starts cawing and doing his crow dance. He wants his peanuts. That much is clear.

I go back into Nutty's kitchen and open the refrigerator, take out the jar of peanut butter and put a big scoop on a plate. It's not the same thing, but I figure it's close enough.

And if Slick is fussy, then he's out of luck.

I put the plate on the top of the garbage can and sit in Nutty's lounger. Slick stays on the roof. He complains a little, but then he plumps himself up and pulls his head down into his feathers.

I do the same thing, and the two of us pass the time, relaxing in the pale sunshine, with nothing to bother us but the freshening wind.

"You know, you're getting harder to find."

Oliver Flood leans against the side of the trailer.

"Not at the school. Not at the hotel." Flood shifts his weight from one foot to the other. "Did you really spend a night at that old factory?"

Slick snaps to attention, his eyes bright with caution.

"And now I find you here." Flood shakes his head. "You're just full of surprises."

Slick has had enough. He caws once, leaves his plate of peanut butter behind, and takes to the air.

"I wanted to bring you up to speed." Flood pulls up the orange plastic chair and sits down. "Things have started to move ahead."

All the people on the list are dead, so I'm not sure exactly what things are moving ahead or where they might go.

"All that publicity about the terrorist group was a godsend." Flood stretches out his legs and folds his arms across his chest. "The Gardeners? Brilliant? Yes?"

Seeing Oliver Flood enjoying himself this much is disturbing.

"Suddenly, personal security has moved to the front of the line. Ms. Locken, because she is concerned with the safety and well-being of the rich, is planning a big get-together to discuss the range of options."

I'm sorry Slick has left. I could use his support.

"It will be, as you might imagine, a very select guest list. Probably hold it in the fall. Utah, Colorado, Alberta. Some remote place with lovely panoramas, a resort perhaps. Very secure, very conservative, with no sense of humour."

And then, suddenly, Slick is back. And he's not alone. He's come with reinforcements.

"But she has a problem."

Flood pauses to give emphasis to the word.

"While she is of the opinion that all billionaires are bad, she is willing to concede that some might be better than others. So, before the invitations are sent out, she needs to know which branches to cut and which to leave."

Flood gives me a moment to appreciate his allusion.

"After all," he continues, barely breaking stride, "it wouldn't do to invite someone to our event who doesn't deserve to be there."

The crows drop out of the sky and land on the roof in a noisy lump. Flood can hear them behind him. But he doesn't look.

"Ms. Locken was hoping that you might be persuaded to prepare a forecast that would aid us in assembling such a list."

The crows huddle along the edge of the roof. I start to count them. And then I give up.

"Of course, there is the matter of compensation. She was thinking that the old B&M plant could be purchased and repurposed as low-income housing. Now that the mayor won't be turning it into a community centre."

Two of the larger crows slide off the roof and take a pass at Flood. I've seen them do this with owls and foxes.

Flood doesn't flinch. "And then there's the matter of the band's land claim. Reserve, school, riverbed. The whole shebang."

Several more crows join the skirmish. They don't come in hard. They keep their distance, as they try to decide what is to be done with this intruder.

"I told her that you would say no, but then, I've been wrong before." Flood stands and turns to the crows. "And just between us, Forecaster, ravens are more impressive."

BY THE TIME I get to the school, the sun is high and bright. I change into my work gear, walk my Little Elephant garden cart to the dry riverbed, and dig up stones.

When I have a load, I haul the wagon up the bank and into the graveyard.

Someone has been pulling up crosses. And someone has been stacking them in a pile.

"Pop-Up. Where have you been?"

Lala is sitting on the ground next to a grave.

"Daddy helped me with the crosses," she says. "Can we burn them now?"

There are still a few crosses left at the far edge near the trees, but now the graveyard looks strangely bare and desolate, no longer feels like a cemetery.

"Mum-Mum is making hot chocolate," says Lala. "And toast. Do you like hot chocolate?"

Emma comes out the back door of the school.

"Come on, honey," she says. "Time to eat."

"Daddy says you might not stay." Lala lifts a flat rock out of the wagon. "But Mum-Mum says he's not always right."

I work the lever, dump the rest of the stones onto the ground.

"Honey!" Emma calls out again. "Before your food gets cold!"

"Pancakes wants you to stay," Lala sings, as she skips back to the school. "And Zoe says you can have third pick of the puppies."

44

Florence and the Three Bears fill me in over coffee at the Piggy.

"The Ankh Foundation proposal came up under new business," says Louis. "But we didn't put it to a vote."

"Sent it back to committee," says Enola.

"Sounds too good to be true," says Louis.

"And you know what they say about that," says Enola.

"Whites always got a plan to make our lives better," says Louis. "They like to pretend they can see the future."

"Future." Wapi pans around the restaurant with the binoculars.

"Residential schools," says Enola. "Reserves. Christianity."

"Last time, it was trailers," says Louis.

"Don't forget the movies," says Florence. "You guys are always getting saved by White guys."

"*A Man Called Horse*," says Enola. "*Dances with Wolves*."

"I could see *Blazing Saddles* again," says Florence.

"They want to build us a new council office," says Louis. "New houses. Dig a well. New septic. Solar panels. You should have seen the list of stuff. What did they call us?"

"A demonstration community," says Enola. "Christmas come early."

Wapi puts the binoculars down. "Christmas."

Louis nods. "Brown paper packages tied up with string."

Florence turns on me. "What the hell do they want you to do? Kill the pope?"

I keep my eyes on the foam at the bottom of my cup.

"You know Billy Tom down in Brantford? Mohawk Construction?" Louis taps his fingers on the table. "He's going to help us build a new band office."

"Doing it on our own will take a little longer," says Enola, "but we wouldn't have to worry about the strings."

"More like ropes," says Louis. "Whites don't give away anything for nothing. There's a bill somewhere that someone has to pay."

Florence looks at me. "You wouldn't know anything about that, would you?"

"So, Emma thanked Mr. Flood and told him that we would have to think about the offer." Enola's eyes are dancing. "Emma says he looked shocked."

I would have paid to see Oliver Flood in a state of shock.

"And then he started laughing. Not a big belly laugh. Emma said it was more like one of those chuckles you hear in a scary movie just before someone gets their head chopped off."

"Whites are crazy," says Florence. "But rich Whites are insane."

"In any case," says Louis, "we'll be okay."

"New city council is making friendly noises," says Enola. "Emma's going to sit down with them next week about utilities."

I'm hoping that Florence will offer me another macchiato.

"You paying attention?" Florence takes my cup and rinses it out. "They're not doing this for you."

"Don't need you running up a tab with some fancy foundation on our account," says Louis. "We can look after ourselves."

"Just what the hell do they want you to do?" says Florence.

THE TESLA IS PARKED in the shade of the graveyard. Oliver Flood is sitting on a folding chair. He's taken off his jacket and rolled up his sleeves. As though he's thinking about doing manual labour.

"I pulled up a couple crosses," he says. "It was fun."

I look around for Spot and Rover.

"I suppose you heard that the band council is thinking of turning us down." Flood gets to his feet. "That's something that doesn't happen often."

The crows are nowhere to be seen. I would have expected them to show up for the grand finale.

"Most times, people fall all over themselves to get to a trough." Flood stretches. "It's mildly refreshing. Though it does present us with a problem. We may not have anything to offer you in exchange for your co-operation. What to do? What to do?"

They've probably found a dead skunk on the road. Or something equally appealing.

"Ms. Locken's gardening plans haven't changed." Flood makes a snipping motion with his fingers. "Of course, there's always the chance that this approach might catch on, might lead to an unbridled enthusiasm on the part of the hoi polloi to cut down the orchard."

The sky is empty. The trees are deserted.

"Wouldn't that be something." Flood's face softens. Sorrow perhaps. Or simply melancholy. "The wholesale slaughter of the insanely wealthy. The best of times, the worst of times."

Flood fixes me with his eyes.

"It's not likely though, is it. You've already considered that possibility, haven't you?"

I have.

"And you would have concluded that the commitment and tenacity needed for such an undertaking does not exist."

Flood is correct. We would have to be crows.

"Which brings us back to the matter at hand." Flood brushes his pants, slips into his jacket. "Who knows. You might find you enjoy pruning," he says. "I know I do."

ADA AND NUTTY, Emma and Roman, and Lala are in the kitchen. There's a big bowl of potato chips on the table, along with a deck of cards. Ada has a green visor on that shades her eyes.

"We're going to play blackjoe," Lala sings out when she sees me.

"Jack," says Ada. "Blackjack."

Next to the bowl of chips is my mother's lunch box.

"Pancakes was in your room again," says Lala. "Sometimes she won't listen to me."

Ada touches her visor. "I'll be house."

"You're always house," says Nutty.

"You're all going down," says Roman. "I've played blackjack in Las Vegas."

Lala opens the lunch box and takes out the photographs.

"Pancakes was licking the pictures, but I saved them."

I reach for the photographs, but Ada beats me to them. She picks up the one of my mother in front of the motorcycle, and turns it to the light.

"Would you look at this," she says. "Would you just look at this."

"That's Pop-Up's mum-mum."

Ada squints at the photograph. "No, it ain't," she says. "That ain't Ruby."

Nutty takes the photograph and holds it out at arm's length. "You're right."

Ada hands the picture back to Lala. "That's me, honey. When I was a young woman."

Lala holds up the second photograph. "So, this is Pop-Up's mum-mum?"

Ada looks at the image and shakes her head. "Got no idea who that is. Maybe it was one of Ruby's friends."

I don't bother to collect the photos. I leave them where they lie.

"Okay," says Roman. "Deal and die."

"You keep eating the chips," says Ada, "we won't have a game."

Emma smiles at me. "It's supposed to help her with her counting. I send my child to school so she can learn card games?"

"Your boyfriend was here," says Roman. "The one with the fancy SUV and the big ideas."

"He scared off the crows," says Nutty. "Slick tried to put up a brave front, but he disappeared as soon as the guy stepped out of the car."

Ada deals out the cards. "Man could frighten pigeons."

"Malibu had her puppies." Lala shows me her hand.

"She had five," says Nutty. "Cute little things. All warm and wiggly. Almost as good as babies."

"If you like dogs," says Roman.

Lala is holding a queen and a jack. "Pop-Up gets third pick."

"You missed the big presentation at council," says Nutty. "Those foundation people had a video with music and everything. Pretty impressive."

"Sure," says Ada. "But I'm not sure I'm going to vote for it."

"What about that WiFi?" says Roman. "Wapi really likes that internet."

"And satellite television," says Nutty. "Baseball sure looks good on that big screen."

"I'm not saying I won't vote for it," says Ada.

"New band office, new houses." Emma takes a hit and winds up with nineteen. "It's a substantial package, that's for sure."

"Imagine that's how Adam and Eve felt about apples," says Roman.

Ada busts on twenty-three, pays the winners, and scoops up the cards. "So, you plan on staying?" she says.

"Of course he's staying," says Nutty. "Where else would he go?"

"He stays if we say so," says Roman.

"Since you're not using that laptop," says Ada, "maybe you want to give it to Wapi."

"His tablet *is* pretty much shot," says Emma.

"You want to be part of the community," says Roman, "then be part of the community."

I don't sit down. And I don't hang around to see who winds up with all the chips. I leave the gamblers, grab my work clothes and my tools.

"Don't worry," Lala calls out after me. "I'll help you pick your puppy, and I'll help you name it."

I SPEND THE REST of the day at the old riverbed, gathering stones, loading them on my wagon, dragging them back to the graveyard. I hear the crows off somewhere in the distance.

But I don't see them until evening.

They float into the trees on the failing light, a few at a time, making sure that it's safe to show themselves. Slick drops to the ground, stands on one of the stones, and waits. As though he expects a peanut. Or an explanation.

Or an apology.

I finish chiselling Mary Camp's name. It's not dark. I could start on another grave. But I don't. I sit back and enjoy the cool air and the soft shadows.

The crows wait patiently. I suppose I could ask them for their opinion.

Stay. Go.

Ash Locken and Oliver Flood.

The school. The reserve. The town.

But I don't. All things considered, I doubt that the birds care.

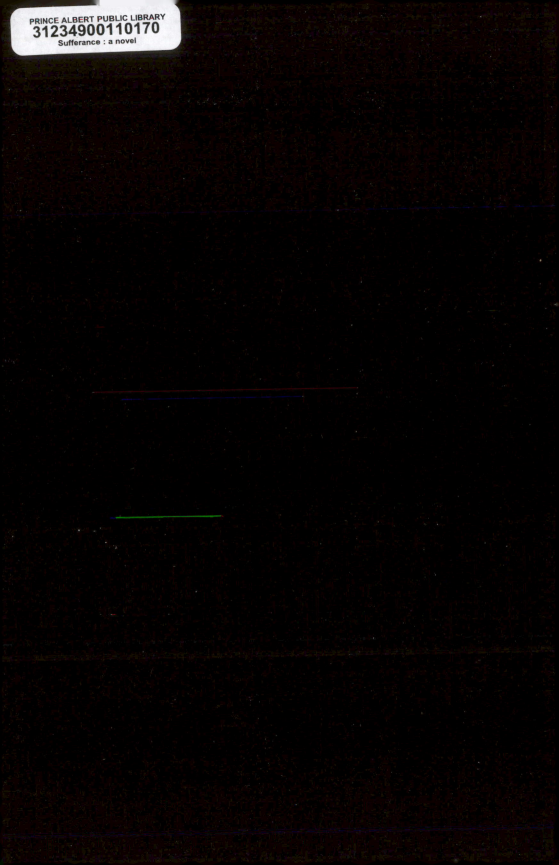